My Dark Obsession

Amber M. Clark

My Dark Obsession.

The Obsession duology.

Amber M. Clark

First published by Amber M. Clark 2025

First edition.

ISBN: 978-1-0681951-1-2

Trigger warnings.

My Dark Obsession is a Dark Romantasy with heavy scenes.

Reader discretion is advised as this book contains:

Sexually explicit discussions and scenes (including rough interactions)

Alcohol consumption.

Abuse.

Blood and gore.

Mental health.

Death.

Obsessive behaviour.

Description of a dead body.

Aggression.

Foul language.

Amber M. Clark

To those afraid of what the darkness brings.
Don't be scared, sink your claws into it and make it your *bitch.*

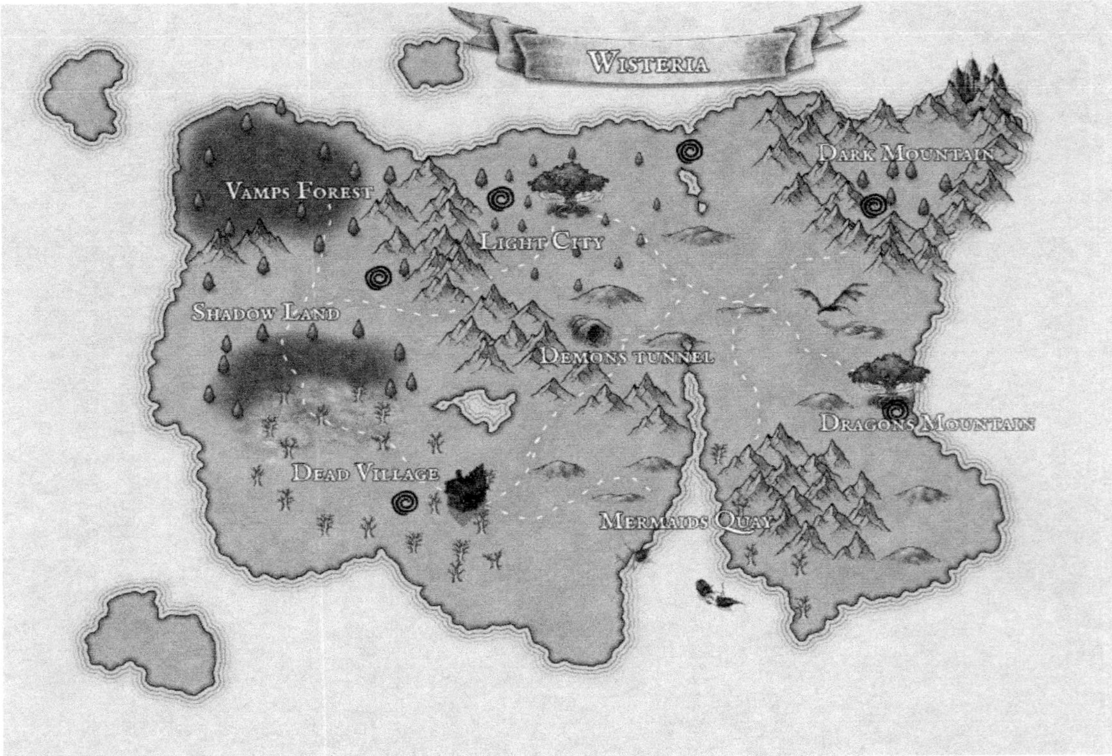
Wisteria
Vamps Forest
Light City
Dark Mountain
Shadow Land
Demons tunnel
Dragons Mountain
Dead Village
Mermaids Quay

One

'Limbo-Limbus'

Amaya.

Crack

That was definitely my ribs; the pain penetrating my lungs had me gasping out in utter agony. Sucking in a deep breath from the pain, I spat out thick liquid as a coppery taste filled my already bruised mouth.

I was choking on my own blood.

This wasn't good.

The heavy pound of his fists wracked my body as I tried to concentrate on getting air into my struggling airways. I slipped on the blood-soaked concrete and fell to my side cringing as a grunt slipped out after landing on my damaged ribs. The white-hot burn was now a sure sign of my lungs being impaled further.

This really wasn't good.

The blows still continued with his punishing hits.

How long had he been at this now? Minutes? Hours? I'm pretty sure I kept blacking out, so I couldn't be sure.

I spat another mouthful of foamy blood to the floor; my head was thrown back and slammed to the dirty ground with an audible thump. Stars burst to life behind my closed eyes.

That fucking hurt.

"Disgusting, vile—" my head was pulled back with force by my hair, the sting making my eyes water as he spat in my face.

And he called me vile.

"-You're. Unable. To do. Anything. Right!" Each word was said with either a slap to the face or a kick to the stomach.

Breathing was now practically impossible. But hey, who needed to breathe when you were about to die anyway? Because that's where this was going; he had never been this angry before. He would have usually worn himself out by now.

The day hadn't even been that bad, not the worst anyway! I mean yeah sure I forgot to pre-heat the coffee pot, which okay, led to me being late to drop the twins off because I was limping from the small beating I then received. Which led to me being late to my first class of the day, History with Ms Roberts. She took great delight in informing the class that the reason I was late and didn't have the essay to hand in was because I had a 'slow brain'.

Yup, that's right the entire town of Bluewater Valley thought I was slow. Like mentally. I mean I very well could have been after all the hits to the head I received daily, but I think it was just a way for them to ignore the fact I lived with an abusive foster father and a set of random twins.

I wasn't stupid; I just wasn't like them. I could give you detailed instructions of how to slice open a human's skin and retract each bone before they bled out and died. I could read an eight-hundred-page book on true crime in half a day and still go on to read a fantasy book on fairy tales and its lore. But apparently that made me sick, psychotic and potentially a serial killer in the making according to the internet.

Not that I care what they thought of me, as I had detached myself from that town and life a very long time ago.

People were like slugs, slowly sliding their way through life full of lies, sludge and sickness and waiting for the escape of death.

I thought the day was going to be like any other with my usual beatings and his drunken slurs thrown at me before bed but nope, after picking the twins up we walked through the door to find Lyal, our foster father, and Ms Roberts sans clothes on the couch.

Turns out her threatening to call my, gag, 'Father' about my tardiness was something else entirely.

Thinking about it made me heave more.

And that's how I ended up on the basement floor concerned for my life for once but still, he was definitely angrier than normal.

More blood filled my airways and had me choking.

It had started to become difficult to get a decent breath in.

I looked over to my usual spot, the dripping pipe that had started to turn green from the years of leaking. It had become my focusing point during those regular beatings.

I just had to get through this. It was going to be the last time I let him put his hands on me. Once midnight hit, I was eighteen and we were free.

Yep, happy fucking birthday to me.

Freedom was so close; waiting for me upstairs were my boys hidden in their little closet. They were waiting for me to open that door, gather them close and tell them everything was fine, that we were free.

I couldn't let him beat me to death; yes, it had always been a literal dream of mine to give in and let the sweet release of death take me away from this sick world, but I had them now.

I gritted my teeth in anger and pain, the rage that boiled the blood in my veins always calling me to answer. I held in the need to climb to my raw knees, lift a piece of that leaking pipe and swing it at his greasy head, to keep swinging until all that was left was a pile of brain matter and his blood staining the concrete of this delightful basement. My head was always noisy, always full of dark and dangerous thoughts that I'm sure would have worried others.

I tried to stave off these desires with the true crime books, immersing myself in their horror and gore, but all it did was feed whatever was inside me. Those books were more like instructions on what you could and couldn't get away with than working out what happened.

My face stretched into what I knew would be a deranged swollen smile at the thought of Lyal and his brains spread across the floor.

"This is funny to you? This is ALL YOUR FAULT!" He roared as he slammed his foot down onto my face. One of my eyes was now unable to fully open. The pain was pulsing through every inch of me.

He was always ranting and raving about things being my fault, how I didn't do anything right. I literally had no idea what he was on about. He was just a disgusting, mean, abusive drunk. When I asked, I always landed up here, staring at that damn leaking pipe.

Another one of my fantasies was a blade to his throat, slicing his chubby neck open and watching as the life drained from his meat sack sounded heavenly.

He wasn't the only person I had those fantasies about; most of the town had their deaths planned out, by me of course. Each one perfectly thought out, each intricate detail planned. I had suffocations, mutilations, acid coffee and so on and so forth. Now I wasn't some kind of head case, as these plans were only for the people who genuinely deserved it: child abusers, bullies, ignorant sheriff's and bitch social workers.

Yes, I know I had a problem.

But I knew I couldn't act on these wonderful thoughts, because the boys upstairs needed me, and we were oh so close to being free.

We had plans, plans to get the fuck out of this damned town. The time we tried to run before had landed up with beatings similar to these, and it had been really damn hard to hide the twins from his anger then. So we figured, once I was eighteen, they couldn't search for us, because I would be legally an adult and didn't need to stay with Lyal. The brothers had no legal paperwork, no birth certificates nor foster forms, nothing. I knew that social worker bitch had stolen them from somewhere and given them to Lyal. I just had never been able to figure out why. There was nothing in his office; I had ransacked the house looking and nothing could be found.

However, it worked to our advantage I suppose, because without them having paperwork, we could run. We just needed to wait until midnight, to get this beating over with and sneak out when Lyal was exhausted and passed out in his armchair with his whisky.

However, it really wasn't going to plan; the beating was taking a turn for the worse and I really feared I was going to pass out or die.

I would never let him put his hands on those boys, so I took his beatings, took his anger and days' worth of labour. And I let it boil inside me; let it fester and grow into a hatred even he would be shocked at. Because one day, I was going to go back to Bluewater Valley, and I was going to act upon every single one of my fantasies.

My ears rang from a swift kick to the head; if he carried on, there was no way I was crawling up those steps to the boys.

The drip from the leaking pipe had now gone silent, as had his raging voice. There was nothing but a muffled screech.

I was pretty sure he'd damaged my ears.

He had to stop.

He was going too far.

I pushed to my hands on the wet floor as I heaved myself to my knees and looked at him standing there with his chest heaving, his hands clenched and his face red and sweaty.

"S-stop." I tried to croak out. My throat was full of blood and I couldn't hear anything but the muffled screech.

His mouth moved but no words reached me. Lip reading was impossible due to my swelling eyes and the blood and sweat dripping into them. I was an utter mess.

I squinted behind Lyal. I swore I could see a black bird watching me from the stair railing.

Was I delirious? Potentially.

Was I panicking that I was dying? Nope.

Was there a cold churning in my stomach at the thought of leaving my boys alone without me?

Abso-fucking-lutely.

I had never been afraid of being alone, of pain or the cold release of death. Of being different. But the thought of leaving them had my heart racing and mouth clenching in utter fear.

Those boys were mine, mine and no one was ever going to take them away from me. Elfyn and Elyas.

I was weak before they came along, weak and pathetic. They made me strong. They needed me to protect them.

More fatal blows came my way, bile and blood pooled around my face as he smashed my head into the concrete.

I'll admit, I was beginning to panic. If I passed out or died, he was going to eventually move onto the brothers.

I told myself to stay awake.

Focus.

Breathe.

Was the bird watching me?

Everything blurred to black as I watched the bird watch me. The heavy blows continued but no pain followed.

Black, everything was black.

Silent.

Time was endless.

So blissfully numb.

No pain.

No panic for the twins.

No thoughts of freedom.

The numb was amazing; we were best friends.

I was floating in an endless black void of nothingness, a vast void of utter peace.

Was I-dead?

My arms floated beside me as I drifted in this nothingness. Something niggled at my subconsciousness, something important. But the numb pulled me back.

So peaceful.

So quiet.

I floated. And floated. I floated until a distance rumble made my almost non-existent heart pump a little harder, a little faster.

I became more aware. But so confused.

I was floating but where was I? Where was I?

Where the hell was I?

My heart hammered as I tried to move my body, but the floating nothingness pulled at my limbs and dragged at my consciousness. It begged me to swim back into the numb.

A tingle in my toes eased up my feet, along my calves, around my thighs and up my back before turning into a scream inducing zap of pain. My back arched as I sucked in a mouthful of lukewarm air. It was agony; everything hurt, every fiber of my being cried for the loss of the numbness as the loud rumble shook my void of nothingness around me.

A voice screamed in the distance; it screamed on and on, piercing my sore ears.

I couldn't work out why my ears were sore.

"Amaaaayaaa!" It screeched.

I didn't know who Amaya was. I didn't know why I was hurt; I didn't know where I was.

And so I floated and floated in utter agony as I wished for death to sing his song and summon my soul.

Unless I was already dead.

"Amaaaayaaa!"

I was Amaya. I was Amaya and the cold churning now pulling at my stomach had my heart hammering in terror. Was I dead? Had I left my boys?

Shit, they were all alone with him.

Lyal, that bastard had killed me.

Well death could fuck off!

Elyas and Elfyn needed me, and Lyal, I was going to kill that fucker.

I fought against the numbness, constantly picturing my boys' faces in my mind to stay alert.

I screamed with my teeth smashed together against the pain in my body and swore to rip death's face apart if I didn't get back to them.

But it was pointless, because no matter how much I fought, the numb took over.

And I floated.

Two

'New Era-Era Novum'

Amaya

Agony. I was in utter agony. Everything hurt, even my damn toes hurt. That was one hell of a beating. The last thing I remembered was seeing Lyals foot come towards my face before everything went black. I must have passed out.

The cold hard ground beneath me did nothing to soothe the aches that covered my entire body. I tried to force my eyes open, but they were swollen shut and sealed with something sticky. I assumed dry blood. I lifted my aching arm to pick away at the stuck lashes, but my muscles screamed at me from the movement.

I sucked in a deep breath, choked on a little blood, forced my arm up and ripped the layer of gunk from my eyes, and in the process tore out all of my eyelashes.

I'm pretty sure the sound that left me was more donkey like then human but shit it hurt!

I opened my eyes as wide as they could go, which was about a centimetre at best, and tried to take stock of my body.

My ribs were on fire, my head throbbed, my arm wouldn't move properly and I'm pretty sure my left toe was dislocated as well as my hearing being muffled. Oh, and I think I was missing a few teeth. So all in all, pretty good.

Grunting in acknowledgement of this being not as bad as I thought, I squinted at the ceiling; the black charred wood looked out of place for the basement.

I grunted again as I lifted my arm once more and pinched the skin surrounding my eye to force it open more.

I definitely wasn't in the basement.

The roof was a burnt unstable wood that creaked and whined above me. I lifted my head slightly and saw that the walls were a soot covered stone. No furniture was in sight in this small dark shack.

Where the actual fuck was I?

Had Lyal thought he killed me and then dumped my body here?

That bastard.

I was actually going to kill him, and I really couldn't wait.

I rolled to my side and a scream lodged in my throat when the sharp pain in my ribs threatened to make me pass out again, and as much as I would have liked to escape from the pain radiating absolutely everywhere, the need to see my twins outweighed it. My stomach churned at the thought of him leaving me half dead and venturing up the stairs to them.

My eyes stung from the soot that drifted down to my face, my cuts itched and my face pulled tight from the swelling.

Creaking from above had my head snapping up. A small part of the burnt roof had moved away from the rest, which whined and groaned causing more dust to settle down on me.

Could I not catch a fucking break?

The entire roof was about to collapse with me under it. There was only one thing I could do; I jumped to my feet, screaming and snorting like a damn pig from the blood in my mouth and slammed myself into what I had hoped was the wooden door.

Thankfully the blackened wood collapsed under my weight, and I smashed through. I collapsed to the floor face first in a heap of unladylike grunts just as a huge puff of black smoke and dust covered me from the now crumbled roof.

Coughing up more blood, I spat it next to me and gave the shack the finger. Or tried too; I think I broke it during the fall.

I squinted my barely opened eyes against the cloud of dust and soot and noticed two things:

One, this wasn't Bluewater Valley, and two, it was at least late afternoon which meant I had been gone an entire night and day. Nausea rose in my stomach. I hoped he had passed out with his whisky; I hoped he had worn himself out with me. I looked at the blackened shack as the debris finally settled and took in my surroundings. Lifting my throbbing head, I saw that there were many more blackened singed buildings and shacks, all covered in that crispy burned char or buried beneath large amounts of sand. It was an entire burned down village.

My hair stuck to my already sticky skin as the humid wind blew small grains of sand to my weeping wounds.

It fucking hurt.

I breathed in carefully so as to not choke on more blood. I slowly pushed to my knees, gritting my teeth as the pain in my ribs throbbed with each jerky movement. The squawk of a bird on a roof drew my attention. Its black beady little eyes watched me as I climbed to my feet. Planting my sweaty hands on my knees, I spat more blood onto the sand without taking my eyes off the stalking bird. I let the red tinged drool dribble from my mouth to the ground in a long slobbery line.

Yeah, that's right bird, enjoy the fucking show.

Straightening up and wiping my mouth on an uncut part of my arm I turned slowly, taking in each building and each sad looking tree.

The grey clouded sky covered the sun and yet it gave no relief from the humid air as sweat began to slowly bead along my skin.

A low grumble from my stomach had me rolling my eyes; it always rumbled and never learned its lesson. I could go days without food, and it had to be on day three by now. What little scraps Lyal gave us was enough to maybe fill one twin, not the three of us, so I always gave my portion to them and waited until I could steal from the school kitchen. If I was lucky, I was able to steal enough bread or fruit and stash it in our hideout in the outhouse next door. You'd think I would be wasting away but I never lost weight; in fact, I never got sick at all. Good genes from whoever brought me into this sick world I guessed.

I needed to get back to Bluewater Valley. Our secret bus tickets were still tucked safely in our getaway bag hidden in old man Jefferys outhouse.

Lyal thinking I was dead was going to be a great advantage, as it gave the twins and I more of a chance to disappear that way. If I could just get back and sneak into the boys, we could still be on our path to freedom.

I was slightly more positive at the prospect of being free, so with that thought in mind I wobbled my way to the sandy trail leading to the barren looking forest in hopes of finding some sort of civilisation.

Not one signpost, car or person was in sight. What had caused this fire and left this village barren and empty? I had no idea how far out of town he had dumped me and finding transport was a must. Something told me I was really damn far away from our town.

Bastard.

I growled to myself in frustration. I clenched my fists and spun to look at the charred building I crashed out of. The more I stared at it, the more the urge to return to it overcame me. Something was calling to me, a magnetic pull that wanted me to—I don't know what, but it wanted me to return to that building.

The loud echoing caw of the stalking bird pulled me from my thoughts. There it was staring at me yet again. It cawed again, its strange croaky noise almost a question.

"What do you want?" I snapped. It of course, didn't answer me, because it was a bird. I was talking to a damn bird.

Ignoring the urge to go back to the charred building, I turned around muttering, "Stupid thing; if you follow me, I'm going to eat you."

Maybe I would. I was damn near starving after all.

I walked towards the drooping dry trees, and saw that the further in I went, the branches were browner, and dark green leaves filled the empty areas. Hopefully there was more life that way. The cold churn in my stomach was my sign to hurry up.

The further I walked, the more I began to realise that I was walking, not limping. In fact I wasn't even hacking up my own lungs; I was breathing with ease. I stopped and gathered a big glob of saliva in my mouth before I spat it onto the thinning sand. It was clear, not a speck of blood in sight. I licked my thumb and ran it over my arm, wiping the grime and dried blood away. Clear perfect skin.

I blinked my eyes a couple of times as I also realised that they were not swollen. I felt around and yep...I had eyelashes.

Now I know I definitely ripped those out. I was sure of it. Not ten minutes ago I was practically dying. I know there had been damage to my lungs, as the blood had been proof of that. The question was, how? How the hell was I walking and breathing with more ease than I could ever remember doing?

Something niggled at my memory, something dark and empty, and just before I could grab it and focus, it drifted away again, leaving me with nothing but an empty wish to follow it. Whatever 'it' was.

A black mist floated and swirled in my peripheral vision and when I turned my head to catch a better view of it, it moved along with my eyes, constantly out of reach.

So maybe there was some permanent damage after all.

The fluttering of wings and a gust of wind behind me told me that the damned bird was still following me.

Growling from the lack of patience and totally not because I was freaking out, I snapped "I will eat you!" as I spun around ready to throw hands at the bird.

But no bird was staring at me, oh no, a giant, a mammoth, an enormous sized man stood in front of me, his thick brows furrowed in an annoyed scowl as I gaped at him with my mouth open.

This man was what you would call lumberjack sexy. With his huge broad shoulders, wide lips, strong jawline, hair so dark brown it almost looked black and sunglasses that covered his eyes in secrets I needed to reveal. He was a walking, talking lumberjack fantasy.

"What are ye' doin' here?" His deep rumbling voice pulled me from my pervy thoughts. His Scottish accent suited his grumpy face. His floppy hair brushed against his deep furrowed brow. Stepping closer so his shadow completely covered me, he asked again, his scowl deepening further.

"I said, why are ye' here?"

One thing about me was that I didn't scare easily. Standing my ground I craned my neck and gave him my own frown.

"Want to take a step back there, Lumberjack Joe?" Making sure my feet were firm on the sand and my hands were loose I breathed slowly, preparing for a fight. There was no holding back anymore; Lyal thought I was dead;

I was eighteen and free. I wasn't going to take anyone's shit anymore.

If it was even possible, his brow lowered even more, "Lumberjack Joe?" He tilted his head, and I knew he was looking at my baggy grey top and my trusty scuffed up converse. I was indeed a total mess.

"Why're ye' covered in blood?" The way he rolled his 'r' distracted me from him taking yet another step closer.

Sue me, I'm a sucker for the Scottish accent.

Raising my hands in a fake sign of surrender I said, "I'm leaving," whilst easing back. The forest behind me was my escape. I needed to find a car, a bus, some way to get back. The darkening sky had a slight wave of panic hit me at how long I had been gone.

"Why're ye' covered in blood Wee one?"

Wee one? I wasn't even that small, I was a good 5 ft 3 inches and if I didn't hunch, I reckon I would be another inch on that! Damn rude if you asked me. I mean I suppose I would seem small to him, as he had to be at least 6 ft 3.

"I fell. Now, if you'll excuse me good sir, I'll be on my way." I answered flatly. He was wasting time I wasn't sure I had.

Turning on my heel I went to march away, thoughts of miraculously healing and my boys crowded my noisy head.

"Wait—" His large hand wrapped around my forearm and as our skin touched an electric shock type pain zapped through my body, settling at my back making me arch and squeak in surprise and discomfort. It ended as quickly as it had begun, leaving me staring at the huge stranger as he looked back at me with his mouth agape.

That was weird.

"Wh-How? I—" He stuttered as he released my arm and ran his hand through his floppy hair messing up the strands.

"Ookay, anywho, as we were." I chirped with a false sense of confidence, I wasn't scared of him but the longer I was away from my boys the more my nerves ran haywire, I backed away once more and started back on my march to the forest.

"Wait! Why're ye' walking away!" He grumbled as he walked behind me, because let's be honest, my march was a slow walk to his giant tree trunks you call legs.

"Look mister, I have somewhere to be. Stop following me." Snapping at him in irritation, I picked up speed. First the bird, now this man. What was with people following me lately? I hated people.

His large hand gripped my shoulder, stopping my march once again. Before I got the chance to yell some obscene things at him, I realised his sunglasses were now rested on his head, leaving his bright red eyes to stare down at me.

That's right, bright red eyes.

Now I was always up for some strange stuff. I couldn't say I was exactly normal with all of my dark thoughts but red eyes on a goliath of a man? Yeah, I was out.

I spun on my heel and raced through the forest.

By raced I mean I ran as fast as I could.

By fast as I could I mean I flayed about and got whipped in the face by a bunch of branches. I had never been the most athletic and my lack of nutrition didn't help.

"I'm no' going to hurt ye'! Please wait!" He called behind me.

Now it could have been the many bangs to the head I had received recently but I had this odd urge to stop and listen. The urgency in his voice pulled at me in a strange way.

I ran faster.

I panted as I ran further into the forest. What were barren twigs were now tall, glorious trees full of leaves and foliage. I jumped over fallen logs and branches, cut through thorny bushes and still I didn't stop.

I'd be damned if I was going to let some giant lumberjack kidnap me and chop me up, even if he was a little bit yummy. Because that's what kidnappers do these days right?

Tripping over another fallen branch I would have smashed my face into the lush greenery beneath me, but his large hand yet again gripped my forearm.

Turning me to him he removed his hands and backed away, showing his hands in a way of friendly surrender.

I glared at him and panted; I was seriously unfit.

"I'm no' going to hurt ye'." He nodded at me as if that cleared it up.

"Then why are you chasing me!" I said as I tried my hardest not to show how much I was out of breath.

"Ye' was the one running!" He rumbled with raised eyebrows, his red eyes bright and slightly glowing in the darkening forest.

"Your eyes are red!"

"Uh, yeah, and ye're my Circle Mate Wee one, ye' felt tha' right?" Lowering his hands, he reached back and rested his hand on his lower back.

Had he hurt his back chasing me? Maybe I wasn't the only one seriously unfit. I also had no idea what the hell he meant by Circle Mate; was it some kind of kidnapping term?

I ignored the small itch at my lower back and growled "You're going to have to find someone else to chop up!"

Exasperated, he threw his hands in the air, "what the hell are ye' on about!" Bending to eye level he spoke slowly, as if speaking to a child.

"I'm not going to hurt you. You are mine." He pronounced each word carefully, so to make me understand.

Welp, I didn't. and I was getting pissed off at red eyes. So I lifted my scuffed shoe and slammed it down onto his massive foot, making sure to grind my heel right into his toes. His face turned a deep red as he jumped back in shock, giving me a head start to race away into the forest.

Except I got about two metres away before I looked back behind me to check on his approach and I slammed straight into a large tree. My head bounced off the bark and I flew backwards to the grounds where my head then bounced off a rock with a crack.

Just before everything went black, I could have sworn I saw that damn bird, that stalking crow, staring back at me from the branch above, the black mist behind it swirling away.

***

I led on clouds; I had to be. Whatever was beneath me was soft and plump. It was warm and my body had sunk deep within its cocoon as I hummed in contentment. I don't think I had ever been so warm, so comfortable in my entire life. And the smell, God it was intoxicating. Warm cake and firewood. It surrounded me, wrapped around my senses and made my mouth water.

Something was very wrong.

I wasn't injured, I knew that much. No throbbing burning pain pulsed through my body like it usually did when I woke up. Lifting my eyelids just slightly, I peaked through my thick lashes…yup definitely had my lashes back. But I'd have to pop a pin in that because I was not in the darkened forest where I stupidly knocked myself out.

I was in a dark bedroom, where thick dark curtains were pulled mostly shut over a window showing it was now night.

Fuck. More time lost.

A large dresser sat next to a stupidly big, overstuffed armchair where the red eye man sat, with his tree trunk legs spread and his elbows resting on the arms of the chair. He watched me intently, his glowing red eyes shining in the dark room.

I couldn't decide if my heart rate increased from waking up in a strange dark room with a giant stranger or the fact that something about his glowing red eyes intrigued me.

I had always pitied the girls in my town for being pathetic when it came to the opposite sex, and I was starting to get annoyed at myself. I needed to get my wits together and get the hell away from this man.

"I know ye're awake Wee one." His voice was so deep I swore I could feel the vibrations of it from across the room.

Giving up on my pretence I sat up, never removing my eyes from his own. I needed to treat him like a large predatory animal.

"Where am I?" I kept my movements slow, never showing any emotion on my face. It was easy for me to do. My mantra had always been 'Show them nothing, give them nothing and expect nothing.'

I squinted at him in the darkness. I just about made out his arm moving before an array of well used candles lit up the dresser next to him. A warm glow lit up the room. I could now see the thick drapes were a deep plum, and the bed that I really did not want to move from was so big it could fit four of the giant; it's plum covers were littered with various purple cushions.

He really liked purple.

"I brought you to my home. I'm sorry if I scared you."

"I wasn't scared." I snapped, probably a bit too quickly. "What happened to your accent."

Although there was a small lilt, his words were pronounced perfectly. Had he been faking it?

He tilted his head at me before standing, his shadow cast across the room, climbing the walls and stretching across the ceiling. "You didn't seem to understand me before."

Ugh, just because a girl didn't like what was being said she didn't understand? Typical male.

"I understood you perfectly. You were just chatting shit. I wanted to leave, I still do. How far from Bluewater Valley are we?" Giving him my usual flat tone and bored expression, I shifted my legs to the side of the bed, already missing its warmth. I wanted to ask how and why his eyes were red and glowing, partially because it was unusual right? But mostly because I was kind of jealous.

His brow furrowed again; his thick brows low as his eyes tracked me. I avoided looking at the glowing orbs.

"Bluewater Valley?" He genuinely seemed confused.

Shit, how far away was I?

"Where are we?" I slid down the side of the bed. It was the only way for me to somewhat gracefully get out of it. The bed was so tall it practically reached my chest.

"The shadow land."

"What's with all the half answers? I don't know where that is. I'm leaving. Stay where you are." Edging towards the door, I kept him in sight. His eyes flashed as a low growl reached me, its small rumble a warning.

"Why would ye' want to leave; we're Circle Mates." His accent thickened with his growl as he took a big step closer.

Okay so I slightly panicked. I had wasted so much time by getting myself kidnapped and I just wanted my boys. So I swung my arm back and jumped up and punched him right in the throat.

As he choked and gripped his throat, I ran through the slightly open door, through a spacious living area and out the door. Running down the dark stairs, I shoved myself through a set of swinging doors and was greeted by a loud noisy bar. Glasses clinked and the low chatter of...animals and people?

I stood frozen; there to the left sat a full-sized fucking brown bear. Its thick fur and plump ass was perched on a tiny wooden stall that creaked under its weight. Its large black snout turned to me, twitching as if sniffing me.

I was about to be fucking mauled by a bear in a bar.

"Fates Above Benny, not in the damn bar!" Shouted a woman. A tall blond bombshell with luscious hair to her shoulders and legs for days came into view carrying a crate so full she shouldn't have been able to carry it; however, she showed no sign of struggling. In fact she lifted it over the bar and placed it down with ease.

Just as the giant's heavy footsteps came behind me, the large brown bear shimmered in front of me. Its huge snout shrunk as its fur shifted as if a breeze blew through. In a blink of an eye, in the bears place sat a large man.

"My bad Cece." He yelled back, lifting his glass of brown liquid and drinking it in one.

"Oh hay there Rí." He nodded behind me.

A Fucking bear…turned into a man. It was a bear. Then it was a man. In a bar.

I slowly turned to the giant behind me. My mouth was wide open, and I knew my eyes were huge.

"Ye' are no' from around here are ye'?" He asked with one brow raised. I didn't answer, I was obviously not from around here, where I came from, bears didn't turn into people!

He placed his large warm hand to my lower back where an instant itch had begun. He gently led me back up the stairs and into the spacious living area over to the set of large armchairs. I sat down wide-eyes and mouth agape.

A fucking bear…into a person…

The giant, Rí knelt in front of me, close but not touching. "What were ye' doing in the Dead Village?"

The Dead Village? The burnt village? Why was he asking this? He hadn't seemed surprised at the bear changing its form. In fact, not one single person in the bar had. No one screamed and ran for the doors.

"That bear…man…how?" I stuttered. I was in shock, I knew this. Who wouldn't be in damn shock?

"Ye' don't have shifters from where ye're from?"

"Shifters? In books or films maybe but not real ones no! Where I'm from, humans. Only humans. The only animals are well…animals."

"Ye're human?" The shock on his face should have been my first sign that I was fucked, but it was when the knock at his door made me jump and twist around to stare at it and his mouth fell open to gape at me like a fish. It was then that I realised I was being like my weak old self-how pathetic of me.

"Mother fucker of all things fucked." He croaked.

Before I could say anything, the door knocked again, and the bar lady's voice called through.

"Rí you okay in there? Are you coming down? I've made you your drink."

Such an innocent question for her to ask. He lived above the bar and obviously knew her, so why oh why, did my stomach now burn with the need to add her to my dark tortuous fantasies.

"I'm havin' the night off." He answered, still looking at me with shock upon his face.

"Oh. Well your drinks here if you want it." As the footsteps receded Rí looked as though he managed to compose himself.

Clearing his throat, he stood up and walked to the fireplace opposite the chairs. Above the large stone was a stunning painting of a dragon, his large black wings spanning the entire painting. Its red eyes shone bright with the flames that were bursting from its monstrous mouth.

"What is ye' name Wee one?" He asked in his deep timber.

"Amaya." It had become hard to keep my tone flat and emotionless with all the shit that had just gone down. And by shit, I mean a bear changed into a man!

Stuff like that only existed in the fantasy books I read; they were well crafted from people with incredible imaginations.

Right?

"Well Amaya, ye're in Wisteria, the first home to the Supernatural."

Son of a bitch.

Three

'Amaya-Everlasting-Eternal'

Rí

A Circle Mate.

I had a Circle Mate.

Sat before me was the smallest, most beautiful, most confusing person I had ever come across.

I didn't do well with people. I wasn't a talker. I liked to be alone. I didn't need the locals to tell me I was grumpy; I already knew that.

My dragon and I barely communicated anymore; in fact, he slept and left me to deal with the misfit locals. I knew the day was coming where he would disappear completely.

But that afternoon whilst loading up the bar I felt it, the huge surge of power that rippled through me and my beast. So I ran as fast as I could and followed the pull towards the Village. The urgency in my veins had my dragon demanding I run faster. He even suggested shifting, but that's when I found her, Amaya. Covered in filth and dried blood and looking as though she was ready to take me in a fight. Me, a 6 ft 3 dragon shifter. It was laughable and I would have laughed if she hadn't tried to run from me multiple times.

The beast within me had reared his head and demanded out. He wanted out, he wanted our Mate and he wanted her bad. It took everything within me to hold him down, to promise his chance but we had to go slow, to be careful with our Wee Mate.

Typical that when he finally wanted to shift and communicate with me again, I knew we had to take it easy so as to not scare the small female before us.

And so she sat in front of me with that small crease between her brows, nibbling at her pale plump lips and making me ache in ways I didn't think possible anymore. Her long black hair still had bits of leaves from the forest and her pale skin was covered in soot and dirt and yet she always glowed in the radiant beauty she was.

It had taken every ounce of strength within me to not run my hands through her hair, to feel the black strands glide across my fingers, settling her mouth-watering fragrance on my skin. My mother would have provided me with the biggest slap to the back of the head had I given in and touched her whilst she lay laid in bed, recovering from her fall. This woman before me, no matter how much her eyes screamed 'touch me and die', was now the most important thing in my long life. I had to tread carefully.

"Supernatural." It wasn't a question; I stayed silent and allowed her to gather her thoughts. Her voice was husky, sensual and I wanted her to talk more. I wanted her to talk for hours and I would listen. Fuck me I would always listen.

"This Wisteria, there are multiple…shifters?"

I nodded and answered "Aye, all kinds, but all supernatural also. No' just shifters."

How she got to Wisteria was a huge puzzle, after seeing her eyes when Cece knocked, the way they completely shifted colour. Fuck me I had worked out what she was instantly. How she came to be, well that was another puzzle entirely.

Clearing her throat she nodded whilst wiping her pale hands on her torn pants.

I wanted to ask, no, demand, how she got so bloody and filthy, but I had a feeling that wasn't going to go down well. My Mate was a feisty one. I could tell that much already.

"I need to leave; I need to get back to the human world. Like now." She stood up bringing us to eye level. Her scent of dark fruits swam around me and had my dragon clawing at my insides. I gritted my teeth and forced him back further. Where I knew I needed to take this carefully, that our mate was obviously a runner, he wanted to chuck her back in our nest and mate her. He wanted her subtle breathing to fill our quarters and calm our souls; he wanted her exhausted and sated.

She wanted to leave. What was so important in the human realm she would want to leave?

"Why?" I grumbled clenching my fists at my side so as to not grab her and rub my own scent on her. The shifters down at the bar would know she was mine. Everyone would. I fought the urge to bare my teeth to show her how sharp they were, perfect to puncture her soft pale skin.

"None of your damn business," she snapped, rubbing at her lower back. The mark was calling to her, asking her to acknowledge it. The longer she ignored it, the more it would call.

We were all born with marks from the Fates Above, two rope like vines that connected into a colourless circle. And when we touched the bare skin of our fated, those marks burst to life, their colour now full and vibrant and connected at the top. Circle Mates. Before the war, most Fated had more than one connected to them, Circle Brothers or Sisters they were called. One Fated was the link, the one to connect them all as one. However after the war, the Fates Above disappeared and those who were lucky enough to find their Circle Mates only found the one.

I didn't think finding my Circle Mate was ever going to be a possibility. My dragon had just about given up on life all together after the war, and me, well I distanced myself from everyone and dragged myself through life hoping and praying that one day, one day my Mate would greet me.

Once I had touched her pale skin my Mating Circle had spread down my spine before settling on my lower back. The world around me had stopped moving, my mind had silenced and everything around me had ceased to exist. She did it for me. Forever more, mine.

So there was no Fates damned way she was leaving me.

Standing to my full height, I relished in the way her lips parted slightly at my size.

My dragon stretched within, proud of our height.

"Ye' won't be going anywhere without me."

Her brow arched high, and she bared her perfectly straight teeth at me. "Want to bet big man!"

Fuck me she was perfect.

She itched at her lower back before snapping and pulling at her top "What the hell is wrong with my back!"

"Ye're Circle Mark."

"My Circle…what is that on my back?" She screeched, her eyes flashed purple as the hair on my body stood on end.

Okay so maybe I didn't do such a good job of explaining things.

Actually, had I even explained anything?

"Wee—" She gave me a heated look whilst scratching at our mating mark "-Amaya, ye're in Wisteria, the realm for the Supernatural. The human realm was shut off a long time ago, eighteen years ago in fact. There shouldn't have been a way for ye' to get here, and there definitely isn't going to be one for ye' to get back. We," Pointing between us I carried on "are Circle Mates, once our skin touched the Fates Above blessed us. I am a shifter, ye'…well I'm still working things out but ye' are not human." I spoke slowly, to make sure she understood each word.

I bared my teeth in what I thought to be a charming smile. I was wrong. Boy was I wrong.

Her entire expression shut down. No emotion was visible on her face, her shoulders slumped, and her eyes seemed empty. Void.

"What do you mean I can't get back?" She said flatly. "I won't be staying here. I have people waiting for me. Urgently."

"Who?" If she said a man, or men I would find my own way to the human realm and snap their necks. But first, I would let my dragon have his fun with them.

She swallowed, and resumed itching her back, this time more insistently. She gouged at it as she began to pant. Her eyes that seemed empty seconds ago were now panicked.

"I need to get back, I need to.." Growling, she clawed at her back.

Grabbing her hands within my own, I held them still, her cold pale skin against my warm tanned. Such a contrast, such a difference. Yet it was utterly right.

"Breathe, Mo Chridhe. Slowly, in and out." She was panicking. And she had every right to be. I had been a terrible Mate so far. I had skimmed around her questions and given barely-there answers. Her mark was calling for her Mate and I stood there and watched her suffer.

"In and out, slowly." I instructed her, pleased with her slowing breath. My touch was soothing the mark, easing its relentless call. I eased her down to the armchair, reached over and blew a small flame into the fireplace.

Looking back at her, her eyes were wide and staring at the now growing flames.

Shit.

I kept forgetting how if she didn't even know about shifters and where she was, then she definitely wasn't going to be used to magic.

"The mark is calling for its Mate. It will be insistent on ye' being close to me."

She looked tiny, sitting in my armchair with a frown upon her pale face. The glow of the growing fire reflected in her changing eyes, her thick dark lashes casting shadows on her high cheekbones.

"If I'm your 'Mate' as you say then how come you aren't bothered by it? Also whilst we are on the subject…mate?"

"As I said, the Fates Above blessed us, we were marked as children. Our touch ignited the mark. Everyone has a Fated, including humans; they just have a smaller life span and no magic so it's harder to find"

Sitting in the chair next to her, I filled us both with a glass of my famous whisky waiting on the table beside me, then changed my mind and left the glasses on the side table. If she really was from the human realm then my drink would make her pass out for days on end.

"Right, like I said I need to get back to the human realm. I don't know how I got here. One minute I was in my basement practically dead, the next I'm here."

Practically dead…practically dead? I would burn the flesh from whomever thought they could touch my Mate.

"Is tha' why ye' were covered in blood?" I bit out, holding onto my anger for when I found whoever did that.

She looked down at her dirty top. "Oh, yeah that's another thing. How am I healed? I had a punctured lung and a good couple of broken bones then I wake up here and heal as if nothing happened?"

Breathe.

Focus.

'BURN THE WORLD TO THE GROUND' my dragon roared his outrage for our Mate. Sweat beaded at my temple from holding him back.

Four

'New Word-Novus Mundus'

Amaya

The giant's jaw ticked constantly under his growing beard; his wide lips pressed into a firm line showing his irritation.

Was it me? Probably-I did tend to irritate people with my presence. I was told countless times not just by Lyal or that bitch social worker but by teachers, shopkeepers and even the good for nothing sheriff and his buddies. We all had a hate-hate relationship-they hated me, and I hated them.

So finding out I was in a supernatural world full of shifters and magical beings and then being told I was apparently not quite human myself, well it didn't fill me with fear as it probably should. I was used to being different. I was used to being the odd one out. But was I different because I hadn't actually belonged to that world? I saved that one for later because the main thing swimming through my noisy mind right then was the fact he said we were Circle Mates? Being as this was a world with animal shifters, I assumed he meant mates as in how animals mated? Or like how in the books I snuck from the library, the shifters mated with their true lovers.

If that was what he meant, he was going to be disappointed.

Again, true love was a creation of someone's imagination.

The giant cleared his throat as his red glowing eyes searched my face. Whenever I spoke, he focused on me with his entire being, never moving, always fully focused. That was a first for me.

"I'm no' a hundred percent sure on tha', but why? Why would ye' want to go back so much when ye' were obviously in a bad position there?" His deep voice rumbled through me, causing goosebumps to line my skin. I don't think I had ever heard a voice so deep before.

I had never spoken with someone like this before now, not including the twins of course. But something about the red eyed shifter man took my usual calm control and stamped all over it. I wanted to yell, I wanted to scream, I wanted to grip that thick hair on his head and pull.

Damn it, focus.

"My foster brothers; they need me. I won't leave them there. They are mine."

It was always hard to hold in the possessive obsession I had for my boys when I spoke of them. I pictured their blond curly little heads pressed together in the small room we shared, curled up in the blanket I stole from the church donation.

My stomach churned with its familiar coldness. I had wasted so much time.

My breath quickened again, once more taking me into a panic I was not used to. Twice in the space of half an hour, I'd complain about how embarrassing that was, but I could only think of my boys.

I needed them. I needed them to breathe.

My vision wavered as I sucked mouthfuls of air into my newly healed lungs, but it wasn't enough.

I couldn't breathe.

The walls were closing in as the ground reached for me.

My heart hammered against my chest as the giant's warm strong arms pulled me into his lap, his warmth wrapping around me as the smell of cake and firewood filled my nose.

"Breathe Mo Chridhe."

His hands slowly ran up and down my arms as I sat on his thick thighs. He was so warm, so big, so strangely familiar. The vibration of his timber travelled through my tense muscles.

I had to get off.

I pushed to my feet and wiped my sweaty palms on my pants. Closing my eyes I steadied my breath and told myself to stop being so fucking weak.

"I have to get back." I repeated.

"Amaya, as ye're Mate I swear to ye', I will help get ye' back to the human realm and get ye're boys. I will protect ye'. But I will no' be leaving ye're side. Whether ye' decide to stay here or there." He stood up before me and held his fist over his heart before bowing low.

Damn. Chivalrous.

"Why exactly can't I just go back?"

"The portals, they're all closed. Have been for years. Tha's why I don't know how ye' got here. But I swear to ye', I will get them boys to ye'"

Portals? Is that how I got here? I would have remembered coming through a portal, wouldn't I? Who was I to argue. I mean once I had my boys, I definitely wouldn't be staying with the giant that was for sure. But there was no denying I could have used the help in getting back.

"So what now?" I asked.

He nodded and walked to the small shelf where he pulled out a pen and thick cream paper.

"I will send word to my connection telling him to meet us tomorrow. We find out how ye're here." He scribbled on the paper before looking back at me "And what ye' are." Just before he rolled the paper up, I just about made out the words

Owe me, so meet at the portal.

Has to be discreet and no involvement of the council.

Why discreet? And who the hell was this council? He obviously didn't trust them. The question was, did I trust *him?*

Taking the paper to his fireplace, he threw it in and whispered 'Libera'. Instead of going up in flames as expected, it caught light then disappeared in a puff of red smoke.

Yep. Actual fucking magic.

I couldn't help but ask, "so what are you?"

"A dragon. The last of them. Soup?"

Seriously? A dragon? I followed him into a spacious kitchen and stood in the doorway watching as he heated a pan of what I assumed was soup over the stove.

Was he a dragon that actually shifted shape and flew in the sky with huge wings? Or was he a dragon as in those cute wiggly bearded dragons? The painting above the fireplace was an obvious sign but my mind couldn't conjure up the image of this man shifting into a mystical beast. I wanted to ask but the smell of cooking food made my mouth water.

I watched on silently as my stomach cramped in hunger. It had been so long since I'd had warm food in my stomach. Any chance of food we had, I made sure my boys were fed first. They always pushed it away and practically force fed me back. They were as protective of me as I was with them.

I couldn't sit in this warm apartment and fill my stomach with food whilst they were in that house with him. No doubt suffering.

The giant slid a huge bowl on the counter and looked at me pointedly.

"Sit. Eat. Then you can wash and sleep. We will find out everything tomorrow." He then filled himself a bowl and waited.

I didn't blink.

My eyes watered.

My mouth watered.

My stomach cramped.

Still, I didn't move.

The silence stretched between us.

He sighed and rested his hands on the counter, hanging his head.

Yep, he was already fed up with me.

"It's not poisoned." He muttered.

Oops. That should have been my first thought, but no, I simply couldn't eat knowing the twins would be going hungry. They relied on me, trusted me. I promised them I would get them when Lyal was done and asleep and I hadn't. How long had I been gone? Two nights? Three? Was the time the same between realms?

My stomach growled loudly.

He sighed again before pointedly sipping from the spoon in my bowl. My eyes tracked the movement. "See, no' poisoned."

Sighing to myself in frustration I wiped my palms on my legs, the urge to grab the twin's hands or to hold a book within my sweaty palms a nervous habit I now had no access to.

"It's not that," I told him, "I can't eat when they aren't."

He nodded his head, eyes full of understanding as he walked to stand in front of me. Placing a warm finger under my chin he lifted my face, his eyes searching mine.

I should have pulled away, told him not to touch me. Told him I didn't like to be touched. But I didn't. Instead I stared into his glowing red eyes and almost sighed at his warmth.

Something was definitely wrong with me.

"If ye' need to find a way back to these boys, then ye' need ye're strength. So eat. Wash. Sleep. Then we will find a way to them." He was right; he was obviously right. I would need strength to get them and run, I would need my strength for when I smashed that pole over Lyal's head, and I would certainly need it for when I slit his throat.

I sat at the round table by the kitchen window as he brought our bowls over and squeezed himself in the chair opposite me, his legs so large and cramped under the table his knees knocked into mine. The soup smelled of cream and tomatoes. My mouth salivated.

I sipped from the spoon and tried my hardest not to slam my face into it and rub the soup into my skin to get it in me faster.

I was so hungry.

"When did ye' last eat Wee one?" There it was again, that tick tick at his jaw line.

I shrugged and slowly sipped more, trying hard not to create loud obnoxious slurping noises. I'd seen someone dip a crispy, perfectly grilled cheese into this type of soup before. The twins and I had had our faces smushed up against the glass of the diner, mouths watering at the sight. I promised them we would try it one day.

Before I knew it my bowl was empty, and my stomach was now so full it could have popped. Looking out the window I couldn't see much. The dark night was clouded and not one streetlight was in sight. The bright cherry of a cigarette glowed as it was lifted to the invisible owner's mouth.

"Where ye're from, ye' didn't get a chance to eat much?" The giant—Rí-I should start calling him Rí-said.

I nodded, "Not really; what little food we got I gave to them. I have to get back."

"Ye' will." He growled, "I'll make sure of it."

***

I had never been so clean, the term 'squeaky clean' was an actual thing. Who would have thought? Rí's shower was amazing. The hot water never ran out and the shampoo smelled of him, like warm freshly baked cake.

I used half a bottle.

Rolling up the work out shorts he had given me; I tied the waistband with a hair tie I found in one of his bathroom drawers. Before I had swiped it, I had stared at it with gritted teeth at the thought of another female being around all of his things, being around him.

Mentally slapping myself for being stupid, I finished tying the shorts and ran my hands through my freshly washed hair. The long silken strands slid along my back and ended at the curve of my butt. I couldn't even remember it looking this nice before. I had taken the kitchen scissors to it when it had gotten too knotty and tangled but it had always grown back unusually fast.

I wiped the steam from the mirror then yelled, "the fuck?"

Because why the hell were my eyes purple? Leaning in to get a closer look, I could clearly see the brown receding.

How many more surprises could I mentally take before I snapped? What would snapping entail? Would I actually give in and act upon my fantasies? Would that be such a bad thing?

I held my breath as I rose to my tip toes, turned around and twisted to see my lower back.

There it was, that godforsaken mark he kept rambling about, the very thing that had been causing the insistent itching all night long. Four rope-like shapes twisted and wound around each other before linking at the top where a purple swirling link joined them all together. Each rope glided along my skin, searching for something. One rope contained a red glow, standing out against the others. Rí's mark. I didn't know how I knew that I just…knew.

Fuck.

The black mist floated in the corner of my eye, taunting me and the mark as if this was some kind of joke.

Adjusting the too big shorts, I looked at my pale bare legs and sighed, Circle Mates, new worlds, magic and the assumption that I wasn't human. Great.

I rushed to the living area to question the giant about my eyes but I saw Rí sat patiently waiting. I should have felt bad that he slept there the entire night giving me his huge cloud bed. But I didn't. The bed was amazing. Not that I slept, because thoughts of Elfyn and Elyas swam through my noisy head constantly.

My stomach gave its usual cold churn. Too many hours had passed without them.

"Mo Chridhe.." Rí looked in awe. He ran his gaze across my face before sliding it down my body, creating a heat withing my core that almost chased away the cold churning. Almost.

"What is Mo Chridhe?" I tried to pronounce it with the roll in the 'r' as he did, but I knew I butchered it. It hadn't been the first time he called me it. I then remembered why I left the bathroom.

"My eyes—"

"Are changing colour; we will find out why. Until we know why, it's best ye' avoid looking at anyone directly."
Right, of course. Show them nothing, give them nothing and expect nothing. No change there.
"My heart." Bright red eyes racked me as I shoved my feet into the scuffed-up converse. I actually hated how much they were going to ruin the thick white socks Rí had given me.
"It means my heart." He cleared his throat and ran his hands through his already messy, thick hair.
"Come, we have someone to meet. He's going to help us," he rumbled as we trailed out of his living area and down the darkened stairs. Silence greeted us as he held the swinging doors open for me.
The bar was empty, only dimly lit by the scattered lamps and candles on each small table. The smell of strong liquor tickled my nose.
The dark wooden bar and matching tables were aged with well use. The dripping wax of the candles had slid and settled within the grooves on the tables and each wall was lined with pictures of various animals and groups of people. Each one as different as the next. Notes of love and signatures were pinned beneath each one.
A memorial wall.
I trailed my hand down a picture of a man holding something bundled up in his arms, the ear poking through the blanket was a sign it was a puppy of some sort…or a shifter. The note read, 'My darling link, forever tied together'.
There was so many of them, so many notes of love, some stained and smudged as if tears had dripped onto the drying ink.

"The fallen. From the war." His deep timber sent shivers down my back; he stood so close behind me, I could feel the warmth seeping into my back. A tingle spread down my neck as he ran his nose along the length of it, inhaling before he shuddered, and his chest made an odd vibrating click.

Was he purring?

Did bearded dragons purr?

Was I fooling myself by assuming that was what he was?

Pulling away, I pretended it didn't happen; the giant didn't need to know how much he affected me.

Clearing his throat he shoved his hand in his pants pockets and pulled out a key. Unlocking the large, black, wooden doors, he pulled them open and let the humid air and grey light in from the street.

Five

'Memories old and new-Memoriam Veteris Et Novi'

Amaya

The air was warm, and my hair stuck to my face instantly. I hated it. I always preferred the cold, a cool breeze against my skin and a dark sky to match my empty heart.

I was expecting the street to be full of animal shifters, flying creatures and people on brooms. Instead, I couldn't see past the crowds of people in front of us, their backs to us as they watched and listened to the voice that boomed further on about the greatest deal of the week, fresh vamps blood straight from the source.

Yep, vamps blood. There were vampires here. Why would anyone want vampire blood? Was it magical? Did I want vampire blood? I kind of did. It would have been a pretty cool thing to own, wouldn't it?

Rí guided me with his hand on my lower back through the crowd that parted the moment they saw the surly scowl and red eyes. Nosy onlookers stared at me; I kept my eyes to the old stone path.

The second we eased out of the crowd I gasped; there it all was, the magic, the mystery, the surrealness. The supernatural. The same bear as last night strolled by with a sack hanging from his neck, a couple walked hand in hand, and both had long thick curling horns atop their heads. A set of wolf puppies ran between legs yipping in their excitement as a tired looking woman ran after them, a smile pulling at her lips. Stall after stall held trinkets and small glass jars of sparkling oddities that I simply needed.

This place was so incredible, I forgot about the humidity. I forgot about the cold churning in my stomach, and I simply gawked at everything. It was like a scene straight from a fantasy book.

"Come, we're going to need coffee to deal with Cole." Pushing gently on my back Rí guided me along the street.

So the person we were meeting was named Cole. That was the first bit of information Rí had given me about his person with 'connections'. The itch on my lower back was soothed by his touch once more and I simply hated that. I hated that I need him to help me get back, so the fact that he soothed my discomfort almost angered me. I didn't need anyone but my boys. I didn't.

I pulled away from his hand and looked through each window we passed desperate for detail, hungry for more information. I wanted it all. Some shops and stalls were similar to my town, such as clothing stores full of fabrics and mannequins. Some stalls held steaming food that made my mouth water. But the rest held so much more, and my brain almost couldn't cram it all in.

A piercing squeak had me covering my poor recently healed ears and wince. Some animal must have been hurt; it must have been dying and screeching its pain for all to hear.

"Dragon man! Who is this?! Oh. My. Fates. Above. You're simply stunning. I love the look!" The rushed ramble took me off guard. A woman with a bright pink apron stood in front of a coffee shop. Her short curls bounced around her head as she jumped up and down in excitement. She clapped her hands and squealed again.

Oh, it was a person. Not an animal.

Rí's sigh had my lips twitching. He really wasn't much more of a people person than I was.

"Come on in. Come on. Hurry up! Tell me everything. Oh you must be special if you have the grumpy dragon looking so happy!" My brows raised as I looked up at Rí's deep scowl and thinned lips. Happy?

Still, he followed her in, yet again placing his hand on the small of my back.

The shop smelled incredible, the roasted nutty coffee smell accentuating the sweet smell of baked cakes. Glass shelves full of iced buns and huge rounded muffins shone brightly under the floating ball of light. Yep, a floating ball of light lit up the baked goods.

My mouth watered yet again. The boys would love them. My shoulders slumped.

The ache returned.

My curiosity diminished.

"Are you guys hungry? Here, have some coffee to go! I'm Bri! This is my shop!" The women Bri, smiled with her entire being. She grabbed two coffees from behind the counter and passed us each one before pointing to the cakes with an eager eye.

Rí licked his lips as he gazed at the glorious treats.

I shook my head and Rí sighed.

"So?" Bri rested her face in her hands, her smile wide as she stared at us with something akin to wonder in her big eyes.

"Oh! Your eye—" Rí cut her off with a firm growl as his eyes brightened ever so slightly. He really didn't want people to mention my changing eyes.

Her large chest rested on the counter as she then whispered another "oh". The counter pushed up her chest revealing a large cleavage that any women would be jealous of. Including myself.

Her curves and long lashes deserved to be appreciated and even I got that, but Rí only stared down at me as he finally said, "Amaya is my Circle Mate."

Bri screeched even louder than before, and I tensed at the high-pitched sound.

Great, he was telling people?

"That is AMAZING, oh my Fates Above how Magical."

My ears hurt.

Usually I shuffled away from overly eager and happy people because well, ugh happy people. But something about the curvaceous, bouncy women intrigued me.

For one, was she some kind of shifter? Was it rude to ask?

Rí cleared his throat once more and ran his hand through his hair. "Thanks for the coffee. We ah, have a meeting to get to."

Bri's eyes widened before she bounced back up and started to clear a table full of empty coffee cups.

"Oh! Of course! Silly me! I'll send some treats across to the bar for you both!" Turning to me she beamed before adding, "please come and talk to me anytime! Like, anytime!"

I was ushered out by Ri's firm hand.

"Wow." I muttered, almost missing his grunt of agreement as the same set of wolf puppies ran between our legs before the air shimmered around them and they turned to little boys with black-as-night hair and eyes as blue as the sky.

Eyes so like my boys.

I remembered the day I saw them for the first time, their blank little faces and their curly blond heads.

I stared at the little white oval pills in my palm. The powder coating my fingers as I counted them. Each one a piece of myself that I had lost in my seventeen years of existence.

I was going to swallow each one with no regret, no one to miss and no one to miss me. There was nothing holding me to this damaged world and I was okay with this.

I wanted to die. I wanted to feel death's cold call and I was desperate to answer it.

I never belonged here, not just this house or crappy town. But here, in this world. I didn't know who I was, who my blood belonged to. I didn't know what family was and frankly I didn't care.

My entire life entailed being beaten and serving Him, my foster father. The town, the school, my very own peers looked down at me. Sensed something in me that I didn't understand.

Breathing in a deep breath of stale air I felt something settle within me. This was it. The end for me.

Lifting my handful of treasures towards my bruised mouth, I froze. Voices echoed through the sparse house. A voice I recognized had my shoulders tensing in memory. The social worker. What madness was this woman there for now? The good for nothing bitch only came round when I either tried to run or she had another money scheme for them to try and weasel into.

"It'll be more money, twins Lyal, twins! It'll be perfect for us." The excitement in the voice ended with a happy squeal.

Yep. Money. The word twins gave me an uneasy feeling in my empty stomach. Looking back to my little oval pills of relief I closed my fingers around them and shuffled on my knees to the cracked bedroom window, dragging myself through the dirt and dried blood on the wooden floor, splinters piercing my skin through my ripped jeans.

There, stood on the dried yellow grass in front of the bitch's old beetle Volkswagen were two small, blurred figures. Pressing my face to the dirty glass, I just about made out two little boys, grasping each other's hands and standing perfectly still as if to be unseen. My breath stalled in my throat. I felt frozen. An unknown feeling unfurled in my chest as I squinted at these little twins.

I had to get closer. Something in me screamed to get closer. To take in the detail of their faces. Slowly sneaking down the stairs I peeked around the corner as Lyal and the social worker's murmurs drifted into the kitchen. Seeing the empty hallway, I snuck out the front door.

There they stood. Big wide ocean blue eyes, messy blond curls that looked more knotted than my own rat's nest hair.

For the first time in a long time I felt the urge to speak, my voice raspy from lack of use. "He–hello." one word. All it took was that one word and time stood still. Nothing else needed to be said. The three of us felt it within our very beings. They were mine and I was theirs. My back straightened, my shoulders firmed and the weakness inside of me turned into something I can only describe as pure obsession.

My clenched fist opened, dropping the pills that almost lost me my new reason for living. They scattered, lost in the overgrown dead grass.

"What are you doing outside?" Lyal's grating voice drifted from the doorway.

Usually the tone of his voice sent shivers down my back, knowing I was about to get beaten or be put on another two-day food ban. But not this time, and never again.

Turning to face him, I stood in front of the twins. He wasn't going to touch them. No one was. They were mine.

My hand burned from the coffee I had squeezed from the cup. I shook my wet hand and froze from the intense look on Rí's face.

"We'll get ye' to them."

"I know."

We didn't stop again. Instead, we walked down the street, dodging the busy crowds and nosy passersby. We didn't have to push through and create a path like others; one look at Rí and the people jumped out of the way. Some outright avoided him. One man even fell into an apple cart, creating a mass of angry market men as the apples rolled into the curved stone gutters. Some apples were pinched by grubby well worked hands. I looked away.

The streets became less busy the further on we walked. The humid air now stuck my t-shirt to my back and the hot coffee made me sweat more. However it tasted incredible, and one of those sweet treats would have complemented it perfectly.

The stalls ended abruptly and, in their place, stood empty barren-looking houses, reminding me slightly of the burnt ones in the Dead village I appeared in.

How did I get there? I had originally thought Lyal had dumped my body in some far abandoned village but obviously not. I was unconscious, beaten to near death and then I was in Wisteria.

I hoped that this Cole had the answers.

A strong sweet and slightly sour smell reached my nose, and I looked up from the thinning stone pathway to see a lone figure leaning against one of the buildings. They were completely covered in its shadow, no detail available except the glowing cherry of whatever they were smoking. They flicked the cigarette but never moved from their position.

I felt their eyes on us, following us as we moved further down the path. Rí's slow stomp tried to match my steps but my small legs hurried to catch up still.

As we wound round a corner, the path completely ended, leaving us walking on dried dirt and weaving through thorny bushes.

"Where exactly are we going?" I said as he took over pulling a long thorny branch from my shorts.

"The Light City." He answered whilst offering his hand for me to climb over a small hump. I ignored the hand and powered through the bushes.

I didn't have help before, and I didn't need it now.

He surprised me by adding "The shadow land is home to the misfits, the shifters and the angry. The Light city is run by the council, all White witches." He looked uncomfortable before continuing, "before the war, all supernatural's were equal. Yes, there were bigger shifters and stronger witches, but everyone was equal. The war tore our realms apart; thousands of supernatural beings died and along with them, the peace."

Wars truly did destroy everything, not just in the human world too it seemed.

"How long ago was it?"

He paused in our walk and looked to me, tilting his head as he searched for some unseen answers in the bushes around us.

"Yesterday was eighteen years exactly."

I kept silent. Nothing added up. I needed the how's and whys and I needed them immediately. I wasn't used to not having the information I needed. I hated the unknown.

We turned one last corner before he stopped in front of a blurred tree. I rubbed at my eyes with the heel of my hands, pushing down until stars appeared.

The fuck? The tree was still distorted by the blur. It covered about 6 ft in a full circle.

"Ye' will walk through with me." Rí held his huge, tanned hand out towards me. Waiting expectantly.

I once again ignored it, pulled my big girl pants up and stepped through.

Six

'Dark Witch-Tenebris Pythonissam'

Amaya

Cool air greeted me. Misty droplets settled on my skin and a slight breeze blew my hair from my face. I was walking on water. All sound was muffled as if I had my hands covering my ears.

Two steps were all it took before my feet settled on hard ground. Opening my eyes, I gasped. All around me hung wisteria trees. Their long drooping clusters of purple petals dangling created a shelter from the beaming sun, the leaves a feathered lace that resembled a fern. There were so many, hundreds in fact. I'd never seen such beauty. A cool breeze blew through their swaying delicate blades causing the fallen petals to gather together on the stone floor.

Birds sung in the distance, harmonising with the leaves when they brushed against each other in the wind, so gentle, so serene.

Something within me had unfurled and stretched. My eyes closed against the breathtaking sight before me as I inhaled the fragrant air. The trees' honeysuckle and Rí's mixture of sweet and smoky surrounded my senses. I didn't know what this feeling was, but I could almost say it was what peace felt like.

"These ones are called a Black Dragon Wisteria." Rí had stepped through the portal and stood with his hands tucked into his pockets. Watching me closely as always.

The air was different here; it didn't slap you in the face with a sweltering heat and choke you, its cool breeze was heavenly on my face.

How was it possible to walk through a blur and end up somewhere so beautiful with entirely different climate zones?

Magic. It was all magic.

There was something about those trees, something important in their magnificent structure.

"Wisteria, is that where the name comes from?" I asked as I ran my hand through a cluster, their petals soft and ticklish on my palm.

"Yes, the First supernatural found this realm, and all tha' was here was land and one Wisteria tree. Their Circle embraced its magic and the realm grew, more supernaturals gathered and the population expanded." He hadn't moved from his spot by the portal. His hands were still tucked in his pockets as he tracked me walking from tree to tree, touching, smelling and exploring the beauty. Nothing had ever drawn my attention like that before.

When a tree's roots dug into the ground and held on with all its might and it grew and expanded, its branches reaching far and wide and its leaves and petals vibrant and strong, it was a sign of life. A sign of a past, a present and its future. It had time. It had viability. Its essence was creation itself.

I hated that.

Hated its freedom to grow.

Hated its healthy future.

Was I jealous of a tree's ability to set roots and grow?

Maybe.

Snatching my hand away from the petals I muttered, "Where do we go now?"

He gestured to a small path covered in fallen purple petals. We walked under the Wisteria in silence. I had no urge to fill the quiet and neither did he.

We didn't walk for long before Rí lifted one dangling full branch and nodded for me to duck under. We entered a small hidden clearing. A circle of trees surrounded us, the floor covered in its petals and a small empty wooden crate rested against a large protruding root.

"He'll be here soon. He's usually late." He grumbled and nudged the crate with a shake of his head, his brown messy hair flopping onto his deep furrowed brow. Something about this giant of a man called to me, with his bright eyes that followed me everywhere and softened whenever they settled upon my face. It was unnerving the way my stomach summersaulted with feelings I was unused too.

I gritted my teeth at my own emotions.

"What is this 'Cole' able to do to help me exactly?"

Sighing, he scratched at his beard before turning those glowing red eyes my way.

"Cole is a White witch, a good one," sneering as if it pained him to admit that he carried on. "He can work out how ye' got here, and if there is a way back. He'll also know what ye' are."

And what was that exactly? What was I? I had thought I was human. Yes, I was peculiar, I couldn't deny that. My morbid fantasies and my tendency to become obsessed with people, well let's just say I'm not normal. But to be told I was something else entirely?

"Why did you seem shocked before, when I said I was human?"

"Because no humans can live in Wisteria."

No humans? So everyone in that busy street we had just left was supernatural. Including that overly happy coffee lady, Bri.

Rí's firewood scent grew stronger as he stepped closer to me. He towered over me with his broad shoulders and tree trunk thighs. "What are ye' thinking Wee one?" He rumbled.

I don't know why I answered. I don't know why I kept giving in to his questions and his touches, but I found myself blurting out, "If I'm not human, then what the hell else could I be? I definitely don't shift into an animal."

And that's when I realised, he hadn't been completely honest with me. The red of his eyes dulled slightly, his jaw clenched shut and he avoided looking into my eyes.

That bastard knew something and hadn't told me.

"Tell me," I growled.

For the first time since I saw him in that burnt out village, the giant turned away from me. It pissed me off more.

"What aren't you telling me?" I snarled again. He had me hiding my eyes, had shut down Bri when she saw them, and now had us hidden in this clearing. He was definitely hiding something.

"I have my theories of what ye' are. But I can't be certain." Turning back to me he ran both hands through his hair and gripped it at the top. His huge arms bulged, and I had to drag my eyes away.

He definitely ate his protein.

I gave him my death stare. The one I reserved for those I created my dark fantasies about. If he didn't start giving me honest answers, I was going to have to put him on my list. And that was a damn shame.

"Ye' might be a Dark Witch Mo Chridhe, not that it's an issue with me. Ye're my Mate no matter what ye' are." A Dark Witch.

Weren't we meeting a White witch? What was the issue with dark ones?

"Why do I need to hide my eyes?"

"Only the Dark Witches have Ye' eyes. Purple eyes."

"Right, so why do I need to hide them?" I asked firmly as I stepped closer to him. I poked his hard chest and pretended it didn't hurt like a bitch. The man was solid.

He wrapped his large hand around mine and held it to his chest. Trapping me to his warmth.

I held my breath.

There it was again, that warm tingle in my core.

"As I said, It's no' an issue to me. But the Dark Witches, they…they started the war. Killed thousands and shut the portals. Trapping all tha' were in this realm on Wisteria. Cutting off everything from the other realms."

Oh. Okay so I could potentially be hated by all and frowned upon. Same shit, different day.

Pulling my hand from his grasp, I rolled my eyes.

"Okay, so I may be hated so on and so forth. How am I a Dark Witch in the first place?"

"Ye' said ye' had a foster father, so you have birth parents somewhere. The question is, where? There aren't any Dark Witches alive. Well, except ye' maybe."

I had never known my birth parents and Lyal had never mentioned them. I could only remember Lyal and his stench. So were my birth parents' Dark Witches?

"If that's so, how was I in the human rea–"

"Human realm? That's not possible." A tight voice behind me said. I spun around and there stood a tall man, with a lean build and neatly styled white-blond hair. His blue eyes were cold as he sneered at me. He crossed his arms, impressing me with how he managed to not create a single crease in his perfectly pressed white shirt.

He was handsome in a way that you hated him. He knew he looked good; he knew he smelled divine with his fresh minty scent, and he knew he was powerful.

What a dick.

He walked further into the clearing, watching me closely, assessing me.

The closer he got, the more details I could see, like the slightly smudged under eyes, the tight pull of his lips, the five o'clock shadow along his jaw even though it was still before noon. This man was tired.

"Cole," Rí rumbled, inclining his head.

"Rí," the man, Cole, nodded back.

I rolled my eyes and sighed.

"If you guys are done, I'd like some answers now."

"As would I. How are you here?" Cole sneered at me once more. I didn't like this man.

"That's why you're here asshat," I sneered back.

He went to take a step towards me but Rí's tan hand on his chest stopped him. I found how quickly Rí moved in front of me quite impressive.

"I called ye' for a reason. We need this discreet."

"And you thought I would play along in your secrets because.." This man was going to be a problem, I just knew it. Why the hell did Rí think this man was going to help us?

His low rumbling growl caused Cole to step back further. His lip curled at him before he said, "tell me what I need to know."

"Amaya appeared in the Dead village. She was passed out in the human realm. She was...beaten" Rí's voice lowered another notch, his jaw ticked as he took a slow breath and continued. "She has no idea how, no power has emerged, no animal. Only her eyes. They were brown. Now they are changing. More and more as the day draws on."

At the mention of my eyes the sneering man snapped his head to me and stared at me in shock.

"Thats not possible."

Obviously was if I was stood there.

"We need to know for sure, and we need to know how she got here."

Cole looked irritated yet intrigued. He walked towards a pile of fallen petals before pulling a glass vial with orange looking liquid out and poured it onto the pile. Steam rose as he started to mutter to himself quietly.

Why was Cole muttering to himself over a pile of steaming petals? Rí didn't seem bothered.

I edged closer to try and listen to what he was saying. He spoke fast, low and quiet and all I picked up was focus. I edged closer still.

"I said focus!" He snapped at me, his blue eyes annoyed as he glared at me leaning over his pile.

"On what!" I snapped back.

"Focus on your breathing, on yourself. Focus on how you felt when you appeared in the Dead Village."

Well someone could have told me I was supposed to be doing something. I glared at Rí who shrugged and slid some of my hair from my shoulder.

I moved back and breathed deeply. Slowly.

Okay Amaya. Focus.

How did I feel when I woke up in the shack?

There was pain, definitely pain. Everything had hurt. It had been a struggle to breathe; the blood clogging my throat and filling my lungs should have killed me. But what did I feel? Disorientated, confused. I had been struggling to walk, to breathe, to even think clearly. My thoughts had been on my boys, how if I kept choking, I wasn't going to be able to get back to them. Then I was walking fine, breathing freely. I had felt strong. For the first time in my life, I had felt strong, I wasn't in pain. And I was ready to act out on my dark thoughts.

The black mist that hadn't left my peripheral vision since waking up in this realm floated there. Always swirling and never quite within sight. A soft breeze blew by us, never once touching the mist.

The gentle wind picked the petals up, spinning them slowly around and around as if they were in a tornado. The steam was now a swirling mass of purple petals as they rose higher and higher.

Cole's eyes grew round as he continued to mutter under his breath. Whatever he was seeing or hearing, it couldn't have been good. The more the petals rose and spun, the more he paled, the bigger his eyes grew and the more uneasy Rí seemed behind me.

What were these spinning petals saying?

Then in one swoop, the wind stopped, and the petals dropped to the ground, now shrivelled and burned.

Cole turned to stare at me with anger and pure loathing on his tired face.

"Well?" I prompted.

"What trick are you playing on us? Hm? Where have you been hidden? What are your plans, Dark Witch?"

So I was a Dark Witch. I wasn't human. I wasn't from the human realm. So many new questions swam in my noisy head, I didn't know what to ask first.

A low growl pulled me from my thoughts as Rí stepped closer behind me once more. "Speak to her that way again Cole and it won't be just your liquor supply going up in flames."

"How did I get to Wisteria? How was I even in the human realm?" I quickly asked as Cole's face scrunched up in anger and slight intrigue.

He paced back and forth, his perfect white shirt rustling as he brushed against the clusters of the hanging branches.

"Tell me exactly what happened, what was happening before you appeared here. Each detail." He asked, giving me a calculating look.

And so I gave him each detail; the swollen eye, the punctured lung, the broken fingers and toes, everything going black. To ripping my poor eye lashes off to see. To being able to walk and breathe freely.

The more I explained, the more the clearing became heated. Petals fell faster as small flames burst from Rí's hands as he also paced back and forth. The red of his eyes were bright and glowing more than usual. His jaw clenched so tightly I didn't know if he would be able to open his mouth again.

I would need to keep a wide berth of those flaming hands.

Cole stopped and stared at me; mouth slightly agape before saying, "I don't think you passed out. I think you died. And with your death, your Dark Witch magic somehow opened a crack in the human portal, bringing you to your true home, reviving and healing you."

I died. Lyal had killed me.

That bastard!

That slimy bastard had gone too far and actually killed me!

"I WILL BURN HIS ENTIRE FAMILY! I WILL CUT OFF HIS–"

"He doesn't have any family" I added helpfully.

Rí's chest heaved in his anger. The heat pouring from his body had sweat beading on my upper lip.

Gross.

"What hut did you land in?" Cole asked, ignoring Rí and his tantrum.

"Why?" I squinted at him, refusing to wipe the sweat now dripping into my eyes. What use were eyebrows if they didn't hold back the sweat!

"I need to see if the crack is still there–"

"-if it is, can I go back through?" Hope bloomed in my chest; I was a step closer to my boys. Adrenaline coursed through me at the thought.

His eyes narrowed at me, untrusting and hateful.

"I don't know which one. I fell through a door and the roof is missing, but half of them looked like that." I answered, happy to help now I knew I could maybe get back to the twins.

He sighed and held his hand out, his nails perfectly trimmed and clean.

"Give me your hand. I'll take the memory and find it myself."

Rí edged closer.

I gave Cole my sweaty hand.

Pain zapped through my body and travelled to my back. I arched and whimpered out in shock and pain. My back itched as if a thousand ants were crawling beneath my skin.

What the fuck.

That wasn't…

That couldn't have been.

"No." Cole's eyes were huge, his face pale as he snatched his hand back and took two large steps back before literally spitting at my feet in disgust.

"I will never link to a Dark Witch."

Rí's angry growl echoed around the clearing as he charged towards the White witch. He grabbed him around the throat and squeezed.

"If ye' ever disrespect my Mate like that again, I will end ye'!"

Cole sputtered and coughed before he placed his hand on Rí's tanned forearm and sparks flew across the dragon man's skin. He shoved Cole away with a hiss that was more animal than man.

"So she is your Mate," The witch sneered.

I wiped my hands on my pants, cleared my throat and cleared my expression.

Show them nothing, give them nothing and expect nothing.

The men turned and looked at me, one full of loathing, another full of rage and something else I couldn't figure out.

"I'm not here to find Mates. I want one thing. Are you going to the dead village or not?"

"You want to go back? Then yes, I'll go to the village, and I'll help you get back. I want nothing more to do with you. I don't want your sickness or your taint. You can go back to the human realm and damn well stay there," he said flatly. His face shut down and I would have clapped at his ease at shutting down if I wasn't so detached right then myself.

"The council can't be involved. They can't know." Rí injected.

"Like I want them to know this," he sneered back, then with one final scowl at Rí, the witch kept a wide berth from me and left the clearing.

Turning to the dragon man, I kept my voice flat and face void of emotion.

"The fuck was that?"

Seven

'Hatred Grows-Odium Credcit'

Amaya

Rí ran his hands through his hair before releasing a long-drawn-out sigh. He looked shocked yet not surprised. He picked up the crate and offered me his free hand.

I ignored it.

Still I waited for an explanation.

"Come, we can visit the White library. Maybe there is a book on ye're birth. Before the war, each birth was recorded."

So he was just going to ignore what just happened?

"Why did the same thing happen with Cole as it did with you?" I asked flatly.

What was with this man and never fully answering me. I could see by the look on his face he was about to avoid my answer.

I gave him my death stare.

Sighing again, he lifted the hanging branch for us to pass through and said, "Circle Mates can be more than one. There can be a Link, in this case Ye'. Sometimes there have been known to be two maybe three Circle Mates that all connect as one."

Okay hold up, more than one Mate? Mates...plural? He was joking. There was no way that's what was happening. I was only just finding out there were entirely different realms full of shifters and magic and I was apparently part of it all.

I hated people, I hated to talk about pointless topics, and I hated to smile and pretend the people around me weren't all sick in their own way with their lies and ignorant ways.

"That's not what's happening here." Not a question-a statement-but there was no way I was ever going to accept having a mate.

"Wee one, Ye seem to be the first Dark Witch in eighteen years. The possibility tha' ye' aren't just mated to me is strong. I knew tha' when I saw ye' eyes. I accept tha' ye' aren't just mine." He stopped walking and looked down at me, my emotionless face reflected in his red eyes.

"My dragon and I have been alone for so long; we welcome Circle brothers in our lives."

More than one. The potential for three. I wasn't made for this. I wasn't made for love. I didn't even know what love was. I didn't know how to love.

The boys were my obsession, my possessions. They were simply mine. I didn't love them, and I know they didn't love me. We didn't have the capacity to love. Our obsession was enough.

Cole's anger and loathing towards me and the fact I was a Dark Witch didn't bother me. I had been hated my entire life. One more person wouldn't hurt.

Right?

I ignored the odd ache in my chest and followed Rí further through the Wisteria trees. His tense shoulders and ticking jaw a sign he was agitated.

I only needed these men to get me back to the human realm. No matter what, that would always be my aim.

I couldn't breathe freely without Elyas and Ellfyn, I couldn't live without them.

I would use Rí's help; I would take their help. But that was all. I had no room or need for anything else.

We walked through the trees in silence before we entered a huge circle garden. More wisteria hung all around, some in pots, some trees and some climbing vines that looped and wound their way through a long narrow pergola that ran the expanse of a perfectly polished stone path. In the centre of the garden stood a huge white stone statue. It was carved perfectly, with sharp angles and soft curves. It was a cloaked man standing tall and proud. He was obviously important.

We veered to the left, coming off the stone path and walked through more trees.

"The head of the council," Rí grumbled, the distaste for the man clear in his voice. Looked like the giant had issues with the people in charge.

"We'll go through the back way; we don't want people seeing ye' eyes Wee one." He walked through thickening trees. Slowly the wisteria thinned, and we eased through butterfly bushes that smelled just as sweet and floral as the trees.

The muscles in his back flexed and shifted as he stalked through the bushes, his large feet trampling through the lush greenery.

He was hiding me, keeping me a secret, like I was something to be ashamed about. He said it wasn't an issue to him that I was a Dark Witch, but now it had been confirmed had he changed his mind? He had said he wanted Circle brothers. Perhaps that's all he actually wanted. He wanted brothers he could bond with, a family. I could understand that. Maybe he didn't want anything more from me than to find his brothers.

I reminded myself I didn't care if he wanted me.

I didn't want him either.

I didn't.

***

After walking through more bushes and a dark looking alley, we entered an old stone building, its aged architecture a thing of beauty and history itself. It was one of those buildings that you just knew held ancient texts that held some sort of important significance to the past. And this was just the side entrance. I wanted to see what the main entrance would look like.

I followed Rí down dark corridors and into a small stuffy office. The stale smell of old smoke and cigars burned my nose. Its desk was a mess with scattered papers, dripped wax and opened leather bound journals.

Each corner of the room held books of all kinds, thick hard backs, colourful leather covers. Each stack was piled high and leaning.

Rí aimed straight for the desk and started opening draws and shuffling the papers about.

"The man is a messy son of a bit–" The clearing of a throat cut Rí off. I turned and inched away from the elderly man stood behind me.

Did I mention I didn't like people?

He was hunched over about my height, with a bald head holding one singular white hair in the middle. His watery eyes were huge behind his thick glasses and a black pipe hung from dry lips.

"What are you doing in my office dragon?" He croaked out before shuffling into the room with a heavy wheeze coming from his chest.

"Sir–" Rí started but was cut off once more by the old man waving a wrinkled hand and shuffling over to the desk, ignoring me completely.

Thankfully.

"Pack that in. Why are you messing up my desk?" If anything, Rí's shuffling had tidied the desk up.

I stayed silent.

"We are looking for the birth records. Eighteen years ago yesterday." Straight to the point it seemed.

The old man arched a bushy white brow and started to hack away from the pipe. His lips held tight around the thin pipe stem as he wheezed and coughed.

"Outta my way then boy!" He snapped when he finally caught his breath.

He sat in the big chair behind the desk with a relieved sigh, then snapped, "Light it up for me will ya!"

Rí sighed and waved his hand towards the pipe; a flame flung from his hand and lit the pipe back up, the smoke now swirling from its end.

I had noticed various things about Rí the past day. When he was angry, his body became so heated, the areas around him singed and burned. In fact, the angrier he got, his eyes burned brighter. He could create and cast flames with just a flick of his hand.

He wasn't a bearded dragon. He was an actual dragon.

"Can you fly?" I blurted out.

His brows raised before a small smile pulled at his wide lips, completely changing his face. His eyes brightened and creased around the edges. He seemed more softer, gentle. Why couldn't I look away?

My chest ached.

Ignoring me, the old man said, "Pass me that book. I'll look there. Then you can get out of my office."

Rí passed him the book and we waited in silence.

It stretched on as the man flicked through page after page. His big watery eyes zoomed through the text before licking a thumb and turning the page.

Page after page, thumb lick after thumb lick.

Somewhere in that book were my birth records, somewhere on that book explained who my birth parents could potentially be. Dark Witches hated and loathed. Dark Witches who may or may not have helped in killing thousands of people and closing off the portals, who somehow put me in the human realm with him, Lyal.

Somewhere on that page were the names of the people who gave me to a monster, and in doing so, created one.

Because that's what I was after all; the dreams I had of hurting people, of spilling their blood and watching as it drained the life from them. That made me a monster, didn't it? Because they weren't just dreams. Oh no.

The second I knew my boys were safe, I was going for Lyal, and I was going to relish in his screams.

The slamming of the book closing ripped me from my thoughts. The man sucked on his pipe then licked his lips and said, "No one was born that year. It was the war after all. Now there was a bloom the year after. But nope. Nadda. Nothing."

"That can't be right." I stormed over and snatched the book from his hands and opened it.

Empty.

The book was empty.

I flung each page over, but it was all blank. No ink in sight. Nothing.

"Mo Chridhe, only the Book Master can read the book." Rí gently laid his warm hand on mine where it clutched at the empty book.

"Now get out," the man snapped as he rose from his chair and finally looked at me.

He stared into my eyes, waited just one second before saying, "And shut the damn door. You're letting the cold in."

Was the old man hiding something? Or were there really no records of me? I had so many questions, and all were unanswered.

We left the building and walked back through the wisteria trees towards the blurred portal.

Rí mentioned there were more ways to find out who my birth parents were, that he would figure something out.

I didn't listen. Instead I looked to the clear sky now turning pink as the sun set, the cool breeze slightly tugging at my long black hair.

My stomach churned. Another day without the twins.

Eight

'My Fated Mate-Coniunx Mihi Destinatus'

Rí

Amaya sat in my armchair opposite the fire. She looked so small; the high-backed chair swamped her.

She stared into the flickering flames with a blank expression. Not a word had been spoken between us since the Bookkeepers office.

I knew she must have been struggling. So much had happened to her in such a short space of time.

My dragon was constantly on edge. He fought me every second to take over and meet our Mate face to face. He clawed at my insides to be let out, and I wanted nothing more than to shift and take to the skies. But our wee Mate was more important than anything me or my dragon could possibly want.

We had been alone for so long. Yes, there was the bar, the entire shadow land in fact, but I was the last living dragon, alone and so very angry. I hadn't allowed myself to shift and fly since I found out I was the last.

I was part of a flight, the biggest one known to the supernaturals, hundreds of us flying through the air, hunting together, sleeping together. Then I was alone. And now we had a Mate. My dragon was letting me know he was awake, and he was ready to spread his wings once more.

I worried if I let him out, he wouldn't take it easy with her, and easy is what she needed right now.

She wasn't one to communicate; I had learned that much.

I was fucking it all up. I knew that.

Sighing, I poured myself another one of my homemade whiskies and drank it in one.

My parents were amazing together. They loved each other deeply and it showed. Dragon shifters were possessive, so when they mated with another dragon, it just worked. They found their Circle bond easy.

This wasn't easy.

We naturally ran hot, easy to anger and we craved our Mate's touch. I had to keep stopping myself from running my nose and mouth along the line of her perfect neck. Her scent would be stronger there and fuck I wanted to taste it.

I wanted nothing more than to rub my own scent on her, I wanted to mark her as mine, to sink my teeth into her neck as I slid my cock into her warm wet pussy. I wanted her screams of pleasure; I wanted all those emotions she hid from the world and I wanted them now.

I had been hard since the moment our marks sparked to life, the constant ache and hunger within me. I was ravenous for her.

But Amaya wasn't a dragon, and she wasn't used to the ways of Mates.

So I had to grit my teeth, steal little touches where I could appease my dragon and fuck me...I needed to try harder. Because I could see my Mate was struggling. And I never wanted her to suffer. It seemed she had suffered enough for multiple lifetimes.

I sighed at myself, pushed the glass away and sat in the chair next to her.

"Tell me about them, these boys of ye'er's." If they were important to her, then they were important to me. If…no, when we got her to these boys, they would be a part of my life too.

She looked at me in shock, her wide eyes now a full purple, the irises bright and clear. Beautiful.

"They are twins, Elyas and Elfyn." She spoke quietly, looking back to the flickering flames.

Her thick lashes fluttered as she closed her eyes, "One year ago they came into my life. They saved me." Sighing and tilting her head to face me, she leaned it back against the chair.

"How?" I asked. I wanted to rage, to heat the room with my blaze at the thought of her needing saving, but I stayed calm. For her.

"I was weak, and I was hoping for the release of death. Them turning up on my birthday, standing together in the front yard. It stopped me. Saved me. Made me stronger. I was pathetic before. I thought my...I thought because I was different, I deserved it all." Her eyes met mine and held.

"I have only known my life in Bluewater Valley. Their lies, their ignorance and Lyal's fists. I've been starving, worked to the bone and so badly beaten, well" …turning back to the fire she sighed yet again. I held my breath and waited for her to carry on. I needed to know.

My dragon held so still within me; we needed to know her story.

"He took it too far this time. He took me away from the twins."

That was something my Mate wasn't. Weak. To have lived a life with that abuse, to have been constantly beaten and starved. And yet she still held her head high, still looked you square in the eye and gave you nothing. Because that's what people deserved from her. Nothing. Yet she deserved everything. And I was going to make sure she got it.

I stood, and extended my hand to her, "Come, there is something I think belongs to ye'."

My palm faced up, waiting, hoping.

Her small hand slid into mine, hers pale and cold against my tanned and warm. My heart hammered against my chest as I closed it around hers, holding it firmly. I never wanted to let it go.

I thought by telling her to hide her eyes was for her benefit, to protect her from the council and their wrath. But my Mate shouldn't have to hide who she was.

Never again would I tell her to hide those beautiful eyes. They should be admired by all; they proved her strength, and they showed her potential power.

Because never before had there been a Dark Witch without power.

Nine

'New Me-Novum Me'

Amaya

No one had ever asked about the boys before, no teachers when I had explained why I had been late, no neighbours wondering who the two boys were, no one.

And yet the giant did.

I took his hand, accepted his help to stand. His warmth had been glorious, my cold skin almost sizzled in his heat.

I let go as quickly as I held on, his now empty hand closed tightly before relaxing and gesturing towards the door.

I knew the bar was full of shifters and magical people alike. I could hear the clinking of glasses, the rowdy laughter and the high-pitched voice of that barmaid Cece.

The sound grated on my nerves.

"There are people downstairs," I informed him. He had made it very clear so far I was to hide my eyes, and now he wanted me to go downstairs? I didn't know what this man wanted me to do. He carried on down the stairs and I followed until he was at the swinging doors. He shocked me by walking me backwards until my back hit the wall. The corridor was so dark the only light was his glowing red eyes. They shone brightly and hot.

He was so close; I could feel his heat through his grey buttoned shirt as I craned my head to look up at him.

My mouth became dry.

"Never again, will ye' hide ye're beautiful eyes." His deep timber was so low the vibration caused me to shiver, my stomach clenched in a new feeling.

"But you said–"

"I know what I said, and I was wrong. Ye' don't hide. No' from anyone. Ye're a Dark Witch. My Dark Witch."

Fuck me I was feverish.

But he was right; why was I hiding? Was it time I stopped with my 'show them nothing, give them nothing and expect nothing?'

Maybe it was time to show the world, or worlds, just who I really was.

Show them who Amaya really was.

This man was fine. There was no denying that. No man or boy had ever made me react this way before. But maybe, just maybe this new me liked to explore this deep wanton need the dragon man brought out in me. You could explore your sexuality without it becoming something further, couldn't you?

I could have my fun, sate this burn that was building low in my stomach and walk away once I was back in the human realm, right?

I breathed in slowly and ever so softly placed my hand on his hard stomach, the muscles bunching under my hand as his breath hitched.

The dark corridor heated.

His eyes brightened further.

I ran my tongue along my dry lips. His chest rumbled as his eyes fixed on my mouth, his head lowered.

"Rí, are you coming?" The blond barmaid asked as she slammed open the double swinging doors.

His head snapped up with a low warning growl. I sighed and lowered my hand back down. He growled again, grabbed that same hand and pressed it back to his stomach.

I wanted to smirk at the woman, yet I kept my face neutral.

"No." Rí growled his answer to her, and I took delight in the way her face tightened before she narrowed her eyes at me and walked back into the bar.

"I don't think I like her," I stated, leaving out the fact I actually didn't like anyone.

His chest rumbled with a low chuckle, brushing against my chest and causing a delicious tingle to spread through my hardening nipples.

His chuckle took me by surprise. I hadn't heard him laugh yet, only his deep grumbles and angry roars. It didn't displease me as I thought.

I pushed my hand against his stomach until he took a step back. I brushed my hands along the baggy borrowed shorts I still wore and walked into the bar with my head high and a grumbling dragon at my back.

A few elderly men sat at the bar with half full glasses and raised them with an incline of their head to Rí before they noticed me in front of him.

Their eyes widened.

Rí guided me to an empty stool beside the men, who still had not spoken but openly stared at my eyes.

"Rí, are you and your friend gunna help me tonight? It's nearly our busy hour," Cece said as she sidled up beside us. Her tight deep purple top cut low, revealing a pair of breasts squished together so tightly it looked as though it hurt.

"Nae, just a quick drink before my Mate and I take a stroll."

Her mouth flopped open, and her eyes swung to my own. Her brows lowered slightly before she beamed, did a little jump so her breasts bounced and threatened to spill from her obviously too small top and threw her arms around my dragon's shoulders.

My dragon? I meant the dragon.

"Oh my Fates Above. That's incredible." She smiled wide, her white teeth going together with an audible snap, just as she happened to put her eyes back to me.

Bitch.

Before the strange urge to slam her face down onto the bar overcame me, she fell into the bar as Rí shook her from his body. He took a step closer to me and placed his warm hand upon my shoulder.

Smoothing down her top she forced a smile once more and rounded the bar and filled up two glasses of the same liquid Rí drank upstairs.

She slid them in front of us, pushing mine a little too roughly so the liquid sloshed over the edge.

I wanted to hurt her.

"Mate did ya say!" Came a strong Irish squeak behind us. Looking behind me I saw the tip of bright orange fluffy hair sticking up. I lowered my gaze and there standing at around 3 ft was a damn leprechaun.

He stood with his tiny hairy hands on his hips with a deep green suit and…flip flops? His hairy toes wiggled in his excitement and I was definitely disturbed.

"Aye! I did indeed. This here is Amaya," Rí proudly announced, his chest puffing out slightly as his hand tightened on my shoulder.

The entire bar quietened before all eyes turned to us. The silence hurt my head, and I gritted my teeth.

I hated the attention.

I inched away from Rí's hand.

"Well fook me sideways me 'lad that's grand!" The leprechaun cheered. He then jumped up onto the bar by using the older man's arms as leverage and lifted my untouched drink in the air and yelled "To Rí and his Mate! Amaya!"

A round of cheers and applause echoed around us, but it was the sing-song yell of "Her eyes are purple!" That quietened the room once more. The atmosphere staled instantly.

"My Mate is a Dark Witch, if tha's a problem to ye' get the hell outta my bar." The dragon didn't yell. He didn't raise his voice. He spoke clearly and firmly.

No one answered.

Rí lifted his drink and swallowed it in one gulp. The cheering resumed.

Huh, were they afraid of Rí? Or was it that he was that respected in this community that no one would argue with him? Either way, my stature of being a Dark Witch was an issue with some of these shifters; I could sense it in some of their stares, the still postures and I could definitely sense it from the hatred stabbing at me from the woman's eyes behind the bar.

"Come with me." Rí's warm breath in my ear caused a shiver to travel down my spine and settle low on my back, circling around that mark and made it tingle.

So far, the itching had been manageable. It had slightly increased after that ordeal with the stuck-up White witch but again, it had been manageable. The heat it gave off the more Rí touched me was almost, nice. I wasn't used to feeling.

Hopping down from the stool, I followed Rí through his bar doors and out into the humid night.

The difference in the temperature between the portals blew my mind, but I definitely preferred the cooling breeze from the Light city.

Here, the sky was covered in thick clouds and covered the bright moon and stars I knew to be above us.

Typical, that something so bright, so beautiful was covered and trapped by something so grey, so bland.

"I have something to show ye'," he said, offering me his hand once more.

Part of me wanted to. It wanted to hold that warm hand and accept whatever he was offering.

But the other part of me, it wanted to shut down, wanted to refuse and give him my death stare.

What would the new Amaya do?

Before I could make that decision, two shapes emerged from the shadows and clicked their fingers, and with the snap a rolled-up scroll appeared in one of their hands.

I squinted at them against the dark and tried to make out their faces, but something, magic perhaps, covered them and made them unrecognisable, almost unfocused and blurred.

Rí made a sound of displeasure before stepping in front of me, shielding me from these shadowed men.

I peeked around his arm.

"Amaya and Rí are hereby summoned by the White council for withholding valuable information–" the voice was cut off by Rí reaching forward, snatching the roll and spitting a flame at it, causing it to burst to light and burn within seconds.

Huh, guess he didn't like that.

"Tha' son of a bitch," he snarled.

Looks like Cole hadn't kept it to himself in the end. He had ratted us out. That prick.

"How dare–"

"Ye' and the council can fuck off." He growled, stalking forward towards the two unfocused people.

They held firm but I could swear I heard an audible swallow.

I snickered.

Wimps.

The dragon man froze and slowly turned his head to look behind at me, his thick brow raised.

I shrugged.

"The council wants the girl. You can stay." The men added in unison, a slight shake to their voices.

"My girl, they want my girl?" His voice dropped an octave, and the humid air became stifling.

This council wanted me, why? Because I was a Dark Witch? Well, fuck them. And fuck Cole and his white magic.

Spotting a piece of sharp glass at my feet, I picked it up, tested its weight and sharpness before gripping it.

The white-hot burn of it slicing into my skin where I held it was utterly delicious.

Something within me settled, the constant churning in my gut eased and my shoulders lowered. A calm unlike anything I had experienced before settled over me. I was going to slice these men up. I was going to finally feel someone's hot blood that wasn't my own splash at my feet.

My face pulled and my dry lips cracked from the stretch. Was this smiling?

"What the fuck.." One of the men muttered before his blurred unfocused silhouette stepped back.

Rí looked back at me again, his angry expression dropping into one of awe.

"Fuck me, Mo Chridhe, ye're fucking stunning." Whilst he was distracted by well, me, the man closest to him took the easy route and reached into his pockets whilst Rí's back was turned and lifted his arm to throw something at him.

I lifted my own arm with my own weapon and went to run forward.

Before I or the man could move any further, Rí's large hand wrapped around his throat, and he lifted him into the air before he threw him across the empty street as if he weighed nothing.

Huh. Okay then.

The one who had eased back before, rushed at the dragon man who was baring his teeth in a wide smile as he essentially took on two men with his bare hands.

He was enjoying himself.

So I dropped the glass, stood back and watched. Because who was I to take someone's fun away? It would have been rude to do so.

It was like dancing, the ebb and flow of arms swinging, the side steps and spins. I hummed the Waltz of the Flowers as I watched him dance.

Just as the orchestra in my head reached its peak, Rí had obviously had enough and grabbed both the blurred men by their heads and slammed them together. Knocking them out and throwing them to the floor.

How anti-climactic.

Rí wasn't even out of breath. If anything, he seemed calmer.

I got that.

His bright eyes sought me out before a huge grin split his face. My face did that strange pulling and stretching back.

It hurt.

"Come my Wee Mate. Let me show ya' what's ye'res."

After walking in silence for a while we stood in front of another blurred tree, this one hidden and overgrown by bushes and thorns. At first, I didn't see it.

Another portal.

I gave Rí a questioning look. Why were we here?

"The Dark Witches lived on the Dark Mountain. Only the true blooded and their Mates could pass this portal. The Mountain will no' accept anyone else. The

Mountain and anything on it are ye'res Wee one. A home for ye' and ye're boys."

I frowned and muttered "How, if they're hum–"

He held my face between his big hands, trapping my gaze to his. "Ye' are a witch Amaya. Ye'll find a way."

A home. For my boys and me. Somewhere safe, somewhere ours.

Somewhere we could be us and nothing less.

Was it a possibility?

My stomach ached for them, for their presence.

Yes. I would find a way.

If I was a witch, I had magic.

Right?

I nodded against his hands and said with conviction. "Yes. For the twins."

Lowering his hands, we stood side by side and stared at the portal, unsure on what awaited us on the other side.

***

My ears popped as we stepped through, my feet sunk into the wet ground and a cold mist blew my hair across my face. The dark sky covered the stars but the moon shone brightly through a break in the clouds. Its light made the green moss that covered the ground, rocks and tree roots vibrant and almost glowing.

The trees were tall, dark with black leaves that dripped…purple liquid?

It dripped onto my hand and ran down my wrist as I held it up to look closer. Its purple smear fell from my skin and landed onto the moss.

The trees rustled noisily before two thick branches moved by their own accord and wrapped around my waist. Holding tight, the leaves tickled.

Rí growled and reached forward to rip them off but I batted his hand away.

"Stop, they aren't hurting me," I muttered in awe. The trees' movement seemed as though they were petting me.

The leaves patted at my skin as the branches circled my waist in a tight hug.

"What are they doin'?"

"I don't–"

A firm yet soft voice answered before I could. "They are welcoming their Lady home of course."

Okay so I'm ashamed to say I froze. Before us stood a man, dressed to the nines in his shiny dress shoes, a long black tailcoat with pure white gloves. His hair was black and slicked back revealing perfectly trimmed black eyebrows, tiny glasses and a jiggling moustache.

A butler.

Except he wasn't just any butler. No no. He was glowing in a huey white shimmer and flickered. He was a damn ghost!

"Um…what?" I gracefully said as I petted the branches gripping me.

Another branch snuck out and poked at Rí's face before sneaking around his thick thighs.

The ghost butler bowed low and spoke smoothly, "I am Jerry. The Dark Mountains assistant. I am now and forever more at your service my Lady Darkness."

What the fuck?

He spoke as if the mountain itself were alive, and Lady Darkness? Yeah, not happening.

He straightened up and before I could blink, he was in front of me. He hadn't walked or ran; he just appeared there. Rí's unsettled growl had the branches releasing us and sliding back into the darkness.

"The Mountain and I have been waiting a long time for you, my Lady. Everything is as it should be. The fire in the master suite is ablaze and-" He looked down to my borrowed baggy shorts and wiggled his moustache. "-clothing more suitable to you has been pressed and hung up for you."

Okay what!

He's been waiting for me? Master suite? I wasn't even going to pretend to know what pressed clothing was. My mind grew noisier as I stood dumbfounded.

"Thank ye' Jerry. I am Rí, Amayas Mate. Ye' say ye've been waiting?"

At least one of us had it together.

Jerry looked at me when he answered, "Of course. We serve the Dark Ladies, always have and always will. We have been waiting for you since your birth twenty-one years ago."

"I'm eighteen not twenty-one."

His moustache wiggled and Rí frowned before looking down at me, a questioning look on his face.

"I can assure you-you are twenty-one. As of yesterday in fact."

He had to be mistaken. I was definitely eighteen, wasn't I? Could there have been a chance that bitch of a social worker and Lyal forged my foster papers? They had definitely taken the boys from somewhere, so could they have taken me too? Why would Lyal have kept me three more years than he needed too?

"This could be why the Bookkeeper couldn't find ye' records." Rí added.

Fuck.

Fuck I wasn't even eighteen? I could have been free three whole fucking years ago. Three years of extra beatings and violence.

But then…if I had been free, I wouldn't have met the boys.

I was torn in my emotions and I hated it.

"Please, come to the house and get settled in." Jerry bowed low again before puffing into thin air, leaving behind a small glow where he had stood.

My stomach hurt, my head was noisy and the black mist in the corner of my eye constantly distracted me and just plain pissed me off.

Every time I tried to catch a direct look at it, it moved with my head. Always out of reach with its swirling mass of blackness.

I looked to the moss-covered stone path, took a breath and followed it.

Because no matter how much my mind screamed that this was all just too much, Elfyn and Elyas were more important.

Always.

Ten

'Deadly Passion-Mortiferum Passion'

Amaya

We walked along the path until we reached huge iron gates, open for us to enter with stone pillars on each side and hauntingly well-crafted stone children atop them. They pulled at the skin of their faces, stretching the skin with their mouths open in a scream.

Through the gates led to an open graveyard, each stone perfectly polished and dated with Latin numerals. The earth around them was fresh with more moss scattered on the ground making it soft to walk upon. Each grave had a sprinkle of the deep purple Wisteria petals. It was obviously well looked after.

It was beautiful here.

Call me morbid but I loved a graveyard, to see the many lives that were here before now gone. To see how many had accepted death's hand and given in to the coldness.

It was peaceful.

I brushed my fingers across the top of the headstones as we passed, and with each brush of my fingertips atop the stone, a vibrating tingle spread through my bones.

Since being told I was a witch just a few hours ago I had been wondering why I hadn't had any magic, why I hadn't felt any buzz of power in my body.

But now, standing amongst the dead and breathing in the fresh air around us, I could sense it. It was thrumming through my veins and begging to be used.

This mountain was my home. I could feel the call of it. I swear I could hear the whispers in the wind, calling my name and welcoming me home.

Looking up from the dead's resting place I froze, Rí's warm torso brushed my back as he stepped close behind me.

Fucking hell.

Stood before us was a huge gothic style castle. Its old stone was perfectly carved with intricate details and high arched windows. More of the screaming children were carved into the stone walls and archways. A set of large dark wooden doors sat dimly lit by floating black dripping candles in an archway. The moss gave way to stone as the trees around us thinned out.

The sound of crashing waves met my ears, and I looked around us for signs of the sea.

Rí gently pressed on my lower back with his hand, encouraging me to go further.

The warmth of his hand sent tingles to spread around the mark, creating an irritating itch.

I ignored it and carried on to the door.

Etched into the wood read, "Sub silentio custodire."

"What does that mean?" I quietly asked Rí without turning around. I knew he was behind me.

"To keep under silence." His deep voice echoed in the quiet.

It was then I realised that it had gone utterly silent. The wind still blew but there was no sound to it, no crashing waves, no birds or rustling trees.

There was no noise in my head. Nothing but utter silence.

My eyes widened. There was no noise in my head, no constant chattering of the voices telling me to hurt, to spill blood and seek revenge. No screaming for my boys.

Just silence.

My eyes fluttered shut, my heart slowed, and my hands unclenched at my sides.

Peace.

The sudden whoosh of air and sound penetrating my ears made me flinch back against Rí. His hands settled on my shoulders as all sound resumed, the wind, the waves. My damn noisy mind.

The double doors swung open of their own accord. Darkness greeted us for a moment, before candles burst into life and the foyer lit up in a warm glow.

Holy fuck this was actually a castle.

"Ah, there you are my Lady." Jerry the ghost appeared bowing low.

"Jesus–please call me Amaya. I'm not a Lady." That title would never stick, and I would never answer to it.

His moustache jiggled but he didn't reply.

I walked to the wall where paintings of women all looking vaguely similar sat in stunning black dresses. Their long black hair was either straight like mine or held a wave or curly spindles. They all wore a necklace with one black jewel nestled between their breasts. Looking closer I noticed that a small glow of purple could be seen in the jewel. Purple like each of their eyes.

Every single one of the women in the paintings held features similar to each other, their dark hair, pale skin and full lips. But it was their eyes that stood out. Purple gazes stared out as if looking directly at me.

Dark Witches.

"Your ancestors my L–my Darkness." The ghost's eye twitched beneath his tiny spectacles.

"Not that either." I raised my brow at Rí as he stifled his chuckle.

"Tell me about them, please." I asked.

"Each Dark Witch born is female, their magic pure and strong. You all came from the same witch, the first ever Dark Witch, Lady Samara." He glided to a larger painting further down the wall, this one held above the biggest fireplace I had ever seen, its stone yet again perfectly polished.

Holy shit.

Lady Samara. I looked just like her. Our pin straight long hair and pale plump lips, our noses, our flat expressionless faces. If I didn't know better, I would have said someone had painted me and put it up there.

The cold empty look in her purple eyes sent a shiver down my spine.

Her soul had been empty. Cold and barren. I recognised that look in my own gaze.

Rí must have assumed my shiver was from the cold as he waved his hand towards the fireplace and started the flames. I preferred the cold, always had but I actually enjoyed the heat it created on my cold skin.

"Lady Samara discovered Wisteria, and along with it, portals to the other realms. Where she went on to meet her four Circle Mates. She is the only supernatural to have ever had four within their Circle."

Shock had me gaping at Jerry. She discovered Wisteria. I was a descendant of someone who discovered the entire realm.

If I was part of a line of powerful purebred witches, how had I landed up in the human realm, weak with no magic and beaten daily by a pathetic human?

"Why was I in the human realm? Why wasn't I with the Dark Witches to begin with?" I had to know, I needed to know.

Rí's hand rested upon my shoulders once more. I didn't shake him off, which surprised us both.

"Why, you were with them at first of course, until your third birthday. Then you were taken to the human realm. But I'm afraid that is all I know. All I was allowed to know. Rightfully so of course." He bowed low once more before sweeping his arm to the side where a winding stone staircase led down somewhere cold and dark.

"Please, your suite awaits where you can settle in with your Mate."

All he was allowed to know? I was three and with the Dark Witches? Was I with my mother? Why had I no memory of this? Nothing at all. Not even a hint. I gritted my teeth as my head began to throb once more.

It had been an incredibly long couple of days. My stomach cramped in hunger, and I realised that Rí and I hadn't eaten since the soup.

I frowned at him and asked why he hadn't eaten.

He tilted his head; red eyes glowing in the candlelight and mussed his hair. "If my Mate won't eat then nor shall I."

Okay, there it was again. That word. 'Mate.' It infuriated me. I had never actually agreed to be his mate. Not once. And he and everyone else was throwing it about as if it had been accepted already.

I couldn't help snapping, "stop saying that. Mate. I never said I would be your mate."

Jerry stood still, his glow still and unwavering with his arm still swept to the side.

Rí leered down at me and stepped right into my space, forcing me to crane my neck up at him. "Ye' are my Mate. End of. No discussion needed. Now, do as the nice ghost said and go to ye' suite." His eyes blazed bright and heated, his jaw ticked, and I could have sworn his teeth looked slightly sharper.

Something was seriously wrong with me. Like seriously. Because why did I find that hot? Why oh why did my core heat and my thighs clench at his assertive tone?

I kept my mouth shut so as to not embarrass myself and stomped off down the dark staircase.

We entered a large room, with floor to ceiling arched windows with the view of a dark sea smashing its waves against the rock around us.

The fucking castle was built into the side of the mountain. My mouth dropped open as I took in the sight before me. A bed so large it could hold six large people easily. The four posts held thick black drapes that held silver threading. The deep wooden headboard had a circle carved into the wood, with winding ropes linking at the top.

Another stone fireplace with a crackling fire and two plush armchairs sat in front. Right in front of the huge windows was a small table and a loveseat. Candles were lit everywhere, every surface they could rest on, the wooden dresser and wardrobe, the shelves and bedside tables. Candles hung from a black stained-glass chandelier and somehow provided no dripping wax.

"Wow," I breathed.

Jerry bowed once more before poofing from the room. Leaving us alone and heated.

A hand slid around the back of my neck, gripped it and pulled my head back. Red narrowed eyes stared down at me. Sliding his hand round to the front of my neck he gripped it tightly. His hand was so large, his fingers met at the back.

I could breathe, but not as freely. My mouth dried as my eyes grew heavy.

I said nothing.

His chest expanded as he inhaled deep, before releasing in a shuddering breath. His eyes closed as his head leaned down and inhaled again.

"Fuck, I can smell ye', smell ye' want for me Wee One." He growled, the vibration of his voice causing me to pant. I was needy. I was hungry for something I hadn't had before.

I wasn't naive. I was a grown woman. I just hadn't allowed myself to want this before. But I was the new

Amaya, right? I was the Dark Witch and could take what I wanted.

And I wanted this.

I placed my hand on his hard chest, then slowly ran it down to his stomach and leaned into his grip around my throat. Cutting off my air completely. My eyes closed and I licked my dry lips. My chest burned; lungs searched for air.

He released my neck, air whooshing through my lungs as I gasped and opened my eyes.

He looked down at me, a question in his eyes.

I nodded.

"Say it." He growled.

"I want you. Now."

His hands gripped the back of my thighs and lifted, wrapping them around his waist. I gripped his hair, and I looked into those red eyes. So warm, so heated, so ready for me.

Slowly I lowered my mouth to his. Pressing my lips to his ever so gently.

His hold on my thighs tightened.

I breathed in his firewood and cake scent, tasted it on his breath. I was soaking. I almost hurt with how much I needed him.

Gentle wasn't enough. It wasn't what I needed.

He sensed this and smashed our mouths together, our tongues tangling, teeth clashing. I pulled his hair to angle his head better. My legs tighten around his waist as his hard stomach rubbed against my heat oh so perfectly.

I needed more.

He walked backwards whilst running his tongue down my neck before sucking at my thundering pulse.

A slow low moan escaped me. Surprising me.

He spun us around before dropping me onto the top of the dresser, candles and various bottles clattering to the floor. Scraping his teeth along my neck, my back arched as a moan escaped me again.

I was on fucking fire.

My back was burning up, screaming for his touch on my bare skin.

He slowly brushed his fingers along my thighs. I shivered and clenched them tighter around him. Sliding his thumbs into the crease of my thighs he stroked them back and forth. My skin burned everywhere he touched.

Ever so slowly his hand slid further up my shorts, before his fingers found my aching heat.

I shuddered as he growled, "So needy for me Mate." I couldn't register what he was saying. I needed his hand to move, to slide into my wet heat and cause friction.

He had to have read my mind, because he then slid his finger along my slit before sinking it into its heat. Moaning deeply I gripped his hair tighter as my eyes slid shut.

"Look at me Mo Chridhe, look at me when I make ye' feel good." He rumbled, low and oh so perfect as he circled my bundle of nerves. His growl of approval had me moaning low and needy as he opened my mouth with his tongue seeking my own to tangle in a wet hungry dance.

"Please," I whimpered against his mouth, shocking myself. God, I needed more.

His fingers ghosted across my collar bone, trailing between my breasts before circling my tight nipple. He lifted the aching mound, bent and sucked my nipple through my top. The friction of the wet material pulled more moans from me. I held his head to my chest as his fingers slid against my soaking pussy. Circling that bud so slowly before he finally slid a finger down to my opening. I waited oh so impatiently. Still he didn't move.

Growling, I tilted my hips, causing his finger to slide into me. My eyes closed as I moaned a slow, "fuuuck."

"Greedy little Dark Witch," he chuckled against my chest. Looking me in my eyes he slowly began to thrust his finger in me. His large thick digit stretched me, but I was greedy. I wanted more.

He knew what I needed, as he slid another finger deep inside me. Thrusting harder now, pulling deep moans from me as he circled my bud with his thumb. Something was building within me. It was unfurling and spreading; its string was lit and the bomb was ready to explode.

My heart hammered and matched his in tempo. My back heated even more as the Circle mark swirled. I could feel his red rope moving under my skin.

He leaned down to my neck, before nipping at the skin there and finally oh fuck me finally he bit down hard, not enough to break the skin but enough to make the whirlwind within me to explode. I shattered. Stars shone behind my closed lids as I sunk my nails into him, holding onto him tightly as my body floated in exhilaration.

The sound of shattered glass and crumbled rock had me flinging my eyes open.

The room was in disarray. The window had shattered, the chandelier had crashed to the floor and the walls held a huge crack.

"How.." I breathed.

"Ye' Wee One. It seems we woke up ye're magic." Baring his teeth in a wide grin, Rí placed a gentle kiss to my lips before lifting me up and placing me carefully to the floor.

I looked at his solid length straining against his jeans before reaching for the button. I wanted it. My hands ached and my mouth watered for its attention.

I really was greedy.

"Nae, until ye' are ready to accept tha' we are Mates, I can only give ye' pleasure. It was hard enough to hold my dragon from marking ye' then. When your tight little pussy gripped my fingers…" He licked his lips and growled "Until ye' can accept what we are, I can no' give in."

Not give in? Then he was never going to enjoy me fully, because I would never accept him fully. I would never give in and allow a man to fully have my soul. I barely had enough soul for myself.

A knock at the bedroom door had us both turning. Jerry appeared with a scroll in his hand.

I rolled my eyes at the same time that Rí growled.

"The council has summoned you, my Lady."

I wasn't going to hide. I wasn't going to run. If the council wanted to see me so badly…then fuck them.

"Remember my Lady. You are a Dark Witch. They have no hold on you. No one does." Jerry surprised me by looking me straight in the eyes, his mouth set in a firm line. "You have magic." He carried on, "Find it within you. It was always there. Always waiting."

Then poof. He was gone, leaving me staring at his left-over glow.

Inhaling deeply, I searched for that angry buzz within my veins. Once I found it, I held on tight, gripped it with everything I had and pulled it forward.

I released my breath. And with it, the magic I had found within me.

As quickly as I found it, it dwindled away, hiding from me in the depth of my soul. But I knew it was there now, as I could feel its life within my veins. I would bring it forward. I wouldn't stop trying until I could bring this power forward and finally fight back. I wasn't weak; I was strong. I was a Dark Witch.

Slowly Rí looked down at me, his mouth stretched, and his teeth flashed as he smiled wide at me.

Mother fuckers better be ready for me.

Eleven

'Death's Warrior-Bellator Mortis'

Ziel

The smoke climbed my throat and drifted from my mouth, floating up into the humid night. The effects of the forbidden drug eased my muscles and created a cotton-like barrier around my brain, quieting the constant noise within.

I was born for war, Death's warrior, his soldier. To serve him is to serve a God, yet he was gone, leaving me with a dangerous power that begged to explode and coat anything and everything in its glorious flames. They wouldn't just burn; they would sear them from the inside out, killing them slowly, shattering their soul and providing me with its broken shards. I'd claw it from their melting bones and swallow it, devouring everything they were and more. Leaving nothing left.

Smoking Mayfeaver was the only thing that kept my mind exploding with the flames, the only thing that kept me semi-sane and everyone around me alive. I was an abomination. Feared by all.

My Circle link was different to other supernatural's; because of my deadly nature the second I laid eyes on who was to be mine the mark would come to life. I didn't have to place my hands on their bare skin. Simply being in their presence was enough for the Fates Above to be their bitch selves and mark her for death.

The fact that my mark slithered under my skin when that scrap of a girl walked through the Dead Village was laughable. The Fates Above were a joke. They were laughing down at me like I was some fool. I had smelled her dark fruit scent through my smoke and my mouth had watered. It pissed me off that I reacted too easily.

I didn't need a weak little girl to protect. I didn't want to swoon over some simpering female. If I had to mate, then I wanted someone strong and dark, someone well matched in the pain I was willing to give.

And so I watched her from the shadows. Watched her with that dragon and the way he couldn't help but touch her. I watched and I stalked but I never showed my face. Never approached her. Why would I?

Then that stupid leprechaun had announced she was mated to the dragon. Rí. He was a grumpy shit, equally feared and nearly as equally powerful. He was well suited for her, as he was strong and could protect her. Her delicate features and tender skin needed to be cherished.

I didn't 'cherish'.

I gave pain.

And I loved it.

But something about her called to me, called for me to mark her and take her as mine. My skin crawled and itched with the need.

I wouldn't give in.

I wouldn't touch her.

But that didn't mean I couldn't watch from afar.

It didn't mean she still wasn't mine.

"I'd like to see her on her knees. Damn. That mouth around my cock. Yeah, I'd show her who her daddy was." A nasally chuckle had my eyes flicking up bringing me from my thoughts. There at the end of the alley, taking a piss against the wall were two greasy vamps. Hand leaning against the wall, and the other holding his tiny dick, he hung his head as he laughed.

"Ooh yeah, that long hair. Fuck-you could choke her with it. Fresh meat." They both groaned.

Flicking the end of my smoke to the floor and blowing out that last remaining hit, I rolled my shoulders. Oh I knew who they were talking about. My vision flickered, the dark alley becoming clear, my night vision casting the two vampires in clear sight. Each detail of their dirt-ridden clothes to their hanging unwashed hair could be seen clearly.

Oh yeah, I definitely knew who they were talking about.

Stepping forward, I let them see me, emerging from the shadows.

The fear in their eyes was delicious; I could taste it, sour and cold. Their eyes widened, their screams lodging in their throats as I gripped their necks in my now skeleton hands. Black vines slithered from my leather jacket and wrapped around their faces; my blue flaming skull-face reflected in their eyes. It would be so easy to just exhale the flames right now. So easy to coat them in its soul-eating heat. To sip on their vile poisoned souls. But I didn't think I'd be able to stop. So instead, I crushed their throats in my hands, their necks crunching and squelching as their blood burst free, covering my bony hands in their cold vampire blood. The life drained from their eyes, as I looked on, transfixed with the dwindling life before me. So easily taken, so easily lost. All mine to take. So. Damn. Easy.

The slow drip of their blood shook me from my thoughts. Dropping the vamp in disgust, with his tiny dick still dangling out, I pulled an empty vial from my jacket, uncorked it with my teeth and filled it with the remaining one's blood. You never know when you might need it.

Throwing him to the floor, I called my magic back and stepped over the bodies, wiping my bloodied hands on my black jeans as I made my way down the darkened street. I had a Dark Witch to find and watch. The Fates Above had provided me with entertainment, and who was I to say no?

Twelve

'Living Power-Potentia Viventem'

Amaya

Jerry provided us with a huge spread of food. He laid it all out on the small table in front of the floor to ceiling windows, which were now perfectly intact thanks to the ghost and his grand show of magic.

Cheeses, fruits, breads, meats and various fillings for sandwiches were piled high.

I told Rí to start eating while I changed. And boy was I shocked when I found a perfectly stocked wardrobe full of clothes that were exactly my size. I chose a pair of ripped black jeans, a long sleeve black top and black biker boots. I'd never worn new clothes before; they were soft to the touch and smelled untouched. As I laced my boots, my mind wandered to the boys.

No doubt, they were huddled together in our small room, in their tatty goodwill clothes, silently waiting.

I internally heaved.

I forced the food down my throat, not tasting a single thing. I didn't get to enjoy it. I didn't deserve to.

This castle, with its dark secrets and power within its very walls would be their home, and when they were by my side, I would truly enjoy its true meaning of home.

"Let's go," I said to the dragon. He was reluctant to go to the council, but after telling him I wasn't hiding, as he encouraged me not to do, he gave a stiff nod of his head, and we made our way back through the graveyard.

We walked slowly and silently as we weaved through the headstones. The trees around us still wept that odd purple liquid-tears-Jerry had told me as he laid out our food. The trees wept for what once was and the great loss it endured.

A loud caw had my head snapping to the direction of a rustling tree. There, sat on a moving branch was that damn crow. It flew from the branch down to the ground and pecked at the dead animal below the tree. Its insides bursting from its stomach and eyes empty of life was obviously a perfect meal for the crow.

"Are you following me?" I asked it flatly. Rí looked at it with a scowl, ready to squash it in his giant hands no doubt.

It pecked at the roadkill, pulled the eyes with its beak as the meat stretched before snapping from its tendon.

I bent down to its level. Not once had it removed its eyes from me, always watching. It pulled at more meat.

"I'm going to keep you," I decided as I petted its head gently. "I'll call you–" looking at the roadkill and its squashed half-eaten eyes, I clicked my fingers "Ravioli. I'll call you Ravioli."

Swallowing its last bite it surprised me by jumping on my shoulder and digging its talons in sharply to hold on.

I had a pet.

The strange swirling in my gut and warmth in my heart was unrecognisable.

The dragon shook his head and grinned at me. He kept silent.

That odd need to stretch my mouth and bare my teeth pulled at me. I wanted to smile.

How odd.

***

The streets of the Light City looked so normal, so human. The night was now ending, the day was rising and the pink glow from the sun created beautiful shadows along the tall buildings. People were starting to rush about and looked like everyday businessmen. No children wandered about and there were no signs of shifters. It was so different to the shadow land, where magic was obvious and the people changed their form in the street, where children's laughter could be heard from all angles. Perhaps further into the day it would change?

One thing was the same however, and that was their reaction to Rí; they gave us our space and avoided his angry stare. My own eyes caused gasps and I sneered as two well-kept women gave my outfit a disgusted look.

Fuck them.

I didn't care what I wore before, and I didn't now. But these jeans, these super comfy boots…they were mine, provided by my ghost, from my castle on my Dark Mountain. I had things for the first time in my life and I wasn't going to let some stuck-up bitch make me feel out of place.

Not anymore.

Or perhaps I was completely wrong, and it was the crow Ravioli, my new pet, still gripping my shoulder. I reached up and smoothed his little head as we walked towards what I thought was a large greenhouse, but once entering and walking past the growing fruit trees, we came to a random wooden door. Right there in the middle of the warm glass encased room. I walked around it in a circle. No walls supported it. It just stood there.

I gave Rí an arched brow.

He sighed and turned the handle, but before he could push the door, it flung open, snatched from his grasp.

There he was again, with his perfect white-blond hair and eyes that hurt to look at. With his deep purple under eyes and stubble, he looked even more tired than a few hours ago.

It felt like days ago we had stood in that Wisteria clearing but it had in fact only been hours.

The dragon growled loudly and reached forward for Cole, gripping his uncreased white shirt in his grasp.

"If you're quite done you brute. I did not tell them." Cole snapped.

"And why would we believe that?" I asked.

His blue ocean eyes snapped to me.

My back tingled and itched, asking for attention from the leering man. I told it to stop being such a whore and glared at the White witch.

Cole ripped himself from Rí's hand and smoothed out his shirt. "Not that I care what you think. I didn't tell them."

I didn't believe him. The twitch in his eye was shifty. I narrowed my eyes further at him. This man was untrustworthy.

Shit my back was so itchy.

I couldn't help but reach back and rub at it, which was a mistake because I then noticed Cole doing the same before he snatched his hand back and closed his expression off to me.

Good, hide your emotions witch. You're not going to get anything from me either.

I shut my own face down.

"I'm here to take you to the council," he muttered before spinning on his heel and walking back the way he came.

Sighing, I followed him through the door before he turned to me once more and sneered, "the bird stays."

Ravioli jumped off; his widespread wings were quite majestic as he flew from the greenhouse.

We walked through a pure white corridor. The floor, walls and ceiling were all pure white and at the end waiting for us was another door. This one almost unnoticeable with it being also pure white.

I detested the colour.

Cole stopped and waited for us to catch up from our slow lazy stroll with an irritated look upon his tired face.

"I don't know what they want. My plan hasn't changed. I don't want you here. They don't know about our mark. So just answer their questions and then leave so we can find your answers and send you far fucking away."

I had no plans to inform him my plans had changed, that my boys were going to be coming to Wisteria with me, that I planned to find a way for them to stay on the Dark Mountain with me.

We entered an oval room. Above us was open sky, the morning sky bright and fresh. In the centre of the room stood a huge wisteria tree; the winding trunk led to the largest purple clusters I had seen yet. A white table spanned it with four white chairs that held three people in white cloaks, their faces hidden by the hoods.

What was with these people and white?

They each rose from their chairs and stood in a line before us. Cole moved to stand beside them, his shoulders back and his face tense.

What a dick.

Rí edged in front of me, shielding me from their view. I huffed and moved beside him.

"Amaya. Dark Witch. You have been summoned here for hiding your identity and magic source from the–"

Yeah, fuck this.

"I've hidden nothing," I called out.

The cloaked person in the middle removed his hood, revealing a middle-aged man with long salt and pepper hair tied at his neck. His cold dark eyes stared at me intently. My throat dried up the longer he stared at me.

"You have–"

"I have been stuck in the human realm and only just found out about the supernatural. I had no idea I was a witch. I don't know how I got here."

The other two figures removed their hoods, their bright red hair and matching green eyes just as cold and just as assessing as the first man.

"The human realm has been lost to us for eighteen long years. The portals have been shut. Closed off to all. Even us council members have been unable to open them." The salt and pepper man said sharply. He raked his eyes down my body and sneered "How is it a girl was able to open it and travel through?"

Something about this man's eyes hurt to look at, the coldness within them so familiar to the hatred I had seen in Lyal's daily.

"I died. Then I woke up here and found out I was a Dark Witch." I answered flatly.

His forehead creased as he raised his brows, mouth slightly parted in shock. "You died?"

I stared at him quietly as he assessed me in his own silence. The red-haired men hadn't said a word and Cole's eyes stared holes into my head.

The atmosphere was wearisome to me. The humans from my town avoided looking at me. They avoided me at any cost and ignored any sign of the abuse that was inflicted on me.

But here in Wisteria, everyone stared, everyone looked at me and I hated it just as much as being ignored.

This is why I hated people.

"It would explain the sudden shift in power," he muttered, obviously speaking to the other council men. No one answered him.

The three of them stood still and silent once more.

"Umm.." I raised my brows at Cole and bit my lip at the awkwardness. The White witch looked at my mouth and froze before giving me his normal sneer.

"They are silently conversing. Quiet."

The warmth at my back shifted as the low vibration of Rí's displeasure caused a shiver to shudder through me. My mind wandered to his hungry grumbles as he kissed along my neck, the deep groans as he touched my–

The dragon's loud deep inhale brought me back from my thoughts as his hands slid to my hips and gripped me tight before whispering in my ear in his low timber "Careful little one, there is only so much I can do to hold him back."

I swallowed back my reply and edged away from those tempting hands.

What would it be like to see his dragon? What colour would he be? Would he have glowing red eyes like his human?

"We have come to a conclusion and a plan," the Council man said as he clapped his hands together.

A conclusion and a plan? For what? I frowned and waited.

"Due to you not showing any signs of actually containing the Dark Witch's pure power, we think that an arranged marriage to a quiet, yet well respected White witch would stop the fear that's going to tremble through the realm."

The room heated instantly as the dragon growled loudly and stalked towards the councilman.

Fucking marry me off?

Yeah, I wasn't going to stop Rí from eating these audacious men. No one controlled me; no one told me what to do anymore and I definitely wasn't going to marry some random witch.

"Gather ye' urns, it's time ye' was incinerated," Rí rumbled as he reached forward to grip the cloak of salt and pepper man.

It would be the perfect time to reach forward, grip salt and pepper man's hair and pull his head back. This would give me the perfect angle to grip his overused, presumptuous tongue and pull with all my might. God, it would be glorious to feel the tendons tearing beneath my fingers as the muscles tore and parted in their-

"Hold on, hold on." Cole sputtered as he stepped in front of the men, pulling me from my vivid imagination. Rí's hand was engulfed in orange flames and the room became unbearably hot. Sweat beaded at my curled lip as I glared at the White witches.

"Damn it Rí! I said hold on!" A rush of cold air burst from Cole as he pushed it at Rí, cooling the room and diminishing the flame in its wake.

"No one is having an arranged marriage." He gave the councilman a questioning look and carried on, "Amaya wants to go back to the human realm; she wants to leave. So, instead of allowing her 'pure' magic to scare our people, let's help her get back then all is well. Right?" His tired eyes met mine and I tilted my head at him, a nod of agreement. I didn't have to tell them I was planning on returning and that it wouldn't just be me this time.

"You want to return to the humans?" The red-haired man on the right of salt and pepper asked in confusion. The utter disdain dripping from his face and voice as he said humans was a sign he hated them.

Well I hated them too, but I wasn't going back for them.

"Yes." I bit out.

Silence resumed as Rí walked backwards until he was next to me once more, his big muscles tense and ready for a fight. I laid my hand on his forearm to calm the beast. At my touch his entire frame relaxed and he edged closer to me still.

This dragon was one needy beast.

"We need time to discuss this, your lack of care towards our messengers last night and your inability to refrain from allowing the beast to control himself are signs we can't leave you to roam the realm without being watched." The original councilman spoke with a cold sharpness that had me gritting my teeth.

Control the dragon? Watched? Wow the more this man spoke the more pissed off I got.

"Until we have made a permanent decision, you will reside at the–"

I cut him off there. I wasn't having any of this and I couldn't hold my tongue anymore. The utter disrespect from these men and Cole-good fucking lord that man was on my hit list for sure.

Yeah, he may have potentially stopped their idea for an arranged marriage, but I didn't trust him. Not one bit.

"I will be staying at the Dark Mountain. Not that it concerns you where I will be because my life has nothing to do with you. You cannot and will not make a decision on behalf of me."

I was angry. I was tense and my stomach churned with the tell-tale sign another hour had passed without the twins. The now clear blue sky and bright sun peered down at us through the tree's clusters.

How could such a beautiful tree be the centre of something so ugly.

The three men before us sputtered and looked at each other in outrage.

"The Dark Mountain is not yours to claim!" Salt and pepper gaped.

"The Dark Mountain is the home to all Dark Witches, and my Mate is a Dark Witch."

"Mate? Now Rí surely you will not be continuing this charade with the Dark Witch, if you only joined our–"

The loud roar of a pissed off dragon shook the room; the vibration had the clusters falling to the white floor as the room heated up again.

"Do no' disrespect my Mate like tha' again!" He roared.

The hairs on my arm stood on end as the tingle of magic filled the air. The power that was spilling from Rí sent a familiar buzz through my veins, my idle magic was responding to its Mate.

The councilman began to yell at him to calm down as the air shifted around the dragon.

Holy shit. He was shifting.

He turned his blazing red eyes to me and spoke through gritted teeth, "The mountain–return...to the mountain Mo Chridhe."

"Hell fucking no. I want to see the beast!" I said excitedly. I'm not ashamed to say I was slightly giddy. This was the most fun I had ever had. I was going to see a real-life dragon and he was no doubt going to eat these annoying men. All for me.

So chivalrous!

A hand on my arm sent an irritating itch along my back as my mark swirled beneath my skin.

"Come on. Out!" Cole snapped as he tried to drag me into that long white corridor.

That was the final straw for Rí as his skin blurred and a loud snapping crack filled the room. The councilmen ran past me, knocking me into the wall as they ran like little bitches down the corridor, swearing about uncontrollable dangerous shifters as they went.

"Amaya?" A shrill voice gasped as I looked from the blurred shifter in front of me. Bri the coffee lady stood with a tray of paper coffee cups with her logo on.

"The fuck.." Cole squinted at her through the sweat dripping into his tired eyes.

"Get out, the both of you." Grabbing my arm and then hers he caused her to drop the coffee all over the pure white floor. He dragged us quickly through the corridor and out the green house, just in time to see a monstrous black dragon with huge glowing red eyes rise from a strange white mist.

He was the deadliest, most beautiful thing I had ever had the pleasure of putting my eyes on. His shimmering scales slightly shone like stars against the sunlight, his huge sharp white teeth dripped with something that burned a hole into the roof below him.

I breathed out in utter awe as the screams around me turned the streets into chaos.

Cole grabbed my arm once again making the itch become almost unbearable, but the dragon's enormous roar of rage punctured through the air and pierced our ears. I clapped my hands to cover them and bared my teeth in what I knew to be a smile up at the dragon.

He was truly glorious. My stomach flipped and my heart raced at the sight of him. So angry and filled with rage. All for me.

Only for me.

Cole let go of me and spread his hands wide in surrender and backed away.

"Wooooow." I jumped and looked at Bri still beside me, her face also stretched wide with a smile as she looked from Rí to me. "That's so damn cool," she squealed before holding onto my arm and jumping up and down, her bouncy curls flying all around her head like a floating halo.

No roar greeted us when she touched me. It looked like he just didn't want Cole to touch me.

I grinned once more.

"Come on, let me walk you to his bar. You can wait for him there while he has his fun." She happily chatted to me as she guided me away from a glaring Cole.

"I'm staying at the Dark Mountain."

I flinched from the screech she gave as she squealed a "Of course you are, you powerful bitch you!"

There wasn't a sign of a councilman in sight.

Pathetic weak men.

Bri walked me the entire way to the portal that led to the Dark Mountain. She chatted the entire way past the nosy onlookers and screaming, panicked people. Her constant chatting filled my noisy head, and I found I kind of liked it. She had so much to say, so much to laugh about and it covered the screams of my begging boys and constant need to bring pain. She blocked it all out.

"I will send over some sweet treats; I can't come to the mountain of course, but you can meet me here and grab them. In fact, I'll send some right away. Rí's going to be super hungry after this shift!" Nodding to herself she smoothed down the orange sundress she wore.

I tilted my head and asked, "Why after this shift?"

Her mouth opened in an 'O' before answering, "Well he hasn't shifted since the war. He's the last dragon, so he and his dragon have been without their Horde and well...that's a bit lonely for a dragon. So they haven't shifted."

Eighteen entire years he had been holding his dragon in. Eighteen years he had been alone without his kind. Eighteen years he had been alone. I had started to wonder if Rí and I were more alike than I thought. Both so very different, so very alone, so very out of place in our worlds.

I hadn't believed in these Fates the dragon spoke off, but could they have chosen him for me because he understood me? Not once had he forced a smile from me, not once had he forced me to be something I wasn't. In fact he had been in awe at my excitement to bring pain to those messengers.

Were we matched together because I also understood the feeling of being alone and lost? Until my twins, they healed me, made me strong. Became my obsession.

Was I that to Rí? Was I his dark obsession?

So were these Fates right in pairing us? Were we supposed to find each other? Was Rí really and truly…mine?

Thirteen

'Soaring Free-Altivolus Libre'

Rí

We were free.
Soaring higher and higher into the clear sky, I whooped inside like I was a young boy enjoying his first flight once more.

We hadn't flown in so long, the stretch in our wings, the ache in our neck, the fire in our belly. It was glorious.

I should have known the anger I felt for my Wee Mate would bring my dragon out. His anger had almost trumped my own and boy was I glad he did burst free. Because this was peace, I had my Mate. I had someone to share my life with and my dragon and I were finally communicating once more.

We were one, my dragon and I. We were one mind, one soul, one powerful beast with two forms. One Mate that we were already so possessive of.

We roared into the open sky in excitement. My parents would be so proud, so happy that I had found our Mate.

Our Mate.

So dark, so closed off and yet so open to our heat and passion. The way she had moaned against my mouth was the sexiest thing I had ever encountered. The sheer pleasure on her face was now forever locked in my memory; the smell of her arousal had flipped a switch in me, and I simply couldn't turn it off.

Her soft yet lithe body against my hands, her silky long hair sliding along my skin. Her reaction to my touch. Fates Above, it had been so hard to stop my teeth from sharpening and sinking into that pale neck and thrusting my cock into her wet heat, claiming her as mine for all to see and smell. Our Circle mark would be final, linked forever as one.

But I knew she wasn't ready for that, knew the thought of forever was different in her eyes. Knew she didn't think herself deserving of my need and possessiveness.

I was glad when I saw Bri guide Amaya away from the chaos my dragon and I had caused. The screaming panicked White witches had my dragon chuffing in laughter.

They were always so weak, so reliant on their spells and 'clean' living. And I don't mean healthy foods. I mean unlike misfit shifters, witches thought that if they didn't have perfect control, and people who weren't seen as ‘respectable’ by the council's standard, were *not* fit for society.

The hatred I had for them burned deep inside of me, begging me to set them all alight and then they would have something to scream about. My parents were open to the love of *all* supernatural, as was the entirety of Wisteria. But that was a long time ago now.

Once many years ago, the Dark Witches and the dragons had been close. They had worked together to build a realm for all to gather and be at peace. They made somewhere to go where there was no misfit, no uncontrolled shifter. No ‘purity’. It was a realm for all supernatural no matter what you were.

I grew up in that peace, in the love of all around us. Then came the war, the betrayals, the anger and pain. The deaths.

I watched my realm crumble before my very eyes, I watched the dragons soaring the skies in a panic before my mother pushed me through the portal with all her might. As I fell the portals closed, and with it I saw the dragons fall to the ground and my mother. My beautiful, strong mother. I saw her eyes slide shut just as her last tears fell.

And so I was alone, the last dragon in a world convinced an order was needed. The Council was formed and the realm divided.

My dragon had grown depressed, without our Brood we were empty. Cold. Angry. So very angry.

Until just a few days ago a surge of power had coursed through my veins, and I finally had a reason to smile. To love. To *fly*.

I flew to a mountain far from the city, speeding through the old dragon-sized portals and landing with an ungraceful thud on the lush green grass. I shifted back, allowed the power to guide clothing back to my body and stretched my arms above my head, an audible pop in my shoulders making me grin. I was exhausted.

It was amazing to be with my dragon once more. Our bond and love for each other warmed my heart as he internally sent his own devotion my way.

I looked down at the cliff edge, the Mermaid Quay shining in the sunlight. Turning around, I walked to the one and only Wisteria tree right at the peak of the mountain, its branches reaching far and wide. The beautiful deep purple petals and deep brown trunk were so stark against the green grass.

I placed my hand upon the trunk, closed my eyes and breathed deeply, hoping desperately to sense some magic. The dragon portal once resided there. Right where they could fly through and head straight for the skies. Straight into the open space.

Nothing. Nothing but bark and fallen petals.

Sighing, I ran my hands through my hair and straightened my slumped shoulders. I may not have my Brood, my family. But I had my Mate now. Even if she hid from me. But not for long, I'd get her to open up to me, and it was going to be oh so glorious.

I ran and flung myself from the edge of the cliff, spinning so my back was to the water and allowed my dragon to take over with ease yet again.

We had a Mate to get to.

Fourteen

'Acceptance Of Life/Love Fate-Amor Fati'

Amaya

After spending some time amongst the dead, I finally forced myself to go back to the castle. I stood staring at Lady Samara's painting when Jerry appeared and asked how the council went. After explaining their boring demands and Rí's dramatic leave, Jerry's eye twitched in sync with his moustache. I dragged my tired body to the bedroom, and I found myself curling up on the love seat opposite the huge windows.

The clouds had darkened, and the waves below crashed with so much force against the cliff I was surprised that the castle hadn't even shook from its force. The wind had picked up, and rain had started to splat against the windows before coming down in a heavy downpour. It matched my sour mood. I had been so excitable seeing Rí shift, seeing his glorious dragon take to the sky and stretch his wings. It had produced a feeling in my chest I couldn't quite place.

I was tired, so very tired of the pull of life. I was
actually jealous of the dead and their permanent resting
place.

The constant demands of the people who didn't even know me was exhausting. This feeling brewing inside reminded me of the day I met the boys, the pull I had felt with those little pills in my hand. I couldn't allow this feeling to fester. I wasn't allowed to feel this way. I wanted my twins so badly my chest *hurt.*

Their little faces always made everything worthwhile. Their big blue eyes and silent little mannerisms. Their little hands holding mine, knowing I was there to keep them safe. To protect them.

And then I was gone, leaving them alone and afraid. Confused and hungry. How could I sit here and enjoy this warmth, this comfort when I knew how bad they had it?

I needed to find this magic within me. I needed to pull it forward and keep it there. I needed to find a way back to them and I needed to find a way for them to live here.

Jerry busied himself behind me, setting up a bird perch just as Ravioli flew through the open bedroom door. He landed on the perch and turned his beady little eyes to me. Rain drops glistened on his deep black feathers.

How had he known where I was? And also, how did Jerry know I now had a pet bird?

"How–" I began

"I know all that happens on the mountain my Lady"

Huh, the man really was the best damn ghost butler uh...assistant.

"Why can't humans live here?" I asked quietly, never removing my eyes from the raindrops sliding down the windowpane.

He glided over and poked at the crackling fire before saying, "The amount of power in the portals, the sheer pressure would crush anyone without any kind of magic in their veins."

Gliding over to me, he gently placed a blanket around my shoulders, making me jump and stare up at his jiggling moustache in shock.

"However, if someone who had this immense power in their veins could somehow transfer even a drop of magic to the humans...well...I suppose that would save them my Lady."

I frowned at him as my mind raced. I could transfer magic to people. Was that the answer?

To do this I was going to need to get a hold of this power and use it to my will. I was going to need serious control. But first, I had to find a way back. I needed to return to the Dead village.

My eyelids drooped as I asked Jerry one final question, "What was my mother's name?"

"Her name was Isa my Lady."

Isa...

I jolted awake and looked around me in confusion. The dark clouded sky was now pitch black and the rain had stopped. I sat up and rubbed the sleep from my eyes.

"Mo Chridhe, did ye' sleep well?" Rí asked, he sat in a large armchair beside the fire. Jerry must have given him a bigger seat. I held in my snicker at the thought of him squeezing into the small chairs.

Yawning, I walked over and sat in the chair opposite him and scratched at Ravioli's head as he perched on the arm of my chair.

"How long have I been asleep for?"

"Ye' was snoring when I got back from my flight."

I sat up straight and said "Your dragon! He was huge!" Then added less enthusiastically "And I don't snore."

"Ah well thank ye' Mate," he leered.

Ignoring the way my core tightened, I told him of Jerrys idea, "They could come through, live with me on this mountain."

He nodded, his red gaze holding mine, "Then we find a way to make this happen."

I leaned back against my chair, my chest once again tight, my stomach swirling as I pictured them, running the halls, enjoying the dead and the touchy trees. Their smiles would light up the room.

"Tell me about them," he asked in his timber.

And so, I told Rí of the day we met. I told him of the strength they brought me, of that new feeling that had unfurled within me. My obsession with them.

"I didn't know who I was before them. It had all gotten too much, the beatings. The people. The life I lived had clouded my mind and made me weak. It was turning me into one of the slugs." He frowned at me, his jaw ticking as he tapped his finger on his bouncing knee.

"People in the human world are like slugs; slow, slimy, weak and eat through anything. I longed for death. I needed it. But they turned up that day and I knew; it wasn't time for death to take me. It didn't matter if my soul was barely there, if inside me I was cold and empty, because those boys needed me." I leaned forward to him, needing him to understand.

"It doesn't matter what I want or need whilst I'm alive. The boys will always come first. No matter what."

"The twins will come first to ye', rightfully so. But to me? Ye' will always come first. Ye' worry about ye'r boys' needs, and I'll worry about my Mates."

Could this man truly feel that deeply about our 'Circle' that he would accept my cold damaged soul along with my twins?

How had I landed up so far away from this realm and things that I could have known from birth? How had I ended up with that monster who damaged me so much that I didn't know if I could accept what Rí so freely offered me?

The Fates Above had supposedly matched us together so perfectly, so why oh why would they match me with the White witch? Why was Cole the way he was? If the Fates Above knew what they were doing why even pair me with someone who hated my kind so strongly, who would want me gone so much? Maybe they had made a mistake and Rí was supposed to be my only Mate?

We sat in comfortable silence next to the fire until the sun began to rise. Its orange and pink glow spread through the darkened room and with it awoke a determination to find out who exactly I was, and just how strong I could be for the twins.

We ate breakfast as Jerry brought in book after book on Dark magic and its source. Everything I would need to know on harnessing the power within me.

I flicked through the piles of books now lining the table and looked at Rí and his huge plate of food. Mid mouthful of eggs and bacon, he froze before mumbling, "It takes a lot to feed a dragon."

I rolled my eyes and picked up a leather-bound book that looked like more of a journal. I unwrapped its leather string and opened it.

'The journal of Lady Isa of the Dark Mountain.'

"Jerry–" I stared at the journal; I didn't know how to feel. The journal had been my mother's, the woman who had given birth to me, who kept me for three years before taking me to the human realm. How were you supposed to feel?

"I thought you might like it my Lady, so you may gain some answers not even I can give you."

Answers.

That's what I wanted.

Wasn't it?

Rí's gentle hand guided my face to look up at him, a soft smile on his wide lips, his usual furrowed brow uncreased and relaxed.

"In ye'r own time. There is no rush."

There was a rush to me. I needed to know why, because the second I had met Ellfyn and Elyas, there was no way I would purposely leave them with a monster.

I put the journal down, promising myself I would read it when I was alone. Whenever that was. I found I wasn't alone very often these days.

"If these are not enough, perhaps a visit to the library or archives would be better," Jerry said as he stared at the pile of books with a frown and his hands on his hips.

Not enough? Piles of books now gathered around the chairs, the love seat and any table surface. There was no way I would be able to read all of them. I mean, I would give it my best, books were the world's best knowledge-full of secrets and unknown answers-and my hands itched to gather them and grip them in my grasp.

"I think we'll try to tackle these first, thanks Jerry." Giving the ghost a nod I perched at the end of the huge bed with a large cream coloured book in my hands. The leather was smooth and seemed to be real. Inked on the front red 'To Harness, To Gather, To feel.'

Perfect, right?

I opened the book with Jerry beside me pretending to adjust the curtains on the bedpost. I looked at him in my peripheral vision and jolted.

Holy shit, the black mist.

How had I gotten so used to it being in my sight that I just forgot about it? Giving myself a mental shake, I looked back to the book in my hands. If I could harness my powers, maybe I could finally heal the damn issue. Whatever Lyal did to my eye really did cause some serious issue.

The pages of the book rustled as I settled further back on the bed and frowned at the messy handwriting. How was I supposed to understand this?

"It seems the skin was still warm, and the ink smudged." Jerry said as he peered down at the book.

"I thought animals' skin had to be fully cooled before use."

"It's not an animal."

"Is it…human skin?" I asked slowly.

"Yes." He adjusted his tiny glasses then poofed from the room leaving behind his glow.

This book in my very hands had once been someone's skin, and they had inked it whilst warm. So, it had been freshly skinned…

That was so damn cool!

"Rí! This book is made out of skin!"

He raised his brows at me from where he dug through piles of books. A small grin pulled at his wide lips causing that swirling in my tummy.

Squinting back at the skin in my hands I tried to make out the words.

'Rule one of Harnessing: Acceptance. Without acceptance, expect no results.' I didn't even get to rule two before I slammed the book shut with a snap and moved onto the next book. The ink had been so smeared and messy I couldn't even make out the rule two.

I knew I needed acceptance now, but acceptance of what? The world? The people in it? The council and their ways? What did I need to accept?

We flicked through the books for hours, only stopping for Rí to eat more meats and cheeses all whilst commenting how he hadn't eaten a good steak in a while.

"You'd happily eat a big, juicy, no doubt bloody steak after touching books with real skin on?" I asked flatly.

"Does it bother ye'?" He asked with another one of those new grins.

"No." I answered honestly. Things like this had never bothered me: death, blood, gore. None of it fazed me. It was the way of life and the way my mind constantly whispered at me to be part of the darker side of it. Well, let's just say I know I was definitely a little on the morbid side.

Now, friendships, love and bright colours freaked the shit out of me.

I shuddered and slammed the book down on the table; we were getting nowhere. All the books went on about was acceptance, how to use the power once you could harness it. However, there was one little book I had snuck under the mattress that informed me more about Circle Mates. It was now in my TBR pile along with Isa's journal.

"Maybe we should revisit the Bookkeeper or even look around the Dead Village." I sighed as I stood and stretched my arms above my head. The top I had changed into pulled from my jeans and exposed my stomach to the cool air. I closed my eyes as the crack in my back released some tension from sitting for so long.

A warm hand softly rubbed down my waist before circling and holding my stomach, pulling me back into a heated hard body.

My legs instantly turned to jelly as my mouth dried. His small growl of appreciation had me turning around and looking at him under my lashes. My breasts grew heavy with need as my thighs clenched in anticipation.

I licked my lower lip as I turned around, pulled a chair to him and stood on it, bringing me to nose level.

Slowly, I placed my hands on his big broad shoulders, stood on tip toes and placed an open-mouthed kiss to the pulse on his tanned neck. His firewood and cake flavour coated my lips and made me so damn hungry for him. He moaned low and gripped my hips in his hands before sliding them to my ass and squeezing.

I kissed along his jaw before ever so slowly running my tongue along his lower lip, enjoying how his red eyes became brighter and heavier at the same time. His hard cock pressed against my stomach, and I shuffled closer, rubbing myself on it and pulling another drawn out groan deep from his chest.

He gripped my face and pressed his lips to mine. Drinking me in, our breathing became gasps of pleasure as our tongues caressed, chests smushed together, and I continued to rub against him in desperation.

I wanted him and I wanted him now.

I tore my mouth from his, placed my hand on his chest and felt his hammering heart. I stretched my face into a grin before I pushed with all my might, causing him to fall backwards onto my huge bed.

He looked up at me in shock and excitement. I swore I could see his dragon peeking at me in those red eyes. I jumped from the chair to the bed and sat with my legs on either side of his waist.

His hands slid to my hips as he breathed "Ye' are fucking glorious."

I pushed my long hair to the side and leaned down pressing my lips to his. I pressed my core down on his throbbing cock and gave a small whimper at the pressure it provided against my now wet pussy.

His hands slowly pushed my top up, his heated palms causing me to shudder.

"If you're quite done, I believe we need to talk."

Before I could even blink Rí was standing in a slight crouch and a growl rumbling from his chest in a warning.

I looked around his large body and saw Cole leaning against the bedroom door, his arms crossed and face sour.

"How the fuck are you in my Castle?" I demanded, ignoring the fact I had already started with the 'my'. Funny what having stuff can do to you huh?

My body still thrummed with need and my mark was almost dancing in happiness at having two Mates so close to me.

Rí's chest heaved as he straightened before he gripped my hand in his. I didn't feel the need to pull away.

"Seems the rumours are true; the Mountain grants all the Mates access." Sighing, Cole rubbed at the stubble on his chin before aiming his tired blue eyes to me. Why was he so tired? He was starting to look sick.

"I couldn't find anything in the Village. I couldn't sense any Dark magic, any surge of power, nothing."

"I'm not ly–"

He held his hand up and said, "It doesn't mean there isn't anything there. Just that it may be hiding from me. The council aren't backing down." He dragged his eyes from mine and looked to Rí, "They have a suitor ready and waiting, and let's just say, even *I* detest the man." He curled his lip, turned on his heel and left the room.

"Wait!" I called out and followed him up the darkened stairs to the foyer.

"Why are you helping us?"

"I told you, to get rid of you." He answered, still walking from the castle. I still followed, my bare feet now getting wet from the cold moss as he entered the cemetery.

"Yeah yeah, we hate each other." Rolling my eyes, I grabbed his arm to stop him from walking further. I swallowed at the coldness of his skin against my own. His coldness held no comfort to me. I sensed only despair within him.

"Why are you even here? Why are you so tired? Why do you even work with those assholes?" The questions just fell from my mouth, and I couldn't stop; the cap had popped from the bottle and the explosion was real.

"Why are you telling us any of this? Why–"

"Fucking hell stop. Just stop," he yelled, ripping his arm from my grasp and rubbed at his lower back. He paced back and forth in front of me as I mentally screwed my lid back on.

I didn't like it when I exploded like that.

"I have to get rid of you; you have to go back. I can't..." He stopped his pacing and faced me; his tired face became pale the longer he stood before me.

"Cole, are you sick?" I questioned. I didn't know witches could get sick. I had assumed we were immune to the human illness. I had never been sick a day in my life and yet Cole looked pale, tired and thinner by the hour.

"Yes. Yes, I'm fucking sick now if you'll excuse me. The Council are expecting me." He stormed away. Just before he reached the trees he called out, "go and check the Dead Village," leaving me amongst the dead.

They usually brought me comfort, but something about our interaction was off. More than usual.

Something was wrong with the White witch.

Fifteen

'Fates Be Damed-Damnari Fates'

Amaya

I couldn't stop thinking about Cole and his tired eyes. Something was seriously wrong, and it added to the noise in my head.

"I know of a quicker way to the Village than the portals if Ye' want to try."

I looked over to the dragon stood in the castle doorway with his arms crossed and a mischievous grin playing across his face. Squinting at him I made my way back into the castle in search of my shoes.

Jerry waited by the fire in the foyer, my boots in one hand and a thick black cloak in another.

"This may be of use to you this evening my Lady."

Sliding my feet into the boots, I took the cloak from the ghost, its thick splendorous material soft to the touch. With a deep purple clasp at the neck and an opulent hoop, it fell to my calves.

It was stunning.

Smoothing my hands down the front, I noticed a deep embroidered ***L.A.*** on the right breast.

"Lady Amaya." Jerry bowed low before straightening up and tucking my hair into my hood. Freezing, I stood still as he fussed over me.

"I know this realm, magic and well…everything is a lot for you right now. But I hope you know my Lady; that the Dark Mountain and I have waited a long time for you to return to us. I cannot pretend to fathom the life you had in the human realm. But know this; *you are* a powerful Dark Witch, with more strength and love in your soul than you could ever imagine." Brushing off the invisible lint on my shoulder, he stood back with his jiggling moustache and something suspiciously like a tear in his eye.

Could ghosts cry?

To think that someone had been waiting for me this entire time. All those years of being alone and not knowing I was needed, not knowing I had a home. Not knowing I had a family waiting for me.

Elyas and Ellfyn were going to be so happy here, so welcomed.

Rí's rumble of appreciation by the door had me grinning with a warmth in my chest.

"Thank you, Jerry," I said quietly as I turned back to the ghost. And then I did something unexpected even to me, I laid my hand on his arm, and I gave him a real smile, one I know was full of gratitude as something akin to affection filled my cold heart.

His moustache jiggled like crazy and that's when I knew.

Jerry the ghost butler was also mine. Mine to protect, mine to keep. Just as my boys were.

I strolled over to the dragon, my cloak billowing behind me like the badass witch I was going to make sure I became and waited to be told of this short cut.

A loud rustling out the front door had the dragon grinning as he jumped out, a bounce in his step as he moved into a now clear space. The trees had created a clear area with enough space to fit a shifted dragon.

Holy fuck.

I finally realised what Rí had meant.

His large body blurred and cracked before a monstrous black dragon stretched its long scaly neck. This close I could see everything, including the humps along its back, the long tail that ended with an orange flame glowing and bright. Its huge talons dug into the stones before releasing, bringing up tufts of dirt.

Slowly, I walked forward, my hand outstretched to touch him, his huge head lowered to my level, resting his scaley chin at my feet.

"You're amazing," I breathed out in awe. Before me, with his head at my feet stood a real-life fucking dragon. His bright glowing red eyes stared at me. I knew it was Rí of course, but something else stared out at me, something primal.

Hot air blew at me, blowing my cloak and hair around my face as he chuffed at me, his teeth bared, sharp and dangerous. They were longer and thicker than my damn thigh. I reached my hand forward and smoothed it down his black glistening scales. They were almost hot to the touch. My fingers tingled as a loud humming came from his chest. Was he purring again? His red eyes were closed in contentment as I continued my exploration of him. I ran my hand along the ridges on his nose leading to his eyes. He was taller than the trees even laying down as he was now.

He was absolutely magnificent, a true mystical creature I thought only belonged in the books I used to steal.

He surprised me by standing up, lifting his head to the sky and letting loose a long loud roar. It echoed around the mountain, and I could just tell, this wasn't an angry roar like before. I covered my ears and smirked at his showing off.

"How am I supposed to get up?" I pondered as I walked to his side and stared up at the hump-like seat on his back. Before I knew it, his big claws grabbed me and threw me up into the air. A small screech escaped me as I flailed my arms about, waiting to fall with a crunch to the floor. Instead, I landed with a "humph!" on his back as my heart tried to escape through my chest.

"A fucking warning would have been nice," I snapped and slapped my hand down on his scaly neck.

He made another chuffing sound before his wings spread out on either side of us; they were even bigger that I had thought. They stretched out almost as wide as the front of the castle before he slowly began to rise into the air. I gripped his hump with both hands and enjoyed the warmth his scales provided me. His dragon form was solid, impenetrable, powerful. You would be really fucking stupid to piss this dragon off. I understood why people avoided him.

We flew through a large portal in the thick clouds, its blur almost unnoticeable in the wind that blew around us. It was unlike anything I had ever experienced before: the pure freedom the open sky provided, the peace that had settled over me. I wanted to close my eyes and enjoy the sensation, but I couldn't stop my eyes from taking everything in. The sky cleared as we flew through the Light city, the stars clear and vibrant above us. I looked down at the city, at the near empty streets and the contempt on the few people that did rush about.

The people that resided there couldn't truly be happy, could they? Or were they stuck in the same sluggish slime as the humans were? Wake up, work, lie, deceive and wish for a better ending. Sleep and repeat.

It was as if they were missing something, something so very important. But what was it? What was missing from all their lives?

I squinted into the night sky as we neared another portal. Rí's wings glided effortlessly, his red eyes a beacon in the dark night. I slowly let go of his hump, spread my arms wide, tilted my head back in the wind and closed my eyes. I embraced this freedom and peace. I embraced the moment and held it deep within like a hug.

Because you never knew when you would need to relive it, to bring the memory forward and hold it tight when there was nothing but horror and pain in your life.

I had wished for a memory such as this growing up, something that would take me from the beatings I had endured. A memory that was peaceful, an escape from reality. Books had been my only saviour. The story I wished I had lived amongst. I never wanted to be a princess. I just wanted to be me. But in a land where I *could* be me. Books weren't just knowledge or stories; they were my escape from reality…until reality ruined them for me. Who knew I would actually find somewhere I could be free, somewhere my twins could be free?

The wind whipped at my cloak, pulled at my spread arms and yet no fear, no weakness and no pain pulsed through me. I was safe here, riding on the back of the last ever dragon.

Lowering my arms, I held back onto the hump as Rí's purr vibrated along my body just before his body tensed and he shot forward. Wings folded in, he aimed towards the ground. I screamed as the thrill buzzed through my veins,

He landed more gracefully than I expected and before I could even wonder how I was going to slide off his back, he changed with a loud click and an oddly familiar hum. I began to fall towards the ground but landed up in Rí's arms bridal-style.

"Ye' did no' think I was going to drop ye' did ye'?" He grinned, his hair wild and unkempt, eyes bright and zoned in on me. As always.

I raised my brow at him and noticed we were in the streets of the Shadow land, just a few steps away from his bar. The red glowing 'Kings Liquor' shone brightly in the dark streets.

Patting his hard chest for him to put me down, I frowned, "Why are we here?"

He placed me down as if I was an unchipped diamond and smoothed my hair from my brow. I knocked his hand away and took a step back. He loved to touch, to be near me at all times. I had noticed his eyes never left me, constantly searching me out. It was...different. Different to being avoided, ignored and hated. To being judged. Everything was becoming a lot. Rubbing my hands down my clean jeans, I looked at my perfect boots, tugged at my thick warm cloak with my initials embroidered so neatly.

Everything was so different.

I was different.

"I thought we could check on my bar first, perhaps a drink, then we will make our way to the Dead Village."

I swallowed the lump in my throat, ignored the cold churning in my stomach and nodded. I didn't take his outstretched hand, but I did walk beside him with my head held high. I walked with my eyes bright and clear; I walked with the knowledge that I, Amaya of the Dark Mountain, was different to the first time I had entered this bar.

Loud greetings cheered for Rí as we pushed through the crowded bar. Half full glasses were raised in welcome; music continued to be played from the petite women strumming on a guitar in a small corner, two burly men enraptured with her every move as she smiled lovingly at them: Circle Mates.

I looked at Rí behind the black mist in my peripheral vision.

Circle mates. I remembered the book hidden under the mattress back at the castle, waiting to be read.

"Rí!! I heard you shifted!" That grating voice had my back tensing and teeth grinding together in seconds.

Cece the barmaid threw her arms around the dragon's neck and beamed up at him. Her thick lashes fluttered, and her low-cut top revealed her bright pink bra.

I had her face smashing into the bar with a loud bang and a smashed piece of glass to her throat in three seconds flat. Her yell of anger and pain had the entire bar in silence.

Rí stood with his arms crossed and his grumpy expression back in place.

If the dragon thought I was going to just stand around and let this slut throw herself at him when we were…well whatever the fuck we were, he could think again.

"Get this bitch off me!" Cece growled, her eyes changing to the yellow of a wolf. Made sense, she was a bitch after all.

I snickered to myself internally as I gripped the glass tighter slicing my skin open oh so perfectly.

"I will slice your pretty little head clean off if you touch him again. Understand?" I said flatly. I was the new Amaya, right? The Dark Witch who took no shit? Well that Amaya certainly didn't hold back anymore.

"Rí, she's crazy! Get her—"

I growled and slammed her head on the bar again. Her nails gripped my arm and dug in; her claws peaked through and drew blood.

I bared my teeth and growled at her.

"My mate can do as she pleases in our bar; if she wants to chop ye're head off because ye' touched what was hers, then so be it."

That's not what was happening...was it? I wasn't claiming him as mine. Was I? No no. Nope.

I let her go with a shove but not before I let the glass slice into her skin. Just a little yanno?

"I wasn't claiming you," I said flatly as I looked to Rí, the glass still in my hand with my blood dripping to his deep wooden floor.

He threw his head back and let out a deep booming laugh. Others joined in as I stared at him in bewilderment.

What the fuck was he laughing at?

"Of course ye' aren't." He chuckled once again before he pulled out a chair by a small empty table. Cece had disappeared and the bar had resumed their chatter and merriment. "Looks like I will have to cover the bar tonight," he muttered as he looked around the room.

"I'm not apologising," I muttered back as I leaned back in my seat, mesmerized at the slice in my skin as it slowly knitted itself back together. I wiped the blood on my jeans and ran my finger along the now healed skin.

That would have been so handy in the human realm.

I sat and watched as Rí bustled about the bar, filling glasses, chatting to the loud leprechaun and other shifters. His grumpy frown had smoothed out and he seemed…happy. I observed the room- the Circle mates were obvious, as they stayed close to one another, their constant touches and smiling eyes a sure sign of love.

It made me nauseous.

"Sickening isn't it."

I jumped in my seat as a deep voice rasped beside me.

I squinted at the figure hidden by the shadows as he leaned back against the wall covered in pictures. The bright glowing cherry of whatever sour-smelling drug he smoked lifted and glowed brighter as he sucked on it, inhaling deeply before releasing the smoke and letting it drift over me.

Sixteen

'Magnetic Pul-Tractio Magnetica'

Ziel

I had been watching her for days, never allowing her to see me, never allowing her to know I was there, always watching in the shadows. The Dark Mountain had allowed me to enter the portal and shocked me when the trees had been so welcoming. They had wrapped around my arms and snuck into my leather jacket like curious children. My deadly vines had slithered out and wound around their branches in their own greeting.

I had expected her to be weak, to beg the dragon for his protection and power, to cower from the Council and that dimwit White witch Cole. But so far, I had seen nothing but irritation and boredom. The distaste and anger that had soaked the air when she had spoken with the council, my my, it had awoken a hunger within me I had to fight control for. The Council thought they could control a Dark Witch? It was laughable. And an arranged marriage? Oh I was going to enjoy the pain I brought to whoever that witch would be.

It seemed I had been very wrong about this little slip of a woman. The utter depravity I saw in her eyes as she held that glass to the wolf's throat was mouthwatering. It seemed that perhaps the Fates Above weren't so wrong after all. It seemed that they had provided me with a Circle Mate potentially as dark and soulless as I.

Did this mean I was accepting her as my Circle Mate? Absolutely not, but that didn't mean I couldn't watch the darkness within her unfold and spread through Wisteria. And it certainly didn't mean that I couldn't join her in the chaos.

"Why are you lurking in the shadow?" She asked, her voice huskier than I expected. I stepped forward and sat in the empty chair next to her. The Mayfeaver hung from my lips as I tapped my fingers on my knee. The exposed pale skin from my ripped jeans was almost luminous in the low lighting of the bar.

My lower back itched and tingled the closer I got to her. It begged for me to touch her, to run my hands through her long silky hair and claim those plump pursed lips.

"Not the talkative type?" She muttered as she looked away from me, surveying the bar silently.

"And you are?" I asked quietly as I stubbed the drug out on the table, the effects already leaving my system, the noisy bar adding to my noisy mind, the whispers that only I heard getting louder.

I tapped my fingers harder.

I tapped my foot.

Anything to ignore the whispers.

Kill them all.

Let your flames go.

Strangle the life out of them.

Swallow their soul—

"Why are you sitting with me?" She asked making me raise my brows at her.

"Should I not?"

"I don't think many are happy that I'm a Dark Witch." She still hadn't looked back at me, her purple eyes were looking at others, assessing those around her.

"That doesn't bother you," I stated. It would bother most others, but not her, not me. And certainly not her dragon. I knew he knew I was sat there; he couldn't take his eyes off her for long. Constantly watching her. I knew he had sensed me watching her from the trees on the Dark Mountain. There wasn't much that dragon missed, especially when it came to the small woman next to me.

If he sensed me there, he knew I was connected to them both, which was the only reason he hadn't stormed over here and tried to rip my body in half.

I lit the tip of my finger in my blue flame and held it over the candle in the glass jar on the table. Allowing more light to fill our space.

Her silence was refreshing. Two questions and she had gone back to her silent observation; she hadn't felt the need to ask more. I wanted her to ask more. I wanted her curiosity, and I wanted those purple eyes on me damn it.

I tapped my fingers more insistently along my knee.

Release your flaaaaaames.

I reached into my pocket, lit another smoke, inhaled deeply and held it with my eyes closed. I let the drug smother my brain in cotton candy and reduce the voices. Opening my eyes, I tilted my head in her direction. And there they were, those big deep purple eyes. Her thick black lashes surrounded the deep orbs; her perfectly arched brows were crinkled as she frowned at me. She nibbled at that lower lip; I wanted to bite it. I wanted to draw her blood and taste it.

She shocked a small laugh from me when she muttered, "I can see why your voice is so raspy if you smoke this often."

When was the last time I had laughed? Had I even laughed before? I wonder how she would react if she knew that my voice was raspy from losing control of my flames and permanently burning my vocal cords

"You don't care how much I smoke."

She sighed and blinked those purple eyes at me.

"What are you? A shifter? You don't seem dickish enough to be a White witch," she said flatly.

I smirked and blew the smoke from my lungs, "Didn't your mama ever tell you not to ask what people were?"

"She's dead."

I nodded, noting the still flat expression. Of course she was dead. The only living Dark Witch sat next to me, enticing me, making me want things I shouldn't.

"I'm a Mors Flamma." I told her, knowing what she would ask next.

"Which is?" She raised her brow and turned more in her seat, giving me her full attention now she was getting information.

"Death's warrior."

She leaned towards me, intrigued.

"Death's warrior? So you know Death?" Something flashed in her eyes, an interest I hadn't yet seen from her. The spark that burst to life at the mention of Death peaked my own curiosity.

"Death left us all when the portals closed."

Her frown deepened just as a drunken bear collided with her chair, tipping it back and taking her with it. I moved without thought, grabbed her waist and lifted her to her feet all whilst wrapping my vine around the bears ankle and throwing him across the room with a loud crash.

The mark on my lower back zapped me with electricity just as she arched and gasped in my hands, her eyes flashing to my own before she ripped herself from my arms and fell to the floor whilst yelling.

"Are you fucking kidding me?"

The drunk bear roared his irritation at me, and I grinned. I was brewing for a fight. And what better time than now.

I stalked forward, wrapped my vines around his body and threw him to the street.

I rolled my shoulder, inhaled deeply on my smoke and allowed the change to take over. Smoke expelled slowly through each gap of my bones as my skeleton form stood in my glowing blue flame.

I had been stupid revealing myself to her. It had been weak of me.

Now that our skin had touched, my mark had awoken on her back and the pull would be even stronger.

I now just needed to decide if I was going to continue to fight it and watch her from the shadows…

Or take what was now rightfully mine.

Seventeen

'Acceptance Of Mine-Acceptatio Mea'

Amaya

I sat on the floor and watched the lit candle roll towards the puddle of alcohol that had been dripped onto the floor. The liquid caught aflame as Rí's yell muffled in the background and roars of a shifted animal echoed in anger.

Another fucking Mate. That was what…three now? Wasn't that practically impossible? I had one overbearing Dragon shifter, a White witch who hated me as much as I disliked him and Deaths fucking warrior. Were these Fates Above having a laugh at me? Was I some sort of entertainment to them?

The flame began to crawl towards me, following the patten of the drip as I blinked at it, trying to settle my busy thoughts.

Someone really should put that fire out; it was going to create a disaster. I looked around the now chaotic bar as Rí shoved shifted animals out of his way to get to me.

My eyes slowly turned back to the flame that had grown into a full-blown fire; it climbed up the chair I had been sat in and as the heat began to burn, the smoke pulled a small cough from me.

Fuck.

That fire really needed to be put out. Like *now*.

As quickly as I thought it, the flames diminished. Gone just like that. No smoke, no charred wood, no scorching heat.

The fuck?

I looked around once more. Rí had his head tilted at me a small grin pulling at his mouth as he shoved the last wolf out of his way. He knelt down on one knee and offered me his big hand.

"Ye' did amazing Wee one."

"What?" I asked with a snap.

"Ye' put the fire out."

Um, no I hadn't. I would have known if it was me. Wouldn't I?

I stood up and brushed my hands off on my jeans, ignoring the dragon's outstretched hand.

"That man—" I began but stopped and gave Rí my death stare.

"Why are you avoiding my eyes…"

"His name is Ziel. He's one of ye' Mates. My Circle brother."

Okay so how the hell had he known that? He was the other side of the bar when he touched me and even then, the man, Ziel, hadn't said a word about our Circle marks. Come to think of it, he hadn't seemed all that surprised.

I was missing something surely.

Because why would Rí who seemed unable to leave my side be happy to leave me alone with a man that I didn't know. He then knew we were Circle Mates before I could even explain.

"Rí. Explain."

He growled low, grinning as he stood and crowded me. "Say it again." He rumbled, "Say my name again."

Oh for the love of God! Was this man serious right now? Actually, was there even a God?

I shook my head from those thoughts and glared at him and his stupid handsome grinning face. I knew he was trying to distract me, and it was only working a little bit.

I crossed my arms and tapped my foot, completely ignoring the patrons leaving the bar. We were now alone, left with the mess of broken glasses and tumbled tables.

"Ziel doesn't need to touch his Mate for his mark to awaken. He obviously saw ye' and knew. I knew because he has been watching ye' from the trees by ye' castle."

He'd been watching me?

I blew my breath out in an exaggerated sigh and looked around at the mess.

"Why the hell had he been watching me? Why didn't he come and talk to me?" I asked as I lifted a chair and pushed it back to its table. I picked up a fallen glass and took it to the bar.

"Ziel is…particular. He isn't one to talk. He doesn't like people," he answered as he in turn picked up the fallen tables and righted the chairs.

So the Death warrior didn't like people. I understood that. I also understood his dislike for talking. I am, or should I say, was, the same. I wasn't so sure I was the same anymore. Things were just so different. I liked the back and forth between me and the dragon, I liked the knowledge Jerry gave me. And I think I even liked the nonstop chatter from Bri. I had never in my life liked to converse with people. What had changed to make me change?

I stared at the glass covering the floor and closed my eyes. The buzz within my veins was always there, the magic within me waiting to be used.

Sighing, I wiped my hands on my legs and said, "I can't think about another Mate right now. We need to search the Dead Village. Then I need to sleep."

Rí stepped close, his firewood and cake covering the smell of spilt liquor, whilst his warmth made my stomach summersault. He tucked my hair behind my ear, ran his finger down my cheek and pressed his lips to mine.

Just a soft gentle brush, but it had me wanting more all the same.

"Then come my Mate, let's do exactly tha'."

***

There was nothing there; the Dead village was just that. Dead. Nothing but burnt wood and crumbling buildings nestled within piles of sand. The humid air stuck my clothes to my skin as I kicked the sand with my boot in frustration. We had searched for some crackle of power or a sign of magic for an entire hour. All we found was my lack of patience and my hatred for sand.

I stomped over to the shack missing a roof and a smashed door stained with my dried blood. It had only been a few days and yet it could have been weeks. Just a few days ago I was struggling to breathe, in my worn tatty clothing and nothing but my boys on my mind. How long had they been hiding from Lyal? Had he hurt them in replacement of me? Had they taken our secret bag and run? What was I going to find if I managed to get back.

I stood on the crumbled wood much to Rí's dismay and breathed in slowly, closed my eyes and tried my best to *feel* something. Anything.

Nothing. Nothing but confusion and a cold churning in the pit of my stomach. My shoulders slumped.

"Let's go home," Rí said softly.

Home. Would it ever be a home without them?

I took his hand, not having it in me to argue and walked with him from the wreckage. I had no words; I was beginning to fear that I wasn't getting back.

"I was only young when the war started," Rí explained quietly. "Well, young for a dragon anyways. We had our own realm, the Dragon realm, somewhere we could fly for days and be as free as we needed. Our land was massive, large enough to fit many Hordes of dragons. My Brood was the biggest of all." He gave me a small smile and continued. "A Brood is basically a pack of dragons born either together or around the same time. I was the oldest." I could see his throat bob as he swallowed thickly.

"My parents, they were incredible. They were leaders who worked alongside the Dark Witches." I frowned up at him as we slowly made our way through the trees towards the shadow land.

"My mother was best friends with a Dark Witch. I never met her, they only ever met alone. I do no' know her name. They worked hard to make Wisteria a place all supernatural could be themselves. It's said the Dark Witches betrayed Wisteria and wanted all the magic and realms to themselves. Tha' they used too much dark magic, and it had consumed them. It's said tha' they were the ones to start the war, and to end it with their lives and the portals closing."

So my kind were hated not just for a war but because they had betrayed all the realms. Who was it that told people that had been what happened? I had a slight inkling.

"I don't think it's true. My mother and her friend were like sisters. They were happy, strong and always saw to other's needs before their own."

"Then what do you think happened?" I asked.

He shrugged and squeezed my hand. "I don't know, but I don't think it was ye're kind. I was so afraid when my realm died, and the portals closed. I was alone, the last of my kind. I was angry and told ye're kind were to blame." I stayed silent. My kind had taken his family away.

"My point Wee one, is I thought I was going to be alone for thousands of years. I thought I was going to get angrier and angrier until I had no other choice but to end mine and my dragon's life. I thought I was never going to find a Flight, my own family. My own Mate. Then one boring humid afternoon, my dragon woke for the first time in years. Our Mate was here, and low and behold, she was a Dark Witch. I had been granted someone to accept me, to match me in my grumpiness." He grinned as his eyes lit up the darkness. "My feisty Wee Mate who likes to pretend she feels nothing."

He stopped our slow walk, lifted my hand to his chest and lowered his head to mine "I know ye' feel like ye' won't get to ye're boys, tha' ye're magic won't show itself, but it will. This is only just the start, for ye', for me, for all tha' ye' wish to allow into ye're life."

How could this man stand to be around me? I was the only living evidence from those who had taken everything from him. If it was true and the Dark Witches were to blame for everything, then could I really accept this power within me? Would I become so greedy and consumed by Dark magic that I would start a war?

I didn't want any of that. I wanted nothing more than to protect what was mine: my boys, my mountain, my ghost…and my dragon. This man, this giant brute of a shifter with his grumpy face and willingness to accept me, accept me when I had done nothing but fight his affection, and tell him I had no plans to accept our mating. This man who had been nothing but kind and gentle to me, who had done nothing but guide me in this confusing world and agreed to help me get my boys.

It was then in the darkened forest of the Shadow land, that I knew, this man, this dragon shifter, Rí, was mine.

Mine to protect, mine to keep, mine to obsess over.

Mine. Mine. Mine.

And so I said the one thing he had been patiently waiting for.

"I accept you as my Circle Mate."

His eyes widened as he turned to me in shock. He stared at me for something akin to awe before he slammed his mouth to mine whilst holding my face between his big palms. I gripped his forearms and allowed the full extent of my need for him to show in our kiss.

He ripped his mouth from mine, the both of us breathing heavy as he stood back from me.

"I want to take ye' somewhere, somewhere we can be truly alone."

I nodded. I fully trusted this man before me.

My man.

My dragon.

My Mate.

He shifted quickly, ripping the trees from the ground in the process and shook the sand from his scales. I grinned and accepted his lift up, this time more graciously.

I found I smiled a lot around Rí, something my twins were going to be delighted in finding out.

We took off into the humid night, the warm air blowing through my hair as I held my dragon tightly between my legs.

We flew through portals. I didn't take any notice as of where. I only noticed the change of air on my face. I had my eyes closed, the feeling of freedom and acceptance wrapping around me in a bliss I didn't know existed.

Snapping my eyes open, I had a thought.

Acceptance. That skin book had said something about acceptance. Was it of my Mates? Of this world? I didn't know if I would ever accept Cole. He was too much of a dick, too stuck in the council's way to ever see past his hatred, yet his tired eyes constantly filled my thoughts. Why was he so tired. What was making him sick?

Then there was this new man, Ziel. He was completely unknown to me. I had no connections to him other than the fact we both hated people. Was I extremely fascinated that he was Death's warrior? Yes. Was I oddly obsessed with the thought of death and his cold grasp? Yes. Death had been my first obsession, the first time I had realised I was different. To find out that Death, as a person was real.

Fucking insane.

I looked up to see Rí was flying straight towards a cliff, the dark rocks almost unnoticeable in the dark sky.

I tapped his neck "Um…Rí?"

Either he didn't hear me, or he didn't care. He picked up speed and just as I expected us to be slammed into the rock and squashed to death, I landed in a confused heap in Rí's arms. I opened my eyes, not even knowing when I had shut them and stared opened mouthed at the inside of a cave.

Eighteen

'Together As One-Simul Ut Unum'

Amaya

"My den, my lair. All my secrets, all my treasure. Everything I have is ye're's Mo Chridhe."

I peered around in amazement. The cave was huge, big enough for Rí to shift and stand tall. Right in the centre sat a nest of sorts. Many throws and different sized cushions were scattered in a circle. I grinned up at him as he placed me on my feet. "You like purple" I said, noting the plum colour once more.

Huge paintings of dragons and people were lined up everywhere, golden vases and chalices piled in boxes, golden coins piled high. Crowns and tiaras mounted the walls like trophies. Sconces lined the walls, creating a warm glow in the darker parts of the cave.

"Where did you get all this?" I breathed in wonder. It seemed my dragon liked to collect his gold.

"My family were old; dragons age differently to witches and most shifters. By the time the portal closed I had already secured most of my family treasures tha' had been lost over time. When the war ended, I spent my free time searching the entire of Wisteria for anything tha' remained of them."

Wait…how old was Rí? I'd assumed he was around twenty-five, but if the war was eighteen years ago and he had already secured most of this…had he said thousands of years earlier? That he was going to live thousands of years.

"How old are you?" I asked with narrowed eyes.

He grinned at me and ignored my question. I would get him to answer eventually. I couldn't believe how much stuff was in this cave. All neatly in its places. Each item would hold a memory, a story of the people it belonged to before.

I trailed my hand down one painting containing a young boy. He sat dwarfed by a huge throne. His red glowing eyes grumpy as his large crown hung tilted of the side of his head. His messy dark brown curls flopped onto his tan forehead whilst his chubby cheeks were smushed against his small fist.

A baby Rí.

I grinned wide as a warmth filled my chest.

"You were always grumpy then?"

"Possibly. But never with you." He tilted my chin up with his finger whilst searching for something in my gaze. Whatever he was looking for he must have found. He leaned down and pressed his lips to my own.

I wrapped my arms around his neck and jumped, wrapping my legs around his waist, knowing he would catch me. He walked backwards until we were by the nest of throws and pillows. Lowering me to the floor he stared down at me with such intensity that I shivered. I lifted my arms above my head as Rí lifted my top, leaving me in my black leggings, boots and black lace bra. I'd never worn such a sexy bra before; thank God for the wardrobe full of clothing at the castle. I wasn't shy. I had no nerves. Why would I? Rí was mine.

I was beginning to be thankful to these so-called Fates Above.

Ever so slowly, my dragon ran his finger from my shoulder, across my collar bone and between my breasts. A small flame burnt the small piece of material between each cup, releasing my aching breasts to his waiting hands. I moved back before I laid myself down on his soft throws, my arms stretched above my head. Dropping to his knees he pulled my boots from my feet, pressing a small kiss to each ankle before he slid my leggings down, leaving me in only a small pair of lace panties.

His hand ran up my leg before circling my thigh in a tight grip, his thumbs indenting into my skin as he pulled me down to him. His leg spread my own, and I wrapped them around his waist as our mouths met in a slow, possessive tangle. His heavy weight caused delicious tingles to spread throughout my body. My core throbbed, dripped and begged for his attention.

I moaned low as his lips trained down my neck, stopping to lap at the beads of sweat on my collar bone, before placing open mouthed kisses along the swell of my breasts. My back arched up when he wrapped his warm wet lips around my aching nipple, swirling his tongue around the peak before gently biting down.

His hard cock pressed into me through his jeans, I wanted the material gone, I needed his heated flesh against my own.

And just as I wished for it, the slide of his skin against my own had us both pulling back slightly and looking down.

Had I done that?

"Ye' magic is going to come in handy." He smirked as he left open-mouthed kisses down my stomach, causing goosebumps to appear in his wake. I was so wet, so needy for this man I couldn't think straight. I couldn't even think about the fact my magic appeared at random times. The feel of his warmth against my cold skin was clouding all other thoughts.

The wet slide of his tongue along the top of my panties pulled a needy moan from me. Lifting his red eyes to my own, he gripped the material and ripped them from my body. My hips jerked as the cool cave air met my dripping pussy.

His deep rumbling breath exhaled on my exposed skin as he growled "Ye' smell fucking *delectable,*" before he dived on me like a starved man. His tongue licked up my dripping juices before circling my pulsing bud. He ate me like I was his last meal, like I was a cold ice-cream on a hot summer's day.

His hands gripped my inner thighs in an unbreakable hold as he devoured me. The elation of finally having his hands, his mouth on me fully, was bringing me closer to the edge in a matter of minutes. I needed more.

My entrance clenched, begging to be filled, so I gripped his hand in my hands and pulled his head from me. His dragon looked at me through his red eyes and growled like I took his food away.

"I want to touch you," I panted.

I was going to combust just from the look on his face alone.

He growled as I sat up, trailing my pale hand down his tanned chest. The sprinkle of hair gliding between my fingers before I stopped and swallowed at the size of him. He was huge. I know I didn't really have anything to compare him with, but I knew he wasn't average. Not by a long shot. My core clenched in anticipation of the stretch he would provide.

I circled my hand around his throbbing cock. His groan was like music to my ears as I began to move my hand, rubbing the leaking droplet from the top with my thumb. His head fell back onto his shoulders as he groaned deep and loud. I grinned, liking that I could cause him to react like this. Repeating the motion I cupped his tight balls with my other hand bringing another droplet of pre-come to the tip.

My mouth watered.

I leaned forward to lick the tip, but before I could get my mouth around it, he growled and pushed me back onto the throw.

"I will nae last. I want to come inside ye' Mo Chridhe, I want to feel ye're wet pussy gripping me whilst I come."

Fuck me.

I was so fucking turned on my thighs rubbed together, my slick heat dripping onto his nest. Dragging my arms above my head he spread my knees with one of his own before he settled between my thighs, his cock hitting my wet warmth, causing us both to moan in unison.

Releasing my wrists he gripped his cock in his own hand, giving it a slow pump before he lined it up with my entrance. We panted in anticipation as he slowly pushed forward. His head entered me, its thickness stretching me deliciously. Leaning back down he gave me a slow soft kiss before staring into my eyes and whispering "I love ye' my Wee Mate." Before thrusting in deep. The sudden invasion and sharp sting pulled a small cry from my throat. It hurt more than expected. I loved it.

He held still whilst allowing me to adjust. I gave him a small nod and a grin. I wanted more.

"Mine," he growled as he pulled his hips back before slamming into me once more. The pleasure was so intense I could barely catch my breath. I just about managed to growl out my own "mine" before it sent him into a frenzy. His hips continuously slammed into me, his cock dragging along my inner walls, pulling choked gasps of pleasure from me.

Rí's glowing eyes never left mine as his canines lengthened, becoming longer, sharper. My lower back almost stung as I felt our ropes on the Mating Mark swirl and entwine together.

He lowered his head to my neck, right where it met my shoulder, licking there before his teeth sunk deep. There was so much pleasure mixed with pain my release exploded suddenly, causing the sconces on the wall to blow out, before small rocks fell around us within the cave. I tightened and clenched around Ri's cock as he thrust one more time before slamming so deep, so far within me it was almost like he never planned to leave, before he shuddered and growled against my neck as his own release was pulled from him.

Lifting from my neck, his lips coated with my blood he licked his upper lip, leaving the bottom for me to lean up and lick clean. I swore I could feel another presence within my head, another being, watching through my own eyes. Rí's dragon's connection to me was now complete.

Rolling to the side, pulling me with him to lean my head against his large chest, we both tried to catch our breath.

"Ye' accepted me." He wasn't asking a question but simply stating it.

My heart finally began to slow as I thought about my answer before murmuring, "There wasn't any point in running from it anymore. You're mine now. I don't know how to love. So I can't say it back. I don't understand any of this 'Circle' mate stuff, but you are mine to keep now. I hope you realise what you got yourself into." Once I had claimed someone as mine, they were just that. Mine.

I ran my fingers along where he had sunk his teeth into my flesh and shivered at the heat that spread through me. If any of the books I had read in the human realm had any truth to them, then Ri's mark would stay with me forever, as permanent as I now knew the mark on my back was.

The black mist floated in the corner of my eye as I listened to his heart slowing beneath my head. It settled into a patten similar to my own.

His chest vibrated with the tell-tale sign of his contentment; he was purring.

"Ye' never need to say it back. I'm starting to figure out how ye'r mind works and as long as I am part of ye'r possession. I am happy." He murmured back, almost sleepily.

There was one time I was ready to take my own life, to leave the world. I wasn't afraid of death, of dying. I never had been. The thought of its coldness filled me with a buzz that made me feel more alive than actually being alive. But then came along the twins and the snap of a tight string that wrapped around our bodies joining our souls in some messed up protective obsession. I couldn't just go ahead and die, leaving them to Lyal like fresh meat to hammer into. They were mine. And now so was Rí. His need to protect and be around me was so similar to my own obsession of the boys. His confession of love, his acceptance of it was all I needed to finally allow that waiting string to wrap around us and secure his place in my damaged soul.

The flutter of wings drew my attention to Ravioli as he flew into the cave; his eyes trained on me as he dropped a rolled-up piece of paper onto the nest.

"That better not be from the Council. I'm not marrying some random White witch."

"Ye' certainly are no'." Rí reached for the paper but snapped his hand back as the crow pecked at his fingers, drawing a bead of blood.

"Ravioli!" I fake scolded as I grinned at my pet. I tickled his head before he flew to perch on one of the sconces.

Picking up the paper, I saw a note from Bri, offering her sweet treats and someone to chat with. I frowned at the note in confusion.

"Why would someone offer to chat? What does she want?"

Rí sucked the blood from his already healed finger and helped me to my feet, "It's what Bri does. She likes you."

"She said she'd meet me at the Mountain's portal. I'd hoped to go back to the castle." I didn't mention the books that were begging for my attention. And now that I had accepted Rí and his mark, the book on Circle Mates needed to be read now more than ever.

We dressed slowly, in no rush to leave our nest of passion. Rí took his time kissing his mark on my neck, the wound already healed before he walked over to a red velvet-covered box. He opened the lid and pulled out a long silver chain. He hung it around my neck before tucking my hair behind my ears. It held a red jewel and was warm to the touch.

"What's this?"

"Each dragon from my realm provides their Mate with a slice of their scales ensconced into a jewel. So tha' we are forever with them. If I'm no' by ye' side and ye' are ever in danger. I will know where to find ye'"

Fucking. Swoon.

I tucked it safely between my breasts and waited for my beast to shift.

Nineteen

'Sickness-Languor'

Cole

I should want her dead. The problem was, I didn't, and the simple fact was, I was jealous. Jealous of her Darkness, of how she simply accepted its coil of blackness like it was second nature. I was jealous of the men that followed her around, of their freedom. Of their ability to just accept her as their Mate.

I'd never felt so suffocated; I wished for death with every fibre of my being. It would be better than the daily torture I endured to try and rid my soul of the black stain that tried to spread throughout my body with all its might. Once when I was a boy, I embraced the sick and found joy in its void.

I was wrong.

I was weak.

He made sure I knew that.

I could never accept the sickness.

I laid down on the cold metal table as the straps tightened around my wrists, ankles and neck. The last one felt tight enough to almost cut my airways off. Almost.

The orange candlelight above me flickered as the clinking of tools met my ears. My breathing turned shaky as I shut my eyes. I hated this part. I hated it all. But this part particularly. I clenched my teeth as the sharp blade sliced into my stomach.

"I can sense it darkening within you my boy, its poisoning you." I peeked open my eyes as a bloody pair of gloves placed the scalpel on the tray next to us. The hand picked up a syringe full of clear liquid that filled me with nothing more than white hot pain before I disappeared into the cold darkness. I squeezed my eyes back shut; I hated myself for opening them.

Hated myself for the poison running in my veins. I hated him for constantly trying to help rid it from me.

But most of all, I hated Amaya. Hated her for accepting her own poison whilst I writhed in its cold painful grasp. Begging for the warmth my White witch power should but never provides.

"We are going to have to double our efforts." His voice made my stomach churn as he injected into my sliced abdomen.

Burning spread through my body, hitting every inch of my skin and each nerve with its fire.

White witches shouldn't have this darkness, this poison, this illness. That was why I hated Amaya. It didn't matter that my soul called to hers, that her big purple eyes held such pain that she tried to hide so obviously. It didn't matter that my mark that I had hidden by a magic lotion, itched with the need to be in her presence. I hated that her darkness coated her in the most glorious way, whereas mine smothered me.

Unbearable pain travelled across my body, burning me from the inside out. I hated that it was her face that flashed across my mind before I blacked out.

The darkness sickened me.

I hated her.

Twenty

'Secrets And Lies-Occulta Et Mendacium'

Amaya

I stared at the painting of Lady Samara, her cold expression forever frozen in place. What had put that empty look in her eyes? What had caused her final portrait to be painted in such coldness? Was she simply born with the emptiness as I was?
Was I born with the emptiness? Or had it simply started in the human realm?

There were so many questions, and I simply couldn't stand not knowing the answers anymore. I left the portrait and went in search of Jerry. He usually greeted me the moment I stepped foot in the castle, but after Rí had flown off to fix the mess we had left the bar in, I entered a silent empty foyer.

Instead of going down the darkened steps to my room, I veered right and walked down a dimly lit corridor. More paintings lined the walls, and floating candles dripped their wax onto the pristine stone floor and the black runner. I turned so many corners I was pretty sure I had gotten myself lost before a curved stairway suddenly lit up with more dripping candles.

"How daunting," I grinned as I ran my hand along the dried wax on the walls.

I came to a circular room, full of glass cabinets and sturdy shelving that curved with the walls, each one containing objects I couldn't even identify. Glass jars were filled with liquid and what looked like fingers and tongues floating about. I raised my brows as I moved through the room. In the centre stood a lantern holding an opened book. Its thick cream pages were filled with drawings, detailed descriptions of spells, amongst so much more that I could barely understand. I closed the book searching for a title but all it read was 'Sub Silentio Custodire'.

To Keep under Silence. Just like the front door. But why? What needed to be kept in silence? Was this what witches called a Grimoire? Was I holding the very thing that guided all the Dark Witches before me?

I carefully opened the book and turned the first page and read aloud "*Acceptance is key. Embrace it.*"

"Lady Amaya." I jumped and slammed the book shut before spinning around to stare wide-eyed and guilty at the ghost. He stood with his hands behind his back by the stairway and his dress shoes shining in the candlelight.

"I wasn't snooping."

I was a liar. I absolutely was snooping.

"You cannot snoop in things that now belong to you."

Right, of course. The castle was mine. I picked up the book and held it close to my chest. This book was important. I could feel it. The buzz in my veins and the vibrations in my chest were reacting to it somehow.

"In that case, I think I'll take this to my room." I stepped towards the stairs when the book whipped from my hands and landed back onto its stand.

"The Dark Grimoire tends to like it down here My Lady."

Sighing I nodded and left the little circle room, but not before grabbing myself a glass of floating tongues and the promise to come back and read the entire Grimoire.

Grinning at my little gift to myself, I made my way to my room and asked Jerry who glided beside me. "I need to harness my magic. How? If I was born a Pure-blooded Dark Witch, how can I not simply just use it? Shouldn't it be second nature by now?"

We only walked down one corridor and took one corner before we were back at the foyer. I frowned in confusion at the corridor. Why the fuck did it take me so long to get there?

I sat on the big bed and noticed Ravioli watching me from his new perch. His beady eyes tracked my movements as I shuffled to get comfy.

"You will understand all eventually My Lady. I cannot give you the answers. Part of being a Dark Witch is figuring out the secrets to simply *being* a Dark Witch." He lifted the duvet and folded it over before laying a set of silk pyjamas next to me. I changed without a thought. The silky material glided across my still sensitive skin. I sat back against the thick pillows and the ghost tucked me in the bed like a child, patting the sides down smoothly before a steaming cup of what smelled like sweet tea appeared in his hand.

The man spoke in damn riddles. And why was he putting me to bed? I frowned and was about to ask just that when he suddenly beamed at me, his eyes shining down at me behind his little spectacles. "Oh! And a congratulations on your first Mating! I assume Lord Rí will be back shortly?"

Lord Rí? "Uh, yeah," I muttered, still slightly confused with what was happening.

He nodded and finished with his fussing and said, "now drink the tea. You have a visitor in the morning I believe? I'll make sure to have some tea and perhaps coffee made for you both."

"What?" I was so fucking confused.

"Bri, My Lady, her note? I gave it to Ravioli to bring to you. The Mountain will allow her entry if you *truly desire* it," and with a poof he was gone, leaving me with more questions than before and utterly dumbfounded to what just happened.

I just got tucked into bed by a ghost. Shaking my head I bent down, lifted the mattress and pulled the two books I had hid there.

So if I truly desired the person to enter, the Mountain would allow it? Was the mountain somehow connected to me? I looked at the books in my hands and decided the only way for me to get answers was to find them myself. Opening the book on Circle Mates I began to read.

'The Fates Above created the link between soul-bonded Mates when the first supernatural felt the loneliness of life.

After millennia alone, the tears of the supernatural created a river, and in this river swam the need and wants of a lonely soul.

The cries caused the river to overflow, and the Fates Above decided for the first time in their creation, that it was time to intervene.

They wanted the supernatural to have someone to spend their immortal life with, someone well matched with similar wants and needs.

In their search for this match, they delved deep into the soul of the lonely supernatural.

At first, they were unsuccessful, which angered the Fates Above and caused them to argue. They had different ideas as to what would help the supernatural and so they split the soul, each taking their own ideas and separated into separate realms.

The lonely supernatural drifted through their life, ever lonely and spilling tears, creating a great sea, an ocean full of magic and life.

It was only when the supernatural gave up, and succumbed to the sea did they find that, their split soul belonged to another being or beings.

A being that brought them joy, love and laughter. A new meaning to their long life.

This being made them whole, a circle of souls that belonged together.

Each one would eventually connect. Perfect for each other.

Never alone and bound together by the circle of their soul.

Mated for life.

And so the Fates Above decided each supernatural should have their souls split upon creation, so that they would eventually find their other half's and connect as one full circle. With one part of the soul being the link to connect them all together, like a puzzle.

What the Fates Above did not realise was that not every supernatural was lucky enough to find the other half of their souls, and so they drifted through their lives, forever missing their soul and the match that could have been.'

So my soul was ripped apart at creation, and scattered around until it found matches that perfectly suited me?

If that was true, then that would mean Rí, Cole and Ziel had a piece of my soul. That they were perfectly matched as one for me. Cole held a piece of me within him and yet he had shown nothing but hate towards me. Was it because of what I was, or was it just…me? I had gotten used to Rí and his kindness, his need to be around me that I had simply forgotten that people simply just didn't like me. I had never been likeable. And that had never bothered me. So why was Cole's tired yet hateful eyes a constant thought? Why did my chest ache just that much more when I thought of how he wanted me to be gone?

Sighing, I leaned back against my pillows and sipped at the sweet tea. I wrinkled my nose at the taste and put it back down.

"Is it time I gave Isa a true moment? Should I give her a chance to answer for her sins?" I asked Ravioli.

I could have sworn he nodded.

I began to read the journal of my dead mother.

'The secrets we have to swim through are so many now. I don't know how much longer the ropes will hold. The trees weep. I weep.

They are gathering an army, forming plans against us. After everything...

It must be done; my sisters understand the sacrifice. We must do this before it's too late.

The portals need to close. But first I must find a way to hide her. My child. I sense her power; it grows as she grows within me.'

So it was them; her confession was clear as day. They wanted the portals closed. Who was forming an army? I pulled the journal closer to my face and read the words as fast as my eyes would allow.

'My heart breaks to know that she will never know her true self, never know how much her kind and I love her.

Tabatheen has agreed, her flight is ready.'

Tabatheen and her flight…the dragons. Could this have been Rí's mother? The words on the page were more hurried, becoming scribbles that were smeared as if from tears. I read on, vigorously turning the pages as my mind raced.

'They blame us. US for the horrors. THEY are the ones that have brought this upon themselves. Always so selfish in their need for power. They want it all, but they can't have it. We won't allow it.'

The next few pages made no sense. She rambled on about death and the sick betrayal that had started all of this. The utter devastation of the death of her sisters, of the two-day wait for their bodies to decompose before they could be buried in their resting place. I frowned, confused. The last page was hurried, with a lipstick print at the top corner. A kiss.

'My darling child, this is goodbye. I kept you from them for so long. I tried so hard to keep you with me. But I can do it no longer. The portals are sealed; my sisters, my Circle Mates are all gone. All that is left is my love for you. So I bid you goodbye. I hope you live a long, healthy and happy life. I hope you stay strong to yourself. It's within your blood my daughter.

I hope you never come home to Wisteria Amaya, but I know you must. For that, I am deeply sorry. Your mother-Isamu.'

What the fuck. What the actual fuck. I couldn't make sense of it. The noise in my head was like a crowd of screaming people. She loved me. She had tried to keep me. My mother never wanted me to step foot in Wisteria.

Not once had she mentioned who my father could have been. Was he one of her Circle Mates? Was he one of the betrayers? Who were these trusted people that wanted nothing but power? My gut told me it was the White witches. Had they betrayed the leaders and made the realm think the Dark Witches were evil?

I needed to know.

One question kept circulating, had Isa known who she placed me with in the human realm? Her journal made me think she had loved me deeply. Would she have initially placed me with Lyal? If not, how did he come to have me?

She had wanted me to be strong, but how was I supposed to be what she wanted, what the twins needed me to be without having any way of harnessing this power within me?

I sipped the tea again, forgetting its disgusting taste as I shoved it back onto the side table.

"Not a fan of tea?"

I threw my book to the person talking without a single thought, using it as a weapon as I jumped to my feet, balancing myself on the huge bed.

"Firstly, you missed. Secondly, nice pjs." Ziel smirked as he walked further into the room, leaning against the bedpost with his arms crossed and his smoke hanging from his lips.

"What the actual fuck are you doing here?" I snapped with my hands on my waist, still standing on the bed. It gave me more height and put me at eye level with the Death warrior.

"Can't a guy simply enjoy the presence of his Mate?" He sneered, before picking the book off the floor, his brows raising at the title.

Fuck. I threw the book on Circle Mates at him.

Well done, Amaya.

I mentally gave myself a slap as I found myself staring into his green eyes. They were captivating and reminded me of the almost glowing moss in the cemetery.

"We aren't mated." I snapped.

"As of yet. I'm still undecided on that one." He rasped around his smoke. He took it from his enticing mouth and disintegrated it with the flames at his fingers.

I stared at him in unease; he was deluded. He didn't just get to decide if we were going to become Mated.

"I don't even know you. Get out." I said flatly, trying to shut my expression down. For once, it wouldn't work. I couldn't stop my frown or the way my mouth dried as he crossed his arms in that leather jacket.

He tutted as he began to wander around the room, poking at my dresser with the jar of tongues before finally standing and staring out the large windows.

"I'm looking for your dragon. I have some information I think he'd like."

"He's not here. Now get. Out." I growled my annoyance at him. Who did he think he was? Coming onto my Mountain, my castle and entering *my* bedroom.

He walked to the now empty bird perch and flicked it. "Birds are vermin."

I was actually lost for words; this stranger, this man who I had spoken but only a few words to in the bar, was wondering about my room and poking at my things as if he belonged there. I stared at him with narrowed eyes as he picked up the skin book on acceptance.

"Ah, having trouble, are we? The answers are always clearer than we think."

The fuck? "You don't know anything about me or my troubles. Now get out before—"

"Ah! There he is," he rasped, cutting me off.

Rí walked into the bedroom looking every bit of the big brute he was before he stopped in his tracks. His thick brows raised as he looked from Ziel to me standing on my bed. His red gaze travelled down my form as a grin spread across his face.

"Nice Pjs, Mo Chridhe." He purred.

"Can we stop talking about my pyjamas and discuss why this man is in my castle?"

Ziel pushed over the bird perch and lit one of his smokes, inhaled deeply and nodded, "ah yes, Dragon, I have the address."

Address? What was he on about? Rí's face hardened as his jaw ticked. He prowled over, pressed a kiss to my forehead and took a deep breath from my neck before saying, "I'll be back tomorrow. Get some sleep Wee one. We'll work out how to get ye' powers going then."

Nodding once more to Ziel he left the room with me standing there confused and slightly pissed off.

"Ahh, issues with the powers, is it?" He rasped.

"Get. Out." I said through gritted teeth. His raspy chuckle filled the room as he strolled out as if he had all the time in the world.

There was no way that man had a piece of my soul.

No. Fucking. Way.

Twenty-One

'Circle Brother- Circulus Frater'

Ziel

Rí snapped the White witch's fingers with ease as he bared his teeth in his version of a smile. Standing back and observing his creativity, I smirked as Rí heated the room.

I was pretty surprised when Cole sought me out and handed me the paper containing information for the witch that was supposed to marry Amaya.

I drew in the Mayfeaver smoke and held it there in my lungs for five, four, three, two, and blew it out on one. Its drug clouded my brain, wrapping me in cotton and easing the anger I felt with the Council. They were laughable. Thinking they could take our Circle mate from us. She was ours. Mine. The deep possession that burned through me whenever those big purple eyes looked my way was almost as dangerous as my powers.

I wanted nothing more than to claim her, to take what's mine. My darkness could sense hers, withering beneath her skin, begging her to let it go.

I was going to teach her just that. To let it all go.

I'd had my doubts. I'd thought the fates were playing tricks on me, providing me a small quiet Mate that needed constant protection, but I was so very wrong.

Amaya was more powerful than all her Circle Mates; her dark magic was pure, strong and she just needed to accept it. Striding forward with it hanging from my lips, I blew the smoke into his face, watching as he coughed from its sour smell.

We had swiftly found the White witch leaving the council's other building, followed him to his large home a few miles from the Light city and tied him to his dining chair whilst he screamed and tried to trance us with his magic. Luckily for us, Jerry had provided us with charms that would rebel against any white witch's magic. That sneaky ghost had appeared at the Dark mountains portal as we made our leave to find the witch and offered them to us.

Amaya had sunk her lovely black nails into the ghost butler's heart, and he relished in being able to serve the Dark Witch line again.

The Mayfeaver clouded my mind more as I stared, now slightly blurry eyed at the White witch the Council had chosen. He was one of the top diamond finders Wisteria had ever had, spelling the diamonds into magical objects and selling them for top coin in the light city. My lip curled in disgust.

Diamonds were sacred, full of pure healing magic that the Council used as more pull and control over its people.

Using my thumb and index finger, I opened his eye, pulling the skin wide to reveal the curve of the ball as it sat in its socket. Taking one last long draw of my smoke, I pulled it from my lips and pressed its burning end to the white of his eye. The sizzle of its gooeyness and his screaming filled my ears. It settled the noise in my head even more as my vines slithered from my leather jacket and curled around my hand holding the smoke.

The smell of his eye melting reminded me of singed hair. I watched the white goo drip down his cheek as Rí gagged behind me.

"Come on man. Tha's gross." He rumbled even as he gave me a depraved smirk.

Sighing, done with my fun, I snapped his neck with a flick of my wrist and discarded the butt of my smoke on the floor.

We were all depraved, dark, deadly weapons, just waiting to unleash our full potential upon the realms. Amaya had awakened us from our endless dreary lives; things were just starting to get fun.

Fun. Huh, maybe the Fates Above did know what they were doing. And maybe, just maybe, it was time for me to accept the gift they had given.

I grinned wide as the dragon gave one last stomp to the white witch's head, squelching it under his big foot, before he tore from the room and shifted into his dragon. He was obviously ready to get back to her.

I wasn't going to hide our evidence. I had decided to leave it there for the Council to find. Rolling my shoulders, I looked around the blood-splattered room, and decided that actually, I was going to wait right there.

I sat in the recliner by the window, popped my feet up, lit a fresh smoke and waited for the entertainment.

Twenty-Two

'Gossip Reveals Secrets-Fama Detegit Secreta'

Amaya

"He just strolled in? The self-entitlement!" Bri screeched as she placed another ice bun on my plate. Jerry had found her in a pile of welcoming trees by the portal the next morning, giggling and chatting away to them as they wrapped themselves around her. She had been in disbelief when a branch had reached through and pulled her over.

After many gasps and, "Oh my Fates Above" from her, we had settled in the armchairs by the fire with a boxful of her sweet treats.

I sat and stared at her beaming face. I hadn't known where to start, what to say. What were you supposed to do in these social situations? I had never done this before.

"So, tell me everything." She had asked as she peeked over her huge cup of coffee. And before I knew it, I had blurted everything, from the twins, to waking up in the Dead village, Rí and I's mating, Cole, my lack of magic, Isa. Everything down to Ziel poking about my bedroom last night. I told her of everything that had been piling up in my thoughts, all my unanswered questions and more.

She gaped at me, her mouth open with an unchewed piece of bun hanging from it. I took a big gulp of my own coffee and almost moaned from the bitterness. It was still so hot it burned its way down my throat. I was still getting used to a coffee actually being hot. Lyal's stale left over coffee was always going to be ingrained in my mind.

I squinted at her as she hastily chewed and swallowed her bun, sat forward and placed her coffee on the table. She stood up, smoothed down her bright blue dress that was scattered with daisies and…threw herself at me. I had just enough time to stretch my arm to the side, so my precious hot coffee didn't spill all over us.

Ravioli's loud squawk pulled a surprised squeak from her as she squeezed me tighter.

I didn't know what to do.

She was hugging me.

Did I pat her back?

I looked at Ravioli with wide panicked eyes and I swore he was laughing at me, a low cough like noise that sounded like a chuckle.

I gave him the finger.

"Ummm," I hummed as I slowly patted Bri's back with my empty hand.

"I…I'm sorry. It's just. You had such a shit life. You knew nothing of Wisteria. And…and…"

Fuck.

Oh fuck.

She was crying.

I was freaking out.

"Your little brothers..." she sniffled and pulled back slightly; her eyes were watery and red rimmed.

"You deserve the world. I'm so happy Rí found you. I'm so happy that we are now best friends! I will show you everything you need to know in Wisteria! I will make sure you are always filled with hot coffee and iced buns and…and…and when you get your brothers here, I will spoil them with as many cakes as they can eat and…"

"—wait! Hold on."

I pulled myself from her arms, gulped a mouthful of less than hot coffee and frowned at her.

"You're crying for …me?"

She smacked my arm, shocking me with her surprising strength as she picked up her abandoned drink and sat back down.

"Of course I'm crying for you! You lived a shit life! You were dealt a really shit deal and yet you still protected those little boys?"

"Well yeah. Because they're mine."

"Your obsessive side is so cute." She grinned.

Fucking cute? Never in my life had I been called cute before.

Useless, pathetic, vile, mongrel, monster. Never cute.

Had she said we were best friends? We barely knew each other. Is that how being someone's best friend worked? I observed her silently as she chatted away. Not once had I felt the uneasy churn in my gut in her presence. In fact I was actually fairly…settled with her. Her constant chatting hadn't once annoyed me; her happy bubbly self almost out done the noise in my head. Bri was easy to be around; I could talk to her without fear of weakness. She didn't demand I be someone or something I wasn't.

Bri was my friend.

We chatted for what felt like hours; well, she chatted, and I listened. Sitting and simply just enjoying someone's company was…nice.

I walked her to the portal when she claimed the cemetery 'freaked her tits off.' I had laughed and grazed my hands across the well-kept stones as Bri informed me of her plans for the afternoon.

"So I thought I'd slip a little something in his coffee and *then* the shit he'd spew would be real." She laughed; her head thrown back as she pictured her little plan. Apparently, some White witch was trying to shut her shop down, stating it was too "human" and nothing about it reflected their supernatural beings. But so what?

"He still drinks the coffees, so why is he being a douche?" She sniped as we passed the welcoming trees.

"What are you? A shifter? What made you think of a coffee shop right in the centre of the shadow land?" I asked curiously, completely ignoring the fact Ziel had already told me you just didn't ask that question here.

Beaming at me she said "I *love* that you asked me. I'm a White witch. Well, half. But I don't relate to the Light City and their order."

"Wait…you're a witch?" She was the first White witch I had come across that wasn't all about the Light City and the correct way to act. You would never have assumed she was a witch at all.

"Yep, didn't you wonder how you didn't sleep for like a straight twenty-four hours or more after that first coffee from me?"

How did she know that?

She giggled as the tree closest to the portal wrapped a branch around her arm, the purple droplets smearing across her blue dress.

"I make my own coffees, the brew is…different." Winking, she unwound herself as we walked through the portal. I wanted to make sure she was safely through, because there was no way I was letting anyone that belonged to me or was my friend go anywhere without protection. I knew Rí could take care of himself. He could simply eat anyone who annoyed him, but Bri, her infectious laughter and bright happy eyes needed me. I could feel it.

"Amaya. You are hereby summoned by the Council. Your presence is demanded immediately." Standing with his arms at the sides as if preparing for a fight stood a rather boring looking man.

I sighed, the Council outright just irritated me, the way they thought they could make demands of me, how they thought they had a right to anything in my life. Ugh. Men who thought they ruled and were God's fucking gift were the worst.

People like the Councilmen where the reason why I hated people. They were the ground beetles of the world; they mostly hid under rocks scared of the world, but when people challenged their manhood, they'd climb out, eat up the slugs and slide back away.

But all bugs were easily squashed.

"She's not going anywhere with you Gary," Bri said firmly as she stepped in front of me with her hands clenched at her side. She was slightly taller than my 5 ft 3 but damn, that's what I would call *cute.*

Also, ew. Gary? The name suited him.

I snickered at Bri and moved in front of her. I didn't need protecting. Especially from someone like *Gary.*

"It's fine, you head back."

"No way! I'll…" I gave her a firm yet kind-I think it was a kind- look and said, "Bri, I got this."

She sighed, frowning at the messenger before she said, "Okay, fine, but I'm finding Rí and telling him." Walking up to him, she poked his chest. A little zap of electricity spread across his body making the man flinch and wince as she then muttered, "And then I wonder who her dragon will take his anger out on then, hmm?"

The thought of Rí shifting into his dragon and eating someone out of anger for me was…exhilarating. I would never get used to someone wanting to protect me.

***

I walked through the white corridor and thought of my boys. The white walls reminded me of the nurse's room in their elementary school. The school were due their yearly shots, and so we lined up like all the others. The parents stood smoothing the children's hair and talking softly and lovingly to them, discussing what warm dinner they would be consuming that evening. Elyas, Elfyn and I stood staring straight ahead, our stomachs cramping with hunger. When we were next in line the nurse had simply said in her flat sluggish voice.

"The boys aren't down for shots. They aren't registered."

"If they aren't registered, how are they even in school?" I had asked back, no expression in my voice as I stared blankly at her.

After the parents had tutted at me for taking up their time, we had left, and it was that night I had searched Lyal's office and found they had no paperwork. No birth certificates, no foster paperwork. Nothing. They were essentially…not there.

Why did Lyal have the boys? Why me? What about the three of us was important that he wanted three fucked up kids? Could there have been a chance he knew? Knew that I wasn't human?

No, no that couldn't be it, because Lyal was as sluggishly human as they came.

I entered the circular room without knocking and stood with my hands hanging loose and looked at the three figures with a bored face.

"Amaya." The salt and peppered haired man nodded at me, his eyes looking behind me, no doubt searching for Rí.

"It seems we got off on the wrong foot. I am Mikhail, and this is Fergus and Finigan. We are the Council and bring order to Wisteria and have done for the past eighteen years."

He paused; was he waiting for me to gush and applaud him?

I stared at them in silence.

"We understand the confusion you must be feeling with everything if you truly are from the human realm."

Was he trying to trip me up there? They still didn't believe me, and I simply didn't care.

"Now, as the leaders of this realm—"

"Who appointed you?" I interrupted.

"Excuse me?"

"Who appointed you three leaders?" Did I have to spell it out?

"Listen here child, your kind almost destroyed this realm, and in doing so, *did* destroy others and closed off our entire travel system. Thousands are dead and lost to us because of the Dark Witches and their greed." One of the red-haired men sneered, his cold eyes stabbing me with his loathing.

"So you say," I said flatly.

He sputtered in outrage as I fought the urge to grin. The urge now becoming a regular occurrence. They were truly pathetic. Thinking they could simply take over from the dragons and Dark Witches' leaderships. Thinking they could control what was never theirs. I knew I wasn't essentially a true Wisterian, but surely the people deserved to live as they pleased?

"Do you care to explain as to why the gentlemen we had lined up for you hand in marriage was tied to a chair and dismembered last night?"

The fuck?

"You actually thought I was going to take some random man as my husband?" I could feel an odd vibration in my feet as the anger I had been holding back began to spill from the edges. Its white-hot burn was similar to the flame on my dragon's tail.

My teeth ground together as I wiped my hands on my pants, digging my nails into the material.

"I want you to understand something child." Fergus or Fanny, whatever their damned names were, stepped closer to me. Their cold eyes settled on my own as their lips curled in disgust.

Yeah, they really hated my kind.

"You do not have a choice in any matter. You are a monster. You are not wanted in Wisteria. We were kind in finding you a White witch. We thought it would simply defuse a situation before it got out of hand. You are *nothing.*"

Was he trying to hurt my feelings? Was I supposed to be tearing up and begging for their kindness? I breathed slowly to try and ease the boil that was brewing in my veins.

Breathe in.

Breathe out.

The noise in my head became screams. It begged me to delve deep and cause this man to bleed. To make him hurt.

Breathe in.

Breathe out.

I knew I was nothing. Being given a home and more people to protect didn't change my way of thinking of myself. I knew I was cold. I knew I was different. I just didn't care.

"You have waltzed around, claiming the Dark Mountain as yours, putting the last dragon under some sort of spell; it's *disgusting."* Mikhail chimed in, stepping beside the red-haired man, adding his own loathing gaze towards me.

The other man also sidled up, joining in with his lackeys and sneered, "The dragon is *ours—"*

Whatever they said next was muffled; they sounded as if they were under water as the vibration spread through my body. My teeth hurt from how hard I was clenching them and yet all I could think about was them claiming my dragon as theirs.

He was *MINE.*

I'm not really sure how it happened, but the wet tongue of the red-haired man speaking was hanging from my blood covered hand. My chest heaved as I glared at him through a red haze.

The garbled screams from his mouth were oh so satisfying as the other red-haired man grabbed him by the shoulders and pulled him away from me. Mikhail stared at me in disgust and horror. The red that now stained the white floor and their white cloaks was such a better look than before.

"Say that again. I couldn't quite understand you," I sneered at them as I wagged the tongue in their faces.

"You're a monster! You need to be controlled! You…you…"

"Fates Above what's happened in here!?"

Ugh. There he was, Cole. The Council's lap dog. No doubt he's here to join in with their disgust.

Mikhail smoothed out the horror on his face, straightened out his stained cloak, and stepped back away from the garbled screams and me, the 'monster', well I had finally given in.

I had finally let the dark thoughts take over and fucking hell it was glorious. The hot spray of his blood, the screams and the horror on their faces. Finally I was able to be the monster I was aways declared as.

"Amaya, we have decided you will be placed in our pr—"

"My, my. What have we here?" The sour smell of a certain drug and the raspiness of its owner stepped from behind me. Mikhail's face paled to almost as white as his beloved cloak.

"Ziel, this is not your concern." He gulped, pulling his shoulders back to seem taller no doubt.

Ziel tutted around his smoke, his green gaze shifting to me. and raised a brow at the tongue dangling from my fingers.

"Everything about the Dark Witch is my concern," he rasped.

I bristled at that. Why did this man get under my skin? He was irritatingly intriguing to me.

"Guess you didn't like my gift?" He asked them as he reached over and wiped a splatter of red from my chin. The skin where his thumb touched burned, begging for more of his touch.

I took a deep breath and tried to ignore my itching back. Cole stared at me, something wild and unknowing in his usual stoic expression.

"By gift, you mean the hands of a well-respected Diamond dealer?" Cole asked flatly, never taking his eyes from me.

I raised a brow at Ziel and snickered. Looked like we both liked to take people's bodies parts. Maybe he had the same noisy mind as I did.

Interesting.

"What are ye' all doing with my Mate." Growled behind me. The dragon's torso pressed against my back, warming me instantly.

I couldn't help the smile that spread across my face. It was starting out to be a good day. My dragon was here, I listened to my noisy head and now had a treat for my pet bird, and I had made a friend.

"Get out. GET. OUT," garbled the tongueless red-haired man from his knees.

Party pooper.

Mikhail gave me one last loathing look before he helped his Councilmen to his feet and shuffled to a hidden door on the other side of the room.

"Well," I started as I turned, hands on my hips and glared at my dragon and the Death warrior. "You just go ahead and dismember someone without me?"

"Dismember?" Rí raised his brows in question to Ziel, who shrugged and said, "I got bored."

"What is wrong with you all!?" Cole yelled with his hands gripping his hair. We all turned to him and stared. No one said a word as he muttered under his breath about misfits and doing as they please. His eyes were dull, almost lifeless and his skin was sickly pale. Whatever he was sick with seemed to be draining him.

"What's wrong with ye'?" Rí asked what we were all thinking.

"You look like shit," Ziel piped in as he lit a new smoke.

He ignored them and asked me, "Did you find anything in the Dead Village?" He rubbed his eye and scratched at his stomach before wincing.

"Nothing." I answered quietly as I watched him.

Something was seriously wrong with him. Something off. My stomach churned. "What's wrong—"

"Are you really that naive? Of course you found nothing. Access your magic first!" He threw his hands in the air, disgruntled and irritated as if we were naughty children.

He spun on his heel, heading towards the hidden door the Councilmen had left from.

"Acceptance is key Dark Witch," he snapped as the door slammed shut behind him.

Acceptance. There it was again. *Accept fucking what!?*

"What crawled up his prude ass?" Ziel rasped.

I rolled my eyes and left the room feeling confused; why was I concerned that Cole was sick?

Twenty-Three

'Push and Pull-Trudo Et Trabo'

Amaya

Bri had in fact found Rí and informed him I'd been 'taken' by the Council. He had apparently flown over here in such a rage, a few of the Lights Cities buildings had caught fire in his rage.

Ziel had been delivering another present, this one containing a foot, and had sensed me here. I didn't know how I felt about that honestly.

I was feeling a lot of things, things I had never felt before. I was confused by my worry of Cole. His tired eyes and sickly pallor were concerning. He hadn't even been as stiff and snippy as usual. Something was really wrong with him, and I was going to find out what.

And Ziel, Death's Warrior, well he was an enigma. He acted like I irritated him, barely spoke to me and yet he was there, showing up when I really didn't expect him. He had only mentioned us being 'Mates' in passing and yet we hadn't actually discussed it.

Then what happened if we did actually Mate? Was I supposed to be Mated to two men? Were we all supposed to live happily ever after together in the same house, the same bed.

Annoyingly, the thought of them both in my bed with me had my core heating, and embarrassingly, I knew Rí could smell it. The bright flare of his eyes and the way his tongue peaked out as if to taste the scent was a big enough sign.

Brushing away those very interesting thoughts, I thought of my boys. How many days had it been now? I hated myself for every second they were without me. I hated the thought of Lyal anywhere near them. My stomach churned.

So much unanswered, so much to figure out. My head was so noisy, so loud.

We walked in silence to the castle. Ziel's smoke blew out and blended in with the fog that gathered on the Mountain. Everyone seemed oddly subdued, lost in their own minds.

We entered the castle and the words 'To Keep Under Silence' greeted us as normal. The question was, what secrets? I had so much to learn, so much to understand. I kept telling myself I was going to find out what I needed to know, but other than more questions about my mother, the confusing things I felt towards Ziel and

Cole and the unknown 'acceptance', I hadn't found out anything. I was still very much in the dark.

I created a list in my head, getting more annoyed with each one I added.

1: Why had I been placed with Lyal?

2: Why couldn't I simply access my magic?

3: Why had the Council taken leadership?

4: Why did my magic bring me to Wisteria after being in the human realm?

And a new question that had started to rattle around in my rather full head…

5: Who was my father?

Isa's journal hadn't mentioned my father; it had mentioned her Circle Mates but not who they were, and also not that any of them were my father.

It was time I pulled up my big girl pants, took a deep breath and found shit out. So my first stop was Isa's journal. I needed to re-read it to see if I missed anything. Jerry had mentioned there were more of them.

Ziel settled himself in the chair closest to the fire and leaned his head back with his eyes closed, whilst Rí stood close behind me, his hands on my shoulder, comforting and warm.

"Are ye' okay Mo Chridhe?"

How did one answer a question they didn't have the answer to? Was I okay? Had I ever been 'okay'?

Before I could think of an answer, Jerry poofed in with an armful of black leather-bound journals and placed them on the table in front of the love seat.

"My Lady, Lords," he said whilst bowing low and poofing out once more.

Lords. As in plural. I glared at Ziel and settled into the seat after hanging the red-haired man's tongue on Raviolis perch, noting the thick fog coating the entire cliff below us. It was as if the Mountain could sense my moods. I made a note to ask Jerry. It was confusing having Ziel here, making himself at home by the fire. I was still getting used to sharing myself with Rí; was I expected to just accept that Ziel was now a part of my life also?

"If ye' are settling in Wee one, I will see to the bar."

I looked up to Rí and his warm eyes and gave him a small smile. I still couldn't quite believe it. This dragon was mine. All mine.

His low growl at my smile had it stretching wider before he leaned down and captured it with his lips. He kissed me slowly, sensually. This wasn't rushed or filled with passion. It was different yet still toe curling. I pulled back slightly, and he murmured against my now swollen lips, "I have something for ye'."

He reached into his back pockets and pulled out a set of black diamond earrings. They glistened from the candlelight next to him and something pulled at my chest. They were stunning and kind of matched the jewel nestled between my breasts.

"She doesn't have her ears pierced," rasped quietly over by the fire.

I hated the way Rí's smile dropped, the realisation in his eyes actually hurt to look at. I plucked the earrings from his big hands and held them to my chest.

"That doesn't matter. Thank you," I murmured to him, ignoring Ziel and his annoying input.

"Ye' won't be able to wear them—"

Before he finished talking, I reached up and shoved one of the earrings in my lobe, piercing into the skin with ease. The sting was nothing compared to the look on my dragon's face when he thought he had made a mistake in giving them to me.

I brushed Rí's concerned hand away, ignoring his look of frustration at me causing myself pain.

But pain didn't bother me.

I had lived through pain.

This was nothing.

I pierced the other ear and stood to look in the mirror on the dresser. They were beautiful. They hung heavy on my freshly pierced lobes and the bright red blood that dripped from them was almost enchanting.

My purple eyes stared back at me, and I froze. I kept forgetting that my eyes were purple. Not just that, but my hair was thick shiny and healthy, my skin clean and without bruising.

Would my boys even recognise me?

"Ye' look utterly stunning," Rí said in his low timber, making me shiver as he wiped the blood away before kissing each already healing lobe.

He left with a raised brow as Ziel, still in the armchair, and I sighed into the silence. Sitting back down into the love seat, I pulled a journal into my lap; it seemed Jerry really did know everything. I noted Isa's messy handwriting across the first page. The pen had been pressed down hard, as if she wrote in anger. I brushed my hands down the page and closed my eyes and tried to picture her.

I came up with nothing. Because I almost felt nothing towards this woman. This woman who had indeed wanted me, who had obviously been betrayed in some way. I felt nothing because I had this feeling that she had purposely placed me with Lyal. Because if she did, then it was her fault that I was poisoned by a monster and in doing so, it made me into one.

To keep under Silence.
Or are we being silenced?
I can't scrape the filth from my skin.
I'm so dirty.
So unclean.
They are monsters.
Evil.
My poor sisters, I can never apologize enough.

She wrote of monsters as if they were all evil, as if they were all vile. She would have hated me.

The trees are weeping; I weep along with them.
I must be strong; I must carry on.
This isn't about power anymore.
I met them today, today of all damn days.
They believe I betrayed them also.
I would never!

"Her Circle Mates were shifters, a Wolf pack I believe." Ziel rasped behind me, making me jump and drop the journal with a thump to the floor.

I gave Ziel my death stare and bent down to pick the book up. The drag of his finger across my lower back caused me to gasp, my Circle Mark tingling and moving as if reaching for more contact.

"Interesting," he muttered.

I straightened up and pulled my top down to cover my back, glaring at him as I asked, "How do you know that?"

"The dead told me."

Why was this man so infuriating! "Want to expand on that?"

He took his time reaching into his jacket and producing yet another smoke. He went to place it between his lips before I reached up and snatched it from him, squashing it in my fist as I kneeled on the love seat, clenching my hands over the back rest and said, "Enough. Stop dicking around and give me the fucking answers."

His face hardened as he leaned down eye level with me, his green eyes glaring into my purple ones.

"Beg me for it, princess."

Hell to the fucking no. I didn't beg for anything. Ever. Who the hell did he think he was? I didn't ask him to come back to the castle-he just came. I didn't ask him to turn up at the Council-he did it out of his own choice. Yet now he was hinting at things I didn't know and told me to beg for the answer?

I growled as I leaned further in and said through clenched teeth, "why are you here?"

"Why are *you* here?" He asked back, his breath warm and strangely minty against my face.

"*What?*"

He laughed and straightened up, pulled another smoke from his never-ending pocket and lit up and stared at me with slightly glassy eyes.

"Why are you here Dark Witch?"

"This is my mountain…apparently. Oh and I died. Now why the hell are you here?" I said flatly, annoyed and yet…slightly invigorated at the back and forth.

"I go where you go, Mate." He ended the word with a pronounced 'T' as if mocking the word. Neither of us spoke; we both stared at each other in the mocking silence, his cloud of smoke drifting around the room and filling the space with a sourness that was beginning to make my noisy head fuzzy and muffled. I leaned in closer and inhaled deeply; my head was filling with its calmness, and it was oh so fucking peaceful. Who knew having a quiet mind was actually relaxing.

Leaning back down he slowly blew the smoke straight into my waiting mouth. I took it into my lungs, loving that my body was now loose and soft, just like cotton candy.

My eyes grew heavy as I stared at the Death Warrior over the back of the chair. And suddenly I blurted out a question that had nothing to do with my birth mother.

"What do you do as a Death Warrior?"

His brow raised and before my brain even registered what he was doing, his body blurred. His body thinned out and became nothing but bones. Before me, stood in Ziels place, standing in his clothes and leather jacket, was a full-blown skeleton.

The fuck.

Was I hallucinating?

Thick black vines slithered from between his bones and tangled in my long hair. One sharp thorn protruding from a vine sliced into my cheek. The trail of blood tickled as it ran down my pale skin.

I must really be fucked up because I actually found a skeleton sexy.

I cleared my throat and croaked, "Interesting."

He snapped his bony jaw together and shifted back, licked the trail of blood from my cheek, gave me a knowing smirk and swagged back off to the armchair. Throwing himself down and resting his feet on a pile of books, he said, "You didn't die. You were reborn."

"How did the dead tell you?" I managed to ask; my heart had slowed down so much I was unsure if I was actually alive. That drug was so damned strong, I didn't know how *he* was alive.

"I'm Death's Warrior. Everything in the Vale of Death is a possibility to me. You have a cemetery full of dead witches as your garden feature."

He could speak to the dead. My dead ancestors had spoken to him.

I was jealous.

I couldn't even deny it.

He sighed and flicked blue flames into the dying fireplace.

"Your mother, Isa, found her Mates the day she found out she was pregnant with you. They were wolf shifters, from the human realm. Apparently, they had a hand in finding your foster father, whom, might I add, will be tortured by my hands when we find you a way back to these boys of yours."

"Okay, hang on there," I said as I climbed over the seat and sat opposite him, leaning forward with interest.

"Her Mates were wolves, and they helped put me with Lyal? So they knew him? And what do you know of my foster prick?"

Had Lyal known I was a Dark Witch?

"They never mentioned that, just that the pack knew he would take you. Something about deals were made and your safety with the correct ending was involved. And I know everything I need to know about you Dark Witch."

"The fuck does that mean!" Correct ending? Like my life had been panned out for me! This was insane. I chose to ignore his comment about knowing everything about me. No one would ever truly know everything about me. The darkness inside my noisy head would always be hidden.

He shrugged.

This was the most I had been able to find out, so I pushed for more. "But did they mention who my birth father was? Who betrayed them? Why did they shut the portals? What deal? With who—" He held his hand up, cutting off my many questions.

"Ask them yourself."

"I can't. I'm a fucking dud. I have no power," I growled shocking myself at my frustration. I knew being unable to access this so-called power of mine had been annoying, but I hadn't realised how much it had been irritating me. Truthfully, it was damn right pissing me off. How was I supposed to be this strong powerful Dark Witch when I didn't even know how to access it in the first place?

He shocked me by snapping forward and gripping my face, pinching it harshly between his thumb and finger.

"You're a fucking Dark Witch. Stop being so fucking weak."

Weak…he thought I was weak. I was anything but *weak!*

I pushed to my feet and shoved at his shoulder, that angry vibration pushing through my veins for the second time that day. How dare he speak to me like that! I had done everything and anything possible to ensure I wasn't weak. Being weak had stopped being an option for me when Elyas and Elfyn entered my pathetic life.

"I am anything but fucking weak!" I growled.

He grinned, raising his brow as he looked around the room before pointedly saying, "I know."

Every book that had been piled in my room now floated in the air, hanging there in suspense. I gawked at them and looked at Ziel.

"I had to get you angry."

I jumped as every book smashed back down to the floor, gravity now pulling them down.

"You have the power; you just need to feel it." Standing up, he rolled his shoulders and said, "Don't tame those demons, Mate. You never know when you'll need to unleash them."

Then he lit up another smoke and left me alone in my room full of scattered book.

Twenty-Four

'A Day Or Two To Turn Blue-Dies Vel Ut Convertat Bue'

Amaya

Ravioli flew into the room not long after Ziel left, sat on his perch and ate the tongue I had forgotten I had left for him.

I sat by the fire in hopes of it warming the coldness that had seeped into my bones when Ziel had left. Rí was still at the bar, Jerry was off doing whatever the ghost did, and Bri was probably tucked nice and warm in her bed. My boys…I couldn't think of them; it hurt too much, it took the air from my lungs and left me gasping.

My magic had indeed showed itself when my emotions became almost uncontrollable. So it was there. But I needed to use them with ease. I needed a clear head to get to my boys; I needed to be calm when I ripped Lyal limb from limb.

Looking to the floor I saw the books that had crashed back down. I picked up the one closest to me and put it on the table. Frowning I turned it around and read the title, 'A Day Or Two To Turn Blue.'

I flipped through the pages, the old Latin unreadable, but towards the end of the book, just before I gave up, was a few pages in English.

When a pure-blooded Dark Witch dies, her magic intensifies and becomes transferable. This is usually done to help the next generation become stronger. A ritual is done to complete the process.
First a cleanse. The body is washed of any dirt or grime.
Then Wisteria petals are sewn into their wrists-a bracelet of the tree of life. A sign of respect to the First Lady.
Finally, they are buried in the Mountains cemetery with Willow moss roots and Wisteria petals scattered across the fresh dirt.
Once this is done, the power that was once hers, would transfer to the next generation.
However, this power can be stolen in the cruellest of ways. Unless willingly, the only way to transfer a Dark Witches power is when they are deceased. During the early stages of life upon Wisteria, certain supernatural believed that mating with the deceased witch would pass the power onto them.

After multiple attempts, the Dark Witches had to hold off a witch's burial and incorporated a two day to turn blue rule. If the Witch had started to decompose, they would not be touched.
So the Dark Witches would surround the deceased, protecting her body from any male that may have tried to steal her power.
Cremation is not an option for a Dark Witch. In burning their body, they burn their power and along with it, the power of future generations.

I was nauseous. Sick to my stomach. The White Witches, and I knew it was aimed at them, would purposely mate with a witch's deceased form to gain access to her power. And they said that the Dark Witches were the greedy power-hungry ones.

"That's a very heavy read My Lady."

I slammed the book and threw it to the table. I hated when people disrespected books but that one gave me cold chills and a horrid sick feeling deep inside my gut.

"It's sick. Fucking sick."

"Indeed, most history is most distasteful."

Distasteful wasn't enough to describe the horror that the witches had been through. The disrespect and utter fear they must have felt. Knowing what could potentially have happened to their body when they passed. Knowing that their temples of life were going to be violated and stolen from them.

"If all the Witches died during the war, did any of them…suffer this?" I asked frowning.

"The witches that perished in the war disintegrated into dust my Lady and disappeared into the wind. There were no bodies to bury."

Is that why I was having so much trouble finding my power? If they weren't buried and didn't have the ritual, then the power wouldn't have moved onto the next generation. To me.

"The closest bloodline of Lady Samara never needed the ritual to gain their powers."

I frowned again, I was going to have permanent frown lines if this kept up.

"Yes, you are of her bloodline, the closest to it. You did not gain your powers from a ritual. Your power is and has always been inside you."

Part of me had hoped that the reason I couldn't access my powers was because the ritual hadn't been done, that it wasn't my fault that I couldn't find my magic. However, that would have been the easy way out, the weak way.

I wasn't weak.

"What do I need to accept? Everyone keeps telling me to accept, but what?"

"Yourself my Lady. Until you accept yourself, accept who you truly are, your powers will not come forth." He poofed from the room leaving me staring open-mouthed at his left-over glow.

It was that easy? All that time, all that time away from my boys, all this waiting and I just had to accept myself?

"Fine," I called out into the empty room.

"I accept myself. I'm a Dark Witch. I'm from the Dark Mountain. Happy?" I looked to the ceiling as if it was going to answer me.

Nothing.

Nothing but the crackle of the fire and the noise in my head.

Ravioli blinked his beady eyes at me before shuffling on his perch.

I growled out loud and stomped from the room, up the dark stair way, past the cold judgy eyes of my ancestors and out into the cold night. I stomped my way to the cemetery and stood there with the wet moss seeping into my socks and the cold mist settling on my skin.

"I accept! I'm accepting it! Okay!?" The dead didn't answer.

The waves below the cliff crashed against the rock, angry slams of water that created sprays of salty tears. The trees wept their purple liquid and the branches, for once, stayed solid and still.

"Please just…help me get to my boys. Please." I whispered. I had begged. I had begged my ancestors and the Dark Mountain. I had begged for their help and yet they gave me nothing. I screamed at the stone in anger. They would speak to Ziel, but wouldn't speak to me, their only living relative? Was I that much of a monster, that much of a nobody that not even the ancestors would help me?

My shoulders slumped, the anger seeped from my body and my pent-up rage diminished. I was failing. I was failing to protect the twins. I had let Lyal go too far and in doing so, he had killed me and took me further away than I could possibly have ever gone.

I truly was nothing.

"Mo Chridhe, what are you doing out here?" My dragon asked as he walked through the iron gates towards me. His glowing kind eyes and soft smile were a comfort I didn't deserve. I didn't answer him; instead, I let him see the utter soul-drowning sadness and guilt that seeped into my weary bones. Because I was. I was sad for the twins and the life they had to live; I was sad I had missed so many days with them, sad for Cole and his sickness, sad for the witches and the horror they had to live through.

And finally, I was sad for myself, sad that I was everything that everyone had always said I was. A monster, a freak, a dud.

Rí smoothed my damp hair from my face, reached down and lifted me into his arms. I wrapped my arms around his neck as he carried me back into the mountain, into my room and through to the bathroom that I never truly paid much attention to. He put me down to the black tiled floor and turned the shower on behind a huge glass wall. He helped me remove my clothes, placing a soft kiss to each ear lobe before following me into the hot spray of water. Never once saying a word. He washed me with such gentle hands my cold heart warmed under his soothing touch.

"Ye' have so much on ye' mind. So much ye' must do. Let me care for ye'. Let me take some of ye' burdens," he murmured as he slowly rubbed soap into my shoulders. I nodded slowly and closed my eyes, gave in to his warm touch and let him take control of the moment. He was so loving, so kind. So utterly devoted to me. The way he treated me made my eyes sting with tears that wouldn't shed. I had never been able to cry.

The act just never happened; no tear ever spilled from my tired eyes.

I looked at him from under my lashes and placed a soft kiss to his soaking wet shirt. He had taken me into the shower, cleaned my entire body and not once had he made me feel like there was an ulterior motive. Not once had he made me feel we had to do more. He had simply wanted to take care of me.

My dragon had a kind heart.

I unbuttoned his shirt and pushed it from his massive shoulders. Pressing a soft kiss to his chest I smiled at the purr that vibrated from him. I squeezed soap into my hands and began to wash him as he had me. I showed him with this act that I cared; I cared in my own fucked up way.

Once we were fully clean, he wrapped me in a large black towel and picked me back up, cradling me in his arms. He took me to my room, placed me on the huge bed and laid down next to me, pulling my damp head on to his chest. His heart beat slowly as his chest rumbled with his contented purr.

This man had truly taken me as his. Body and soul.

My eyes slid shut as his warmth spread through my body, pulling me into a deep slumber as my twins' faces flashed in my mind. Their big blue eyes begged me for help, begged me for my protection.

"They're gone!"

I jumped up, heart slamming against my rib cage as I looked around the darkened room; the fire crackled and fog thickened outside the arched windows. Looking down at Rí's sleeping form, I noted the small frown and downward tilt to his lips.

Confused as to what had woken me up, I slid to the edge of the bed and picked up the fallen silk pyjamas. Dropping the towel, I shivered as the exposed air hit my cold skin.

"They're gone, you know."

I snapped my head up, holding the top to my chest covering my nakedness. A luminous glow stood floating at the end of the bed. It flickered before focusing into a small child, her pin straight hair and purple eyes an obvious sign of her being a Dark Witch.

"Who's gone?" I asked quietly, hoping not to wake my dragon.

"Everyone," she answered in her small childish voice.

"Who?" I whispered as I quickly donned my sleepwear. Shuffling around to the end of the bed, I stood facing her. So far Jerry had been the only ghost I'd come across.

Her eyes lowered to my chest, where the jewel Rí had given me rested between my breasts, warming the skin there like his touch always did to me.

"They all burned you know. They all burned and now they can't be with us. *You* are all that's left."

She had to mean the witches; Jerry had said they all turned to dust. This could be my opportunity to ask her things only the Dark Witches knew.

"Who betrayed them? Why did they shut the portals?"

She sighed and twirled in a circle, her glow floating off her like whisps of fireflies drifting into the night. The bright whisps glided through the black mist in my eye before disappearing completely.

"Well, they couldn't let them have the humans, could they? Greedy little things."

The humans? The witches were protecting *humans?* The very beings that had looked upon me as a stain on their perfect lives. The very beings who had abused me and created the noise in my head.

Why would anyone want to protect them?

"Why were they protecting the humans? From who?"

She spun and spun, making me dizzy. I wanted to grab her by the shoulders and shake her; I wanted to yell in her little glowing face and demand she answer me. I stood still and mentally told the voices to piss off.

"Why, the humans are innocent of course!" she giggled as her puffy dress spun and flared out around her.

That was something the humans were not; and that was innocent. They all lied, cheated, abused and slid their way around life.

I *hated* them.

"Without them, there is no us." Whispered so close to my ear, the cool breath of its owner made me shudder.

I spun around and stared wide-eyed at the elderly lady stood before me. Her black gown glowed in the same manner as the little girls, and she stared at me with familiar purple eyes. Another ghost.

Were the witches finally answering me? Had they actually heard my beg of help?

"What do you mean?" I whispered watching her as she gazed around the room as if remembering a fond memory. This could have been her room; she could have sat in this very room and lived her life.

"The humans are life; we are them in death."

The fuck? Did all ghosts speak in riddles?

Ravioli squawked from his perch causing the little girl to scream and poof from the room. The old woman pointed her gnarled finger at him and snapped, "What's that?"

"My pet, Ravioli."

"That's not your Familiar," she sneered before poofing away also.

A familiar? What was that! I was now left with even more questions! I huffed and climbed back on the bed, now wide awake as I stared across the room at my bird's beady eyes. He was always watching me with an intensity I couldn't fathom.

"A familiar," I muttered to myself.

"He's watching you child," She whispered coldly into my ear once more. I jumped and my eyes flung open, burning from the brightness of the morning bursting through the open windows. Rí's heavy arm was draped across my waist as I gently pushed it off me and sat up.

Had that all been a dream? Was I now making things up to try and get myself some answers? I pulled at the silk top I wore and frowned. Looking over at Ravioli watching me from his perch I squinted at him, if I really focused, it almost looked as though he also had the smallest of black mist floating around him.

A sleepy yawn from behind me and the toe-curling warmth of Rí's arm sliding around my waist and pulling me back against his chest had my stomach fluttering.

"Wee on—"

"What's a familiar?"

Twenty-Five

'Confusion Of The Mind-Confusio De Ille Mnetis'

...

Darkness called to me, its cold empty arms open and ready to embrace me as I yearned to give in, yearned to release the burn of anger I held in the pit of my stomach. The misty draught of death whispered to me in sinful, silky ways of love. It floated around my seeking soul searching for an opening I kept shut and hidden with the biggest of locks my damaged mind could create.

But all locks erode after time.

I hovered between the scorching heat of Life and the alluring cold of Death. The temptation was constant to give in and join the Darkness in its hunt for revenge and vengeance and release its coiled body of pent-up rage.

It's always there, always with me, assuring me that I was not alone in this anger, not alone in this clouded world of sickness. It slithered across my clammy skin begging for me to answer its desperate call, sneaking in between the cracks that had become more exposed as the years slowly crawled by.

My mind flickered with the different ways of revenge I planned to bring upon my victims like the pages of a book. So many different ways and various weapons to choose from, each one gorier and more gruesome than the other. This however, I would always remember. It would be embedded within my mind and soul forever relaying the turn of events.

A shudder ran through my tense body as the hot lava-like blood flowed to the ground, splashing my clothes like a pretty little accessory I planned to wear with pride. The smell of its coppery iron tang mixed with the humid air, created a stifling smell that caught my breath. My face stretched with a smile as I looked upon my work of art; the splashes of colour spread far and wide and the mangled mess in front of me would be a horror to most. But to me, it was a glorious beginning, a release of creativity and need that had been building for years. Something within me had been let free and it wanted, no, needed more. Tension left my shoulders as a thrill of happiness stretched within me.

The body before me was shrouded in a wet darkness. The voices whispered to me, I ignored them at first, but they became so loud I had no choice but to give in.

Stepping over the spreading puddle of life leaving its owner, I gathered my leaking confused thoughts and shoved them back into its broken box of secrets where even I had no idea what had happened.

Twenty-Six

'The Pleas Of The Weak-De Placitis Information'

Rí

"A Familiar?" I looked from my stunning Mate to her bird and tried to pull my thoughts from her sleep-mussed hair, kissable lips and enticing body teasing me in those silken pyjamas.

The bird only ever had eyes for Amaya, its black empty eyes always trained on her, watching her every move. I didn't blame it; she was enrapturing. Her bringing up a Familiar was a valid point. Some powerful witches were lucky enough to gain a Familiar to help guide and comfort them during a difficult time of their lives. Amaya had been through so much it wasn't surprising to me that a Familiar would seek her out.

I said as much to her and she hummed, thinking over what I said. I found she did that a lot; she liked to process whatever was said to her, not giving a reply instantly like most. She tended to keep her thoughts to herself, though I had noticed her expression was less closed off around me.

The first time I had seen her smile, my stomach had flipped, and my dragon had roared his glee at our Mate. Pleasing her was all we ever wanted; we would live our long life making sure she smiled. She deserved the world and more- I knew it was going to take more than me to make her see that, to make her see that she was utterly perfect and was more than her abuse and pain. I knew it was going to take more than me as a Mate for her to see the love she could have, which is why I didn't bat an eye at Ziel coming back to the castle with us. He had as much right to be by her side as I did; he was just going to be a difficult one to tackle. He was almost as closed off and withdrawn as her.

She needed my love, my devotion and my touch just as much as she needed Ziel and his dark view of the world. I saw the Darkness in her when she ripped the tongue from Fergus's mouth. My dragon had chuffed with laughter and my chest had swelled with pride. My Mate wasn't one to sit idly by and take the words of the Council. She was so strong. She just needed to see it herself.

And Cole?

Fucking Cole. The White Witch had been a pain in my ass since he was a child. Always strutting about in his prim and proper ways and his superior complex. Yet lately, even I had noticed how tired he looked. He looked sick, and definitely not himself. I knew that eventually our Mate's mark would call to him, whether he liked it or not, and to be honest when Ziel had said he'd silently handed him the address for that White Witch, I knew then that he wasn't as immune to her as he let on.

I hated how she worried for him, how he was just another worry clouding her head and pulling her down. I had planned to see what I could find out about him so she could concentrate on getting her powers to listen. There was only so many more days she would be without her twins before she broke. I could already see her steal resolve crumbling under the pressure to get back.

I left her in a pile of books on witches and their Familiars and took to the skies. I allowed my dragon to fully take over for a while, internally laughing at how he spun and flipped around in front of her high arched windows. Her silent laughter as she watched from the chair by the window was euphoric.

We gave one last spin before gliding off in our search for some answers for our Mate. I took back control and flew into the Light City, purposely keeping to the outer edges so to not be spotted. I shifted and walked from a forest of Wisteria and kept to the shadows as I made my way to Cole's home, a stupidly big two-story mansion that screamed 'White Witch' with its perfectly trimmed bushes, white stone path and white door. I walked around the back, weaving in and out of the many bushes containing ingredients I knew he used for potions. I purposely stomped on a few as I passed them.

I had waited so long for my Mate, so long to provide her with happiness and love, to give her everything I had. The fact she had such an awful start to life pained me and filled me with so much rage I constantly had to swallow down the fire that threatened to burst from my mouth. I hated how I had to sneak around this prick's home in search for answers for her; a Mate should never have to be unsure on the feelings of her Circle Mates. I wanted to squash his perfectly shaven face in my bare hands for ever making her worry for him.

Hot steam drifted around my face before I realised how irritated I had become again. Shaking my head and ruffling my hair, I located his back door, made my way towards it and wrapped my large hand around the dainty silver handle. Before I could even twist, the door opened swiftly, the sour smell of drugs burning my nose and irritating my dragon once more.

"We had the same idea it seems."

"He's going to smell the Mayfeaver ye' *Fanan!*"

He laughed at my Scottish use of the word 'idiot' as I shoved past him pinching my sensitive nose to his smoke. I looked around the pristine kitchen. It looked almost unlived in.

"I've looked around everywhere. Nothing interesting. The boring witch didn't even have anything I wanted to steal." Ziel rasped and leaned against the island in the middle of the kitchen. His leather jacket creaked as it pressed against the pure white marble counter. He stubbed his smoke out on it, marking it with a gleam in his crazy ass-eyes.

I nodded once and made my way to the basement door; glad I didn't have to snoop around the prick's house. I trusted Ziel, as much as it annoyed me to admit it. I trusted him because I knew that everything he now did was for her.

Our Circle Mate. Our Link.

We were brothers now, forever more, a family.

The second my hand touched the door handle my dragon's hackles rose. The crackle of black magic lingering in the air was stifling. My eyes jumped to Ziel who had also noticed the change.

We opened the door and walked down the dark stairway. My shifter sight allowed me to see every groove, every mark and smudge along the white wall. I could taste the spicey flavour of black magic. Its burn along my skin had my dragon creeping forward, ready to burst free if needed.

Black magic had always been a vicious whisper among the witches. White and Dark Witches always had the agreement that it was to be avoided at all costs. It had always been the one thing that they had agreed on together. It spread through your veins like a sickness that poisoned you from the inside out. It slithered around your brain and clouded your entire perspective of the world. It turned your veins black with its sickness and completely overtakes your thoughts.

The White Witches had accused the Dark Witches of using it during the war; they had claimed that it was the use of the black magic that had caused the death of so many and had closed the portals, that it was reason of the Dark witches' demise, the reason they disintegrated into black dust and floated into the air as particles.

I called bullshit.

Vines slithered down the wall beside me as I flicked some flames from my hand and casting light around the large basement. The room was completely different to the vibe upstairs; the dirty walls and vile smell of something dead was pungent. I actually much preferred Ziel's sour drug then the one burning through my airways from the basement.

Right in the centre of the floor was a drain, stained and overflowed with thick sticky blood. Beside it was a silver tray, one you would usually see a surgeon with. I frowned, confused as to what we were seeing.

Ziel walked further into the room, knelt down and swiped his finger in the blood. His tongue peaked out as if to taste it, yet before I could bark a disgusted grunt at him, he straightened up, wiped his finger on his pants and aimed his now empty eye sockets at me.

"Something stinks of death here; it's not dead though," he rasped, swivelling his head around the room as if coating his now bony body in the scent surrounding us.

"It smells of death yet isn't dead?" I asked scratching at my beard. I hadn't realised how long it had grown the past few days.

He grunted, shifted back and grabbed another Mayfeaver with shaking hands. He relied on the drugs too much; his Darkness and hunger for souls needed a release and pushing the urges down were only going to cause more damage.

I shook my head at him and walked back up the stairs, my heavy feet stomping against the wooden steps. I needed fresh air, to get away from all the overbearing smells.

Why did Cole have a basement that stank of death and black magic? Why was there a drain overfilled with blood and surgeon tools.

What the fuck was that prick up to?

Ziel slowly strolled out the back door where I stood filling my lungs with clean air. The fucker was lucky the human diseases didn't affect us; the amount he smoked was worthy of death in the human realm.

"I have a source who can help with the location of who used Black magic," he muttered as he stared at me with glassy eyes.

"The location? We have the location. It was that smug prick."

"I dunno." He murmured, seeming unsure as his vines slithered from his sleeve and slapped at his cheek as his eyes lowered as if drifting off to sleep.

The fucker was so high he was falling asleep standing up.

Opening his eyes wider he bent his neck to both sides, a loud crack echoing in the silent garden as he started to walk away.

"Bring Amaya to the shadow land. I have someone who can help," he called over his shoulders.

I growled and stomped on Cole's bushes as I followed after him, annoyed at the way he commanded me and my dragon as if we were his fucking servant. If it wasn't something that would help my Mate in some way, I would have told him to go fuck himself. I flipped him off and shifted in the middle of Cole's path, ripping some of his bushes and trees from the roots as my powerful body took up the space.

There was no point in denying we had been there; anyone who smelt the sourness of Mayfeaver would know Ziel had been there anyways. If Cole had a problem, he could come find me.

***

Flying with my Mate's slight weight on my dragon's back, her cold hands gripped my humps and her thighs clenched around my lower neck. Fates Above, it was fucking glorious. Her trusting me to take her to the skies, to follow me from the safety of her castle and Mountain and to fly with her, made me one lucky fucking dragon. She smoothed her hands along my hot scales, spreading tingles of awareness through my entire shifted form.

Mating with her was better than I ever could have imagined; her body had accepted me in with ease, and although my dragon was still a possessive dick, knowing we had marked her for all to scent, it settled us slightly. Giving her our scaled jewel as my people did, it made me feel closer to them, to her. I wanted to make sure I kept with the traditions of my realm, even if I was the only one left.

We landed with a thud in a clearing a few metres away from the bustling streets of Wisteria and I shifted, making sure she landed in my arms as always. She grinned, her big purple eyes bright from the thrill of the skies.

"The Wisteria trees look incredible from that height," she said as she wiped her hands along her legs. She tended to do that when she didn't know what to do with herself; her hands gripped as if searching for something to hold, something to settle her emotions. Emotions I don't even think she realised she had.

Amaya was a closed off, expressionless person. Her flat tone and silence would come across as rude to most. But to me, I knew it was her trying to figure out her thoughts, her emotions and gaging what to expect next. It was the motions of an abused, neglected person.

My jaw ticked as her hands clenched and rubbed at her legs. I grabbed her hand softly, settling it against my side as we walked towards the busy streets. People swayed out of our way, their eyes widening when they saw her eyes, some nodded towards me before making space for my large form. She hummed beside me before veering off towards Bri's.

My Mate had found a friend in the half witch. The pair were complete opposites, one as morbid and dark as night and the other a damn daisy basking in the sunlight.

Bri had opened her coffee shop only a few years ago; the misfits of the Shadow land were untrusting at first, not seeing Bri as one of us, but instead seeing her as a spy of the White Witches and the Council. Her magic was all pure White Witch and yet not once had she ever used it on the misfits or shifters. Her coffee was enchanted to help strive of sleep, giving energy where it was most needed. You could request all sorts of coffees containing different types of intentions. Bri was truly amazing at what she did and had gained the trust of all of us here.

She was good for my Mate who I believe, never had a true friend before.

The loud scream of happiness that pierced my ear drums and had me wincing pulled a small twitch from Amaya's mouth. She didn't seem bothered by her friend's overly excited greeting.

She was beginning to change.

"OhmyFates! What are you guys doing here! Coffee? Cake? Oh Amaya I have the most amazing book you should read, but first you need to try this coffee—"

Her persistent rambling became muffled as I watched my beautiful Mate nod along and listen intently. Her big eyes tracked Bri as she busily made our coffees behind the counter, adding in her own 'hmm' where needed. The way her body tilted to the movements of the half witch had me beginning to smile widely.

It seemed my little Mate had found herself another obsession, a new need to protect.

"What?" Amaya asked, her eyes looking deeply into my own. I had to kiss her, to press my lips to her own plump ones. I needed her to feel what I was feeling, to understand the happiness she was bringing me.

Her lips parted easily, accepting my kiss with a small sigh of her own. I could have lost myself in her taste. The smell of dark fruits on her skin and in her silky hair begged me to pull her close, to deepen the kiss.

A small squeak had me pulling back; Bri stood with her hands to her chest beaming at us. I looked back into Amaya's now heavy eyes and growled low as she slowly swiped her tongue across her lower lip as if licking up my left-over taste.

I needed to leave; I needed to walk away before I threw her over my shoulder and carried her off to my big bed at the bar.

Swallowing, I rumbled low just for her ears. "I'm going to go, before I strip ye' bare Mo Chridhe."

Her breath hitched and her pupils dilated. I went to grab her and do just as I had feared I would do when she patted my chest and walked towards Bri who stood waiting with a coffee for her.

"Ziel should—"

"I'm fine. He'll get here when he gets here. Go."

Nodding, I dragged myself away. My dragon grumbled within me about our Mate needing our touch. I didn't disagree.

Shifting once more, I took to the skies and made my way to the Bookkeeper. Amaya had concerns as to who her father could be. Now we know her true age, we were hoping there had been record. If not, there were definitely more secrets involved then people were letting on.

Twenty-Seven

'Forgotten Magic-Oblitus Es Magicae'

Amaya

"That kiss was steamy. Like drench your panties steamy." Bri grinned as I choked on my sip of hot coffee. The bitterness and scorching temperature helped to ease the urge to run after Rí and dive on him. My dragon was a constant temptation.

"So this book?" I asked, trying to move on from the dragon and his heated eyes.

"Oh! Yes!" she reached behind her counter and handed me a thin paperback book. Its creased pages and frayed edges from years of use were yellowed. Turning to the first page, I frowned as I read the title: 'The beginning'

"The beginning of what?"

She sat in the chair opposite me and leaned in close before checking that no one was listening.

'Of Wisteria. Lady Samara was the first Dark Witch to find Wisteria, her, a Dragon, a Wolf, and a Fae. They mated! They were Circle Mates."

Holy shit…fae? The Fae was real? Tall sexy long hair men with wings? They were a big staple in the books I used to sneakily read in the human realm.

"Why have you given me this?"

"Because!" she whispered leaning in closer "it holds secrets only a Dark Witch would understand!"

I didn't want to reveal any more secrets. I already had enough on my plate, figuring out how to use my powers, getting back to my twins, transferring some to them. My birth parents, Lyal, why the war began. It was a lot. My noisy mind was already too crowded, too busy.

"Hmm, thanks. Do you have a Familiar?" I asked, the books I had read said that Familiars had stopped finding their way to witches around a century ago, easing away from the new realms and the new ways of life. That only the most powerful were lucky enough to have one.

She tilted her head and frowned before her eyes widened, "Oh! Ravioli? I should have guessed…yes, he could be your Familiar. You said he just kept appearing right? I think he must have sensed your need for him."

I told her of my dream, how the ghost witch said he *wasn't.*

"What else would he be? No, I do think he's yours. What did Jerry say?"

"He said—"

I cut off when the strong sour smell of Ziel floated into the shop, completely overtaking the bitterness of the coffee. He stalked towards me, his green eyes glassy yet focused on me with such an intensity my heart began to beat faster the closer he got.

Nodding to Bri he muttered "Halfling."

Her eyes widened as she stood, wiping imaginary crumbs from the table as she stuttered "-oh hello. Well. Um…the book is here with me Amaya." Giving me a bright smile that faulted as she passed Ziel, she disappeared behind two swinging doors.

Raising a brow at Ziel in question, he shrugged and gestured to the door. I walked out slowly, still trying to catch a better glimpse of the mocking black mist.

We walked in silence down the street, neither of us saying a word. I wanted to ask where we were going, why I had to go with him. Yet the childish part of me refused to be the first to give in and talk.

"You should read that book." He rasped, making me want to grin at him giving in first. I kept my face neutral.

"Why?"

"The halfling was right, it reveals secrets only the Dark Witches will *want* to know."

I swatted the thick thorny vine that had crept from his jacket and lifted my back revealing my Circle Mark. Did he have full control of those vines?

"What would I *want* to know?"

"Ah you know, just why they thought so highly of the humans, why the White Witches wanted to get to them."

I stopped in my tracks and gaped at him, "How do you know that?" Was he in my head? Had he seen my dreams? I wouldn't put it past the nosy fucker.

He raised his brow at me, and tutted. "The dead told me. Chatty lot." Of course, my ancestors seemed to like to tell him everything.

"So it was the White Witches. But why, what did they want? Why did my ancestors want to protect the *humans?*" I pondered aloud, unable to keep the dismay from my voice when I spoke of the humans.

He hummed and shoved his hands in his pockets as we followed a trail that led to a street containing small cottage-like homes. Each one was filled with flowers and life, all except one right at the end. Instead of bright sunflowers, this one had a garden of dead shrivelled up roses. Instead of neatly painted gates and window trims, the wood looked as though it was rotting. The low windows were each covered by thick drapes obscuring our view and making it look all the more abandoned.

"Why are we here?"

He ignored me, opened the gate and slowly stalked towards the door. I followed him, jolting when my body vibrated from the feet up, my noisy filled mind almost screamed as a spicy stale smell burnt the hairs in my nose. I wrinkled my face in disgust. Ziel reached into his pocket and withdrew ...a hand. A real hacked off at the wrist hand. Its bluish hue looked as though it sweated.

I decided then that I was most definitely mentally unwell, because who watched on as someone withdrew a hand from their pocket and didn't scream and question them? I simply waited expectantly as if it was all very normal to me.

"What is that smell?" I asked pinching my nose together.

"Black magic" he muttered as he flattened out the hand onto the glass pane of the door and waited as it began to glow. It vibrated before a click sounded, letting us know the door had been unlocked.

"Why the hand?" I muttered as we stepped over the pile of dead bugs littered by the open door.

"It's a magic hand," he rasped as he shoved it back into his pocket. Somehow it left no smell, no bulge or showed any sign of being unable to fit. I could use a jacket with magic pockets. The amount of books I could keep with me at all times would be incredible.

"It's my damn magic hand," a gnarly voice snapped from somewhere behind a huge pile of dusty books. "Now give it back boy." He snapped the B with a pop of his mouth as he wobbled around the books.

A tiny bald Asian man stood leaning against a stick glaring at Ziel. I sensed the magic there within him and somehow, I knew it wasn't his. It belonged to someone else. This man was utterly human. My heart began to pound as I looked to Ziel, now realising why we were here.

Ziel walked past the man leaving me stood on his bug-riddled door mat as the man squinted at me.

Turning around to follow Ziel, he yelled, "Who's the girl!" before peeking back at me and snapping, "And shut the damn door!"

I hastily slammed the door shut, wafting up that vile spicy air and quickly followed them. His living room was full of books, towers and towers of them, leaning like the leaning tower of Pisa. Each thick book had bookmarks or noted paper sticking out. The elderly in Wisteria sure liked their books, and to be honest I couldn't blame them.

The old man plopped himself into a green looking armchair opposite the small fire that created too much warmth in the already stuffy room. Ziel rummaged around on his knees in a basket full of tea-stained looking paper.

"You're human?" I found myself saying as he adjusted himself in the chair, sighing contently as he lifted his slipper-clad feet onto the little stall in front of him.

"Obviously. But you can already sense that can't you girl." A steaming teacup floated past my ear, the spoon stirring whatever was inside.

"I need to know how; I have two humans that need to be able to stay here."

He never answered; instead he lifted his stick back up and poked at Ziel kneeling on the floor.

"It's not that one Idiot." Without a word Ziel moved on to another basket, this one fuller, bulging with screwed up papers.

"Stop staring at me with those purple eyes witch-it's unnerving." Sipping at the contents of the cup he peaked at me again, squinting and pursing his lips.

No one in this realm gave me answers, always staring with that squint of unease. I was starting to get fed up with it. And the new me was going to start getting stabby if I didn't start receiving answers.

"Got it." Smoothing out a crumbled paper Ziel stood and nodded to the man before walking back to the door.

I stayed put, glaring down at the old man and his stupid teacup. I was so irritated, so fed up with blatantly being stared at and yet ignored at the same time. I wasn't in the human realm; I was in Wisteria. I was somebody here. I had a home, I had people. So why were people still ignoring me?

My anger threatened to boil over as I rubbed my hands along my legs.

"Your anger is not the answer." He sniped as he blew delicately into the cup.

"Then what is the answer. Hmm? Or are you just going to ignore my questions like everybody else? Are you going to tell me I need to accept things? To harness my power with acceptance?" I stepped closer to the man.

My anger wasn't just with him; it was with *everyone.* It was with every single human who had ignored me, sneered at my appearance or turned a blind eye to my abuse. It was at Isa for leaving me with that monster, the Council for their laughable try at controlling me, with Cole and his tired fed-up eyes and stick up his ass. It was with Lyal and the bitch social worker, with *myself* for thinking I had control over the beatings.

Every single person I was angry at flashed in my mind, like a flickering book of images.

With each flicker of face that passed through my mind, a pulse of vibration zapped through my veins. Every single candle within the old man's room burst to life, just as the fire rose higher, blasting the small room with a heat that had sweat dripping down my back and swirling around that damn mark.

"Not my anger huh?" I snapped as I looked around the room.

"Amaya." Rasped behind me, looking back at Ziel and his raised brows, I huffed.

I shoved passed Ziel and stormed from the cottage.

No one had answers. I had accepted I was a Dark Witch, yet I was told I still needed to accept something? And being told my anger wasn't going to help, pfft. So far, my power had only revealed itself during my time with Rí or when I was angry.

A firm grip on my arm halted me. Ziels slightly red heavy eyes caught mine. "Come on," he muttered, leading me out of the dishevelled garden and passed the bright and sunny cottages.

I ripped my arm from his grasp, ignoring the way my mark had itched like mad begging for his attention and gave him my best death stare, meaning every ounce of it and stormed down the street.

Fuck him.

What was the point in taking me somewhere that wasn't even going to help me? What was the actual point of it?

"Will you fucking stop having a tantrum?" he sighed with a smoke hanging from his lips as he easily caught up to me, his long legs strolling whilst I walked with fever.

Stupid little legs.

"That paper I took-it's the spell the Dark Witch used to transfer some of her magic to Yim. They were Circle Mates, but he was utterly human. She wanted to stay in Wisteria with her sisters, and he wanted to be with her. So she gave him some of her magic. Brought him through, kept him hidden but alive. He's the only one its ever worked for. Took a lot of tries a lot of magic. But it worked. This was nineteen years ago, one year before the war, when the witches blew themselves to smoke." I narrowed my eyes at him in annoyance. How long had he known all of this.

"He aged quickly after; eighteen years were more like forty to him. Yes, he has Dark magic within him, its miniscule. The minute its real owner died the magic dies with it."

So if I gave the twins some of my magic, I just needed to stay alive? To live a long life for them. I could do that. I could live for them. Everything I do is for them. Would it be so bad, to spend my life with them running the long dark halls of the castle, Jerry and his kindness, Rí and his possessive passion? Looking up at Ziel, I wondered if it would even be so bad to spend it with him. Would I become…happy? Would I be satisfied with life. Would it matter?

"How long have you known all this?"

Tired. I was tired of the games. Tired of all the secrets. He shrugged, his eyes now clearing from his drug induced smoke. I nodded, because I think I understood. Why would he tell me all the answers? He didn't know me. I didn't know him. We were essentially strangers, strangers who had their souls torn apart and scattered before being shared. We may share a deep soul connection, a mark claiming each other as theirs, but who said we had a choice in this matter? Who gave him the choice?

He frowned down at me, searching my face for some emotion that would make him understand my thoughts. I kept my face neutral, clear of emotions and feelings. It was always better this way. When had I even begun to change? To give away bits of myself to people I *barely* knew?

The flapping of wings had me turning away from the Death Warrior. I waited for Ravioli to land on my shoulder. The sharp sting of his talons digging in were almost welcoming.

I was so tired.

Tired of not being with my boys. I was tired of being silent, tired of holding in my anger, tired of never allowing my true cold rage to seep through. My mind was constantly filled with the noise of life, the constant chatter and ebb and flow of being alive, it was exhausting. The twins saved me, but deep down, very very deep down, I missed that feeling I had when those pills stared back at me. I missed the knowledge that I could be done with it all. The obsession had taken over of course, and with that the rage had built and built and I swore, I swore on everything I was, that one day my rage would be witnessed by the man who poisoned me with it in the first place.

Twenty-Eight

'My Truth-Veritas Mea'

Ziel

She was silent the entire way back to the castle; after stopping at the halfling's and grabbing that book, she ignored me, not once aiming those big eyes my way.

It pissed me off.

I wanted her gaze; I wanted her anger and irritation. It was the best look on her, the way her lips would purse in a pout, her brows would furrow, and her chest would rise in a heated breath. She was fucking glorious.

I didn't like her ignoring me, however, everyone else ran from me, avoided me, feared me. I didn't care if others ignored me, but not her. Never her.

I knew finding the answers were frustrating her; if I had them all I would give them to her…well…some of them.

The dead whispered to me here and there, giving me bits and pieces. Whatever they had told me I had passed on to her, eventually anyways.

I was starting to wonder if I should outright tell her the things I found out. I just couldn't help but poke at her; her anger was so fucking *delicious.*

She laid star fished on her bed; her boot-covered feet hanging off the edge as if she purposely avoided putting them on the sheets.

"Did you know that White Witches defiled deceased Dark Witches to gain access to their powers?" she murmured, her thick lashes settled against her pale high cheekbones as she closed her eyes.

I hadn't known that.

"No," I answered. I unlaced her boots and slid them from her feet, noticing how small they were in my hands.

"My ancestors had to create a rule, to sit with the body and wait until it started to decompose before they could bury them with their rituals."

That was so fucked up even by my standards. The dead were sacred; their bodies had been a temple that held their souls within them.

"Can you imagine, having to watch over your family as their bodies began to rot? Just so that a man wouldn't defile them, all for greed." She spoke quietly, softly, as if fearful of the dead hearing her speak of such a disgusting horrid past.

I removed my own boots, shrugged off my jacket and laid myself down beside her. She turned her head and looked at me. Our faces were so close I could see the deeper purple specs within her eyes. She held such torment within them, such pain.

I couldn't wait for the day she realised the power she held within herself. I hoped I got to see the pain she would bring to those who put that look there.

I don't know how long we laid there, staring into each other's eyes. It could have been hours, but I knew of one thing- my mind was quiet. No angry whispers telling me to kill and suck down the souls of those who deserved pain. I stared in Amaya's eyes with a clear head, a firm focus and not once had my hands twitched to reach for the sour release Mayfeaver provided me.

At some point during the evening, her eyes slid closed, and her breathing deepened. She had fallen asleep and yet I still couldn't look away.

I wanted to scream at the Fates Above for giving me a Mate to protect. I had always thought of myself too far gone, too selfish, too dark to have someone to…care for. But Amaya was more than I ever could have imagined. With her own darkness, I gained…peace.

And so I gave her my truth.

"I needed to know why you wanted to bring them here first. You're sick. Fucked in the head. Obsessed with them. Willing to do anything, kill anyone for them. And that, I understand." I didn't know if she could hear me, if she was truly asleep or just resting. "I understand pain, sickness and obsession. I understand the need to kill, to seek revenge. You're dark, filled with it. I hated the Fates Above for providing me with you. Laughable really. Me, a burning skeleton fighting the urge to swallow everyone's soul, mated to a little Dark Witch. But do you know what really draws me to you? The silence-your soul is quiet, empty except for your obsessions."

Her eyes opened; her pupils dilated, the deep purple drawing me in, trapping the air from my lungs. I reached my hand up and slid it into her black silky tresses. I clenched my fist around them; her gasp of pain was music to my ears.

"So here I am little Dark Witch. I am yours; you are mine. Just know this: I'm not gentle. I'm not loving. I know pleasure and I know pain. And together," I leaned forward and nipped at her jaw, just enough to leave a sharp sting. "Intoxicating."

Her silence beat heavily against my head, before she whispered those perfect words.

"I can handle pain."

I pressed my lips to hers hard, taking everything I wanted from her gasping breath as I tasted her fruitiness. It coated my tongue as we duelled for dominance. My hands pulled at her hair, tilting her head for better access. The action put her slim pale neck right in front of me and I pounced, biting hard and leaving teeth marks as I then licked to soothe the pain.

Her deep needy groan had my vines sneaking out and wrapping around her wrists. They pulled her arms up high above her head before slicing into the skin with their thorns, marking her as ours.

"You should have said no. You should have run, because now you're mine little Mate. Mine to play with as I wish." More vines appeared, tearing her top down the middle before doing the same with her leggings. Leaving her bare to my heated gaze. My lower back almost ached with the need for the ropes to entwine. For us to entwine. And fuck me, I was going to give it what it wanted.

Her thighs rubbed together trying to ease the ache that was obviously building. I knew she was slick with need. Need for me.

I trailed one finger ever so slowly between her perfect breasts, nudging aside the large jewel resting there, down her stomach and stopping right above her panties before tapping there.

"There's no point in wearing these anymore. I want you always bare. I want to constantly smell you. I want to be able to get on my knees and feast whenever the fuck I want. I want you constantly wet and needing." I ripped the offensive underwear from her, wanting her bare and free beneath me. I caught her gasp with my mouth as the material bit into her skin before tearing.

I tugged her to the middle of the bed, her arms stretched tight above her head, and I stared down at her rounded breasts, just big enough to fill my palms, just perfect enough to bite.

I tutted at her as she moaned from my body pressing into hers. My blue flame flickered along my body, touching her all over. Its heat burnt out her cold; it singed her skin in the most delectable way. Patches of bright red skin flared, no doubt stinging but never actually burning the skin away.

"I haven't even touched you yet. You're so needy." I licked along her neck, purposely swirling my tongue around the healed bite mark of the dragon.

"Mmm, it's my time to claim you." My rasp had worsened, becoming more of a gravel. Licking down her neck, right to her left begging tight nipple. I slowly blew on it, tightening it more before I bit down hard.

She cried out, her back arched from the bed, pushing her tight nipple into my wet awaiting mouth.

Lifting my head I saw the blood dripping down the curve of her breast before I leaned down and caught the running trail with my tongue, lapping up her essence with a deep guttural groan.

She tasted like pure darkness, like cold, sinful sickness. It was the most addicting thing I had ever had. Her blood burned like ice as it slid down my throat, filling my body with everything that was her: My Mate, Amaya.

Now I wasn't some filthy blood-sucking vampire, but whatever fills her veins had been calling me, tempting me, begging for me. My Circle mark heated as the ropes swirled together so close to us being connected forever.

Trailing my blood-coated lips down her flat stomach leaving a bright red smear as I went. Stopping at the junction of her thighs, my mouth watered. She glistened, soaked and needy for me. The smell of sweet dark fruits filled my nose, imprinted on me. Oh yeah, she could fucking forget wearing underwear. Fuck trapping this stunning smell from me. I couldn't help myself; I was starving, so hungry my teeth clenched. I ordered my vines to wrap around her lush thighs, tightening until her flesh pinched and beads of red appeared, marking her, hurting her, making her *mine.*

I ate her like my life depended on it, her flavour filling my mouth with her sweetness. I couldn't help the growl of possession that left me.

Her cries of pleasure-pain punctured the room, filled me with more hunger. Her greedy little pussy clenched as I shoved my tongue in as deep as I could go, her wetness soaking my face, covering me in her scent that I planned to wear with pride. I wanted everyone to know where my face had been. I wanted them to sweat with jealousy before I ripped their throats out for smelling her sweet scent. She was mine. I could share with the dragon, maybe even let her suck his dick as I fucked her on her knees.

I could feel that she was close; her thighs quivered around my vines, her chest heaved as she pulled at her wrists, desperate to be free. Just as she was about to reach the heavens, I pulled back. Her scream of frustration was like music to my ears. Chuckling, I climbed her fucking stunning body. The vines slowly released her, drawing back into me.

She dug her nails into my scalp and dragged my face to hers. Our teeth smashed together, tongues fighting for dominance. My dick was aching from within its denim prison.

Wrenching myself from her clawing grasp, I smiled as she drew blood. Removing my clothes I palmed my dick, watching her laying there, covered in my vine's scratches and pierced holes. Droplets of blood coated her thighs, her black hair fanned out around her head like a gathering cloud of darkness.

Her purple eyes watched as I slowly stroked myself, following the movement of my hand before tracing each dark part of my skin that I had inked. My skin was covered in skulls; thorny vines and grim reapers faded into shadows. Her tongue peeked out, swiping at her plump pale lips.

So she was hungry for me too huh.

That was going to have to wait because I couldn't hold on anymore. I needed to be inside her.

Just as I rested my knees at the end of the bed, loving how her legs opened welcoming me within their heat, a fucking bird flew into the room and landed on the bird perch.

"Ignore him," she moaned, reaching forward for me.

I dragged my gaze away from the fucking vermin and slid my hands up her open thighs and tugged her closer to me, lining my throbbing dick to her entrance. We were finally about to be forever joined when she pressed her hand to my chest, stopping me.

I frowned and looked from her pussy to her pain-filled eyes.

"Little Mate?"

She gasped, rubbing at the valley between her breasts, her eyes grew wide as she seemed to struggle to breathe. I slid my hand under her shoulders and lifted her up, confused and worried.

"Amaya, what's wrong?"

"I-fuck I don't know..." she gasped and panted, trying to catch her breath whilst still rubbing at her chest, the jewel being knocked to the side.

"Is it the dragon?" I asked, wondering if her mating mark was calling for her other Mate. Was something wrong with Rí?

She shook her head, a frown pulling at her brow as she inhaled deeply before dropping her hand from her chest.

"I don't know what that was. My chest burned, almost like when my lungs were fucked except this time my chest…" she trailed off, confusion all over her pale face. I stood and pulled on my jeans, pulled a Mayfeaver from my leather jacket on the floor and lit it within seconds. I drew in deeply before passing it to her. She reached for it without a thought, drawing in deeply herself before slowly blowing out with a dazed look upon her face. She handed it back and walked to her dresser where she began to pull on more black clothing.

Something had hurt my Mate, something or someone that was connected to her somehow.

Rustling behind me had me turning to glaring at the fucking bird on the perch.

"Why the fuck do you have a crow?" I muttered as I walked over to it. Something about it was…familiar. Its black eyes tracked me as I walked over. Its feathers were so black you could barely see the slight tinge of purple that mixed within.

My head filled with a calm only Amaya's body and presence had provided me. The Mayfeaver hung from my lips, its ash growing as I fell down a narrow hole. Cold seeped my bones, filled me with pure dreadful sickness. Muffled voices called to me, but I couldn't pull back. I fell deeper and deeper into this hole before a slight sting to my arm had me blinking back into focus.

"I said get your hand off Ravioli asshat!" Amaya snapped as she slapped at my arm again. Blinking, I realised my hand was wrapped around the bird's neck, squeezing. It should have been dead; squashed within my hand, its blood should have been easing between my fingers, but the crow, Ravioli, looked as though it had its eyes narrowed at me, as if pissed off at being choked rather than afraid.

Releasing the bird and drawing deep from the remaining smoke, I stepped back.

"Where the fuck did you get that bird?" It had done something to me, drew me in somewhere, pulled me from the room and placed me in a trance somehow.

"It's my Familiar, I think," she muttered, clearly irritated with me as she bent down and picked up the remaining fucking tongue and gave it to the crow.

The moment between us was over; the strangeness of her chest pain and the strange trance I had fallen in from this bird had well and truly ruined the moment. I couldn't work out what was with this bird, but something about it wasn't right.

Her Familiar? Something about that didn't sit right with me.

Twenty-Nine

'To Keep Under Silence-Sub Silentio Custodire'

Amaya

Just moments ago I had been about to mate with another of my Fated Mates. His passion had been entirely different to Rí's, yet just as amazing. Whereas Rí was warm and loving, soft yet firm, Ziel was about the mixture of pleasure and pain. The hunger in his eyes for me had been so incredibly fucking hot I couldn't help the noises that had escaped me.

Although the passion between us had felt utterly right, I was kind of glad we had stopped. I hadn't fully decided if Ziel was truly mine, because I didn't know how I felt about him. He irritated me most of the time, angered me beyond belief, and made me *want* to listen to the noise in my head. When I was around Ziel, the urge to act upon my dark fantasies grew stronger, and I just didn't know if that was a good or a bad thing.

I couldn't explain what happened with my chest, but all of a sudden, I couldn't breathe. My chest almost felt as though it was being crushed; the pressure pressing down on me had been suffocating. Then as quickly as it had begun, it ended. It wasn't any of my Mates. I felt them within my very being. This…this was something else.

Ziel now sat in the chair opposite Ravioli's perch and watched him with the drug hanging from his lips. He seemed out of it; his usual nonchalant self was confused and weary, which was something I hadn't seen on the Death Warrior as of yet. Something with Ravioli had really taken him aback. But what?

I looked out the windows at the sea below us, the crashing waves against the rock almost hypnotising with their back-and-forth motion. I had never seen the sea before. I had never left Bluewater Valley before Lyal had killed me.

My experience of life had only been from that small town with less than 2000 people and Lyal's house. The abuse from both the towns people and that monster had been all I'd ever known. Yet now I had two men that called me theirs, a friend, a ghost butler and a pet.

So why did I still feel so cold and empty inside? Why was the noise still so loud in my head? Why was I still so fucking *tired?* I knew that even with my boys by my side I would still have this empty void within me, because it had always been there.

No matter who forced their way into my life, no matter who became a part of my unhealthy obsessions, something was missing within me.

I was starting to wonder if it was my soul or heart.

My eyes drifted to the book containing the answer as to why the humans were protected by the Dark Witches. The humans were a piece of shit in my eyes. They were a waste of creation by their Gods.

Sighing, I looked back over to Ziel and his spaced-out face before picking up the book and sitting on my big bed, which had not so long ago been rumbled from our passion.

The book was thin so I was sure I could read the entirety before Rí returned home.

***

I stared down at the book with a mixture of shock and dumbfoundment. The humans were so much more than anyone could imagine. Did the supernatural's of Wisteria know the truth? Where the hell had Bri found this book? Within its very pages was the truth of why the portals had been closed, of why the Dark Witches did what they did. It was all here. Had Bri read it? Did she know?

"What have you there my Lady?" The ghost popped out of nowhere, appearing at my side with a tray of sandwiches resting on his gloved hand.

I said nothing, instead showing him the first page, waiting for him to go into more detail than the book could have provided. Instead he stiffened and his luminous glow faulted.

"Where did you find that?" he asked, placing the tray down beside me and adjusting his gloves as if he hadn't given me that reaction. But I saw it, something about this book made him uneasy.

"That doesn't matter. What do you know about its contents?" I asked with narrowed eyes.

"My Lady, that book had been missing for a very long time."

"And now she has it. I know what's inside. Amaya knows what's inside. The question is there Jeeves…why the shiftiness?" Ziel asked as he walked towards us, his eyes also narrowed upon my ghost butler.

Ziel's chest was still bare. His dark tattoos covering almost every inch of his exposed torso were a work of art. Each one looked as though they had their own story, their own telling of why they were placed upon his skin. Ignoring the clench in my lower stomach, I looked back to Jerry who did indeed look shifty.

I got off the bed, placed my hands on my hips and said "Jerry, what's going on?"

The ghost sighed, his glow faltering yet again as he stepped back and looked at me with unease. "My lady it all began well, at the beginning.

"The first Dark Witch had also been the first supernatural to find her Circle Mates. When the Fates Above had spilt her soul and sent it between the realms far and wide, the Gods of the human realm had intervened. You see the Fates Above and the human

Gods were family, siblings of the sort, whom both created their ideal beings and ideal realms. They declared that the Fates were cruel to do such a thing to their own creations. But the Fates Above didn't think so. They thought they were helping the poor lonely supernatural. Her river of tears had brought them a feeling within their chest that they weren't used to:

Empathy.

They wanted to make the witch smile, to bring her love and joy. The Gods said that splitting her soul was indeed cruel, but they would help them achieve their task as long as they were to help them.

You see, the Gods of the human realm were struggling with where the souls of the humans would go when they died. They wanted the precious souls to live on in some way, to have a purpose.

Well the Fates were of course elated, because if they were to split the souls of the supernatural it wouldn't leave enough within them to live. They would perish at creation without a full soul within their beings.

And so an agreement was set: when the humans died, their souls were placed within a supernatural before they were fully created, or born, if you will. This way, the human soul worked alongside what was left of the supernatural soul and allowed them to live fully. In doing so, this then allowed them to search forth for their Mates, creating a circle of life.

And that is where the name, Circle mates was created."

"None of this was in the book on Circle Mates," I stated as Ziel frowned at Jerry as if he was mentally placing all the puzzle pieces together.

Jerry smiled sadly at me before continuing, "I am not done my Lady."

"The first Dark Witch discovered the truth and kept it to herself, because the human souls didn't just bring the supernatural to life. They held the utmost powerful magic of all, Innocence to what the world truly was. This magic could essentially create another God.

The Dark Witch was of course silenced, sworn to secrecy. The Fates Above threatened to tear her Mate bonds apart, leaving her alone once again. The human Gods threatened to bring death upon all supernatural that would harm their precious humans. This terrified the witch and so before she allowed the Fates to wipe her memory, she wrote this secret down, knowing that one day it was going to need to be revealed. No one knows why she did this.

Until one day, the Dark Witches were betrayed, and this book was stolen. And with it, its secrets were revealed to those full of greed. The White Witches wanted the humans for their magic. They wanted to create new Gods.

If they did this, no matter how many centuries had passed, the Fates Above would rip apart Dark Witches' bonds, and the humans would eventually perish without their innocence within them. And so the Dark Witches vowed to close all the portals, sealing off the greedy witches' path to the humans.

The war began, with plenty of pointed fingers towards the very witches who had saved Wisterias bonds and people, but the White Witches already had their hold of the people of course."

I couldn't move; my heart thudded within my rib cage, slamming against it in a rush to pump blood through my frozen body.

"Holy fuck." Ziel rasped as he stared at Jerry in shock.

"Why didn't you tell me? This entire time I've been searching and begging for answers!"

This entire time I'd been asking and begging and looking for answers. Why had the witches done what they had done. Why protect the humans!

But now I knew; the humans were us, and we were all linked. All so the supernatural could have Mates, so they weren't alone.

I hated it. I hated it all.

Being linked to the humans in some way out right pissed me off.

Why would the Gods even want to save them? They were disgusting, vile weak beings! Beings who treated me like dirt!

Jerry covered my cold pale hand with both of his as he said "My Lady, it is not for me to tell you everything, nor do I always know everything. I am dead. A ghost. I was in fact, a human."

What the fuck! He was human? How was his ghost here!

I opened my mouth to ask but he answered first "I was the soul that connected with the first witch, the first human soul to pass on through the realms. When Lady Samara decided it was her time to leave the realms and leave with her Mates, she released me. I vowed my full servitude to the Dark Witches from then onwards."

"Why! Why the hell would you do that?! You were trapped in her? Like a prisoner!" I pulled my hand back and backed away. My heart wouldn't calm down; why was I freaking out?

"All human souls know that they are within the supernatural, but you must understand, we are given a choice! I chose to serve; I chose to be connected. I wanted my soul to do something worthwhile and meaningful! I have served generations of Dark Witches, and all have been as glorious, as perfectly pure as the last, including you, Lady Amaya. When I am not within the presence of a Dark Witch my mind…wanders. I am ever so old. I am forgetful. But in my age, I know when things should and shouldn't be revealed. You needed to learn and to grow before secrets were revealed. Sub Silentio Custodire"

To keep under silence. Holy Fates Above, Jesus, Gods of the human realm. Holy fucking everything.

I plonked my butt down on the armchair Ziel had just been sat in and tried to process everything.

The humans had magic within them that the witches could harness and turn themselves into Gods, no doubt bringing death and destruction everywhere. Someone had found this book and told the White Witches. So what? The Dark Witches tried to protect the precious humans and closed the portals? The White Witches fought back.

"Why did the White Witches want to do this? Why did they want the human's power?"

"Because they were jealous of the power the Dark Witches had. They were jealous of the purity of it, of the respect from the realms. They wanted it all to themselves," Ziel answered as he lifted shaking hands to light the Mayfeaver hanging from his lips.

"Answer me truthfully Jerry; why was I placed with Lyal. Why was my power non-existent in the human realm? Why did it take me dying for a crack to open and send me back?"

I waited patiently.

"I swear to you on my left-over soul my Lady, I do not know. Lady Isa was gone before I knew. You were three when I last saw you. You sat amongst the dead playing in the dirt there. Then…you were gone, as were the rest of the Dark Witches. I knew you were alive somewhere, otherwise I and the Mountain would have perished along with the rest of the witches."

I slumped down in my seat.

So close, I had been so close to getting all the answers I had been after.

"Where the fuck did Bri get the book from?" I blurted out, the sudden thought bringing me back from my pity party.

"Good point little Mate." Ziel rasped and pulled his top on over his head, careful not to knock the Mayfeaver hanging from his lips as always. He shrugged his jacket on and looked at me in question as I sat and squinted my eyes at him.

"How did you know what was in the book?"

He shrugged and grinned at me, "I break into Bri's place regularly to use her shit and make this masterpiece." He nodded to the smoke he held out to me in his hand.

I rolled my eyes and pulled my boots on.

"Let's go ask her. Whoever *she* got it from could be the person who knows the person who stole it in the first place."

"My Lady, you haven't eaten in a while," Jerry gestured towards the food, worry covering his glowing face.

I shrugged and followed Ziel up the dark stairs and into the foyer. I had begged for answers, something I had never done before. And he hadn't answered me. I knew he told me his reasons. But truthfully, I felt a little betrayed. I stared at the painting of Lady Samara as we passed the paintings and couldn't help but wonder, was that the reason for her cold void-like eyes? Was she holding secrets that were killing her from the inside out?

I was finally piecing together the broken puzzle, and for the first time since waking up in Wisteria, I felt true hope that I was getting home to my boys. I had some answers now, and I wouldn't stop until I had the rest.

Thirty

'Clouded Sickness-Nubilum Languorem'

Cole

Bile dripped down my chin as my stomach cramped with more acidic vomit. I heaved and fell to my knees in my white-stoned garden.

Fuck, the pain was burning me from the inside out. My last session had been brutal. They had been getting more frequent, and my mind was slowly disappearing. I barely knew who I was anymore. The Darkness was trying to overtake my mind and no matter what we did, it never left. It only increased in its sickness.

I couldn't even remember the sessions anymore, only pain and horror then utter darkness.

I knew Ziel and the fucking dragon had been in my home. Their stench was all over the place. The thought of them seeing the basement where my procedures were taking place had slimy panic shake through my bones.

Part of me had hoped they would see it, see the torture I was put through, the pain I suffered just to be pure. Part of me wanted to be saved from this madness, to be told I wasn't sick, to live a life of freedom and free will. To be able to be a true Mate to my Circle Mate.

But that would never be a possibility. Her sickness was worse than mine. Wasn't it?

Muffled conversations echoed like a memory in my confused mind, secrets that could bring an uproar to the Council's well-ordered pureness. As quickly as the secrets spread through my mind, they disappeared, leaving me with an almost agonising headache and even more confusion than before.

I climbed to my feet and began to walk.

I had no idea where.

I fell into the thick trunks of bright Wisteria, their dangling clusters brushing against my face and smothering me in their sweetness.

I pushed back to my feet, kept walking.

I just needed to tell them.

They would understand.

It was never my fault. I'm *sick*.

They need to know, needed to understand.

They have to stop him. Before it's too late.

I walked some more, falling over thorny bushes and brambles.

The flashing red sign of the King's Liquor hurt my eyes, too bright against the night sky.

Why was I here?

"Haaay! Here have a drink on me!" cheered a strong Irish voice before a glass of strong liquor was shoved into my hands.

When did I get inside? It was too loud.

I swallowed the drink in one. Then drank another. And another.

Why was I here?

Thirty-One

'Acceptance Of Darkness-Acceptatio Tenebrarum'

Amaya

Bri's coffee shop was dark and empty. It was pretty late but no amount of knocking had her answering. I knew she lived in the quarters above, so where was she? After tutting at Ziel and his suggestion to just smash the glass and wander in, we made our way to Rí's bar where I knew he was waiting for me. He had spent the day with the Bookkeeper, trying to work out exact dates of my birth and potentially a sign of who my father could have been. The butterflies in my stomach were new; the excitement of seeing the big brute had me picking up my pace.

The king's liquor was bustling with drunken misfits of all kind; Wolf tails knocked full glasses of purple liquor, big burly bear shifters growled their annoyance, and an orange haired leprechaun stood atop the bar pouring drinks.

The atmosphere was insane. It wasn't this busy the other night. There were crowds of people everywhere, and not one table was free of half-full glasses and chattering supernatural.

The fact that this now was completely normal to me was crazy. Just a few short days ago I had thought I was hallucinating when I saw a large bear shift into a human for the first time. Now, although magic was still very much new to me, animals shifting into actual people didn't faze me in the slightest.

Things really had changed in such a short space of time.

I knew where Rí was without truly having to search for him. The scaled jewel at my breasts and both our Mating Circle and bite mark pulsed with his presence. He walked through the door from his quarters carrying a large crate of glass bottles full of his secrecy. His huge arms bulged with the weight. His nostrils flared before his head snapped in our directions, a tooth bearing smile lit his face up. Dumping the crate with a loud clatter, he prowled to me, grabbed my waist with his big hands and lifted me to his eye level.

"Mo Chridhe," he rumbled before firmly sealing his lips to mine.

The possessive bitch in me preened.

The obsessive sickness swirled to life.

The introvert stiffened at the public display.

My mark swirled its happiness at being back in his presence. With Ziel close to my back and Rí plastered to my front, my insides screamed in need.

I knew it, knew the moment I explored my sexuality I was going to become an obsessed sexual deviant.

I mean come on; obsession was my entire personality.

Wolf whistles and cheers pulled us from our kiss. Rí grumbled and growled at them but I saw the gleam in his red eyes; he enjoyed them seeing I was claimed, seeing I was his. I didn't mind too much; I understood the need to claim what was yours.

Grabbing my hand and shoving the slumped-over wolf shifter from a stool at the bar, he guided me to sit and said, "The Bookkeeper still found nothing, ye' birth was not recorded. I got the old goat to check every birth recording book he had, just in case it had been put somewhere else."

The news didn't surprise me; I had a feeling a lot of things were hidden and kept quiet.

I sighed and shook my head at the leprechaun when he offered me a glass of whisky. Ziel took it and downed it in one.

"Do you know where Bri is?" I asked, looking around the room for a sign of her bouncy curls and bright eyes.

Rí furrowed his brow and shook his head, "Nae, she doesn't come to the bar usually."

Ziel hummed from behind me and reached into his pocket for a smoke. He frowned deeply whilst rummaging around and poked about in the other pocket before swearing under his breath.

"I'll be back."

"Whilst ye' break in, see if she's in," Rí said and rolled his eyes.

Ziel wrapped his hand around my throat and pressed his mouth to mine. To those around us it looked as though he gently and softly kissed me, but it was far from it; his vines slipped from his sleeves and tangled in my hair as his teeth bit into my lower lip, hard enough to draw a drop of blood. He licked it away and pulled away with a hungry gleam in his eyes.

I slowly looked at Rí, gauging his reaction to another man kissing his Mate. He smiled kindly down at me and smoothed my hair behind my ear before sighing at the commotion a rowdy crowd had created as they entered the already busy bar.

Their greasy hair and dirty baggy clothes created murmurs of annoyance from the patrons.

"Lemme sort these Vamps out, then I can feed ye' and ye' can tell me what ye' found out," he grumbled and walked towards the chaos in the far corner.

Vampires?! If I was being honest, they weren't what I was expecting. I always assumed that if vampires were real, they would have been something to really look at, and that their presence would have been magnificent and quite spectacular. The stories they could have talked about, their age and the things they had seen. These vampires looked like a bunch of street rats.

"You're sick." A body slid onto the stool next to mine. I didn't need to turn to know who it was; my mark itched as the smell of cedarwood drifted to me. Internally sighing, I refused to look at him, refused to show him that he affected me in any way, so I did what I do best, and closed my face to any emotion.

"You hear me. You're sick. Your darkness is a poison." He slurred as he sloshed his glass of Rí's liquor over his own hands. He was drunk. But as always, the words didn't hurt because I knew this already. I knew I was sick; I knew I was poisoned with a darkness. I hid my dark thoughts and fantasies as best as I could, ignored the constant noise within my head.

There was nothing this man could say to me that would hurt me, as I knew he didn't want me. I knew he hated the thought of being mated to me. And although my body and blackened soul called to his, I knew this was different to Rí and Ziel. We had accepted each other's sickness. We had accepted each other body and soul. Ziel and I had been close to being fully mated. Cole: -he had already told me he didn't want to be Mated to me, had shown his disdain toward my magic and well...just me. After spending my entire life being beaten and talked to as though I was literal dirt on the humans' polished shoes, I just didn't care anymore. I would have my boys. I had Rí and Ziel. I had Ravioli and Jerry. Hell, I even had my first friend Bri.

I just wished my body was on the same wavelength as my head because even with him stinking of strong liquor, a sickness and that weird spicy smell, his cedarwood scent had wrapped around me and had me squeezing my thighs together to stop the heat that was gathering.

Fucking Fates and their stupid games.

"I was getting better, I was...I was losing it." Scrubbing his hands down his face, he huffed when I still didn't turn to him, instead turning my head to watch the leprechaun almost fall from the bar from the alcohol he was now drinking instead of serving.

I watched as Rí literally threw two Vamps from the open bar doors, his bright red eyes glowing in excitement over the fight he was no doubt going to win. I shook my head and gave a small grin. The dragon deserved to have his fun after being alone and grumpy for so long.

I had no idea what Cole was losing but I didn't care.

I didn't.

"You just…just accept it! It's not working anymore. I can't remember…" Slamming his hand down onto the bar he slid from his stool and landed in a heap on the floor groaning as he just gave up and laid there.

I sighed. He was a mess. I peered down at him as his bright blue eyes caught mine.

"Why are you here?" I asked quietly, tilting my head as he just stared at me, mouth slightly open. When he showed no sign of answering me, I rolled my eyes, hopped down from the stool and grabbed his arm. Heaving his heavy ass into a sitting position I snarled, "Give me some help here witch."

He fumbled about before dragging himself to his feet and leaning heavily on my shoulder with drooping eyes.

"Damn Dark Witch–"

"Just shut up," I snapped before I started to drag him towards the hallway leading to the stairs to Rí's quarters.

This drunken idiot needed sleep. I hated that I needed to help him. In fact I was so annoyed at myself I almost dropped him at the bottom of the stairs and left him there, but then he whispered so quietly I thought I'd mistaken him at first.

"I can't...can't get her out of my head. I wish I could just accept it." Lifting a strand of my hair to his nose, he inhaled, before closing his eyes and smiling.

"My Mate, she'll know what to do. She can stop him."

What? Stop who? His Mate? Me?

"What are you on about?" I huffed as I dragged him up the stairs then stopped as I stared at the door handle.

Shit.

I hadn't thought this through and there was no way I was going to drag this lump back downstairs. Looking over my shoulder at the dark stairway, I contemplated just throwing him down. He was big; he'd be fine right?

"I'm weak. Weak and poisoned."

Augh, the damn man had become more trouble than I needed.

Huffing again, I slowly reached for the handle and just about managed to open it with the White Witch leaning heavily against my hip and shoulders. I dragged Cole through the door as he wrapped my hair around his finger and mumbled more nonsense about how he just couldn't remember, but there was so much blood.

After dragging him across the floor and practically falling onto the bed with him, I stood over him panting.

"What blood, Cole?" I managed to get out over my wheezing. I was really out of shape.

Laying on his back he stared at me through tired glassy eyes. The more I stared back, I realised how tired he looked, how pale he was, how he was actually looking quite thin. My mark burned with the need to look after him. My stomach swam with coldness. Something was wrong. I could just feel it.

His hand circled my wrist with more strength than he looked to have and pulled me forward, so I fell on top of his chest, my hair creating a curtain around our faces.

Hiding us from the world. I couldn't help the gasp at our closeness.

"I don't want to hurt anymore. I don't want to do it anymore," he whispered to me, his voice low and full of pain.

"Do what?" I whispered back. My heart began to beat faster as my hands pushed at his chest, lifting my head to frown down at him. Someone was hurting him. I didn't know who, didn't know how, but I could feel his pain reaching out towards me, searching for our Mate bond to heal him.

His eyes were now closed as he soundlessly moved his mouth in a name I couldn't understand.

"Cole." I shook at his hard chest. It did nothing but cause him to groan and wrap his arms around me. He pulled me in tightly as he drunkenly drifted off. My core heated more as I felt his cock grow between us. My breath hitched with the need to reach down and press my lips to his.

Ugh the fucking Mate bond.

No. I didn't want this! But just because I didn't want it, didn't mean I couldn't see if he needed medical aid in some way.

I pulled back from him, pushing against his tight hug as he mumbled more nonsense.

"I'm dark, so fucking dark. My mind, it asks me to do things…sick…so sick."

Frowning down at him, I started to understand slightly that he thought the darkness within him made him sick, made him unworthy of being pure. So someone, I didn't know who, was doing something to him to make him less…dark?

"Being Dark doesn't make you unpure," I whispered down to him. "Being Dark isn't what makes people sick. Having these thoughts or being different doesn't make you unworthy; it just makes you, *you*. You have to accept who you are and fucking embrace it. Let it empower you, enrich you! Allow its Darkness to fester and grow within you!" I trailed off as my eyes grew wide.

That was it.

The acceptance.

I had to accept the Darkness within me.

It wasn't the power, the fact I was a witch or had Mates', and it wasn't Wisteria. It was the darkness within me, the constant noise within my head, my deep obsessions and possessive need towards the people that were *mine*.

That odd vibration began to tingle along the soles of my feet within my thick boots. It travelled up my calves and swirled around my lower back were my Circle Mark resided.

This time, I closed my eyes, breathed deeply and allowed it to continue its path.

It travelled around my waist, up my stomach before settling within my chest, where utter peace consumed my entire body.

I was a Dark Witch, with a Darkness within me.

And I accepted that.

Opening my eyes, I grinned. My skin practically glowed and my long hair floated above me, standing on its ends. I looked bad-fucking-ass!

I pressed my hands against Cole's chest to try and move out of his grasp, my fingertip brushing against his skin peeking through the creased buttoned top.

The second our skin touched I could feel it, that horrid spicy tanginess was smothering him from the inside out. He wasn't sick with Darkness but was sick with a magic that felt wrong; it felt vile and deadly.

The vibration within my chest spread through my arms and heated my hands. This power inside of me wanted to leak out, to delve into Cole and grasp the horridness that was hurting him. So, I closed my eyes and gave it the acceptance it needed. I gave it my full permission to do whatever it needed to do. I let my magic expand around us, allowed it to search out for anything that may need healing on Cole. It spanned out, searching, seeking. There were no visible wounds, but I could sense something, something tearing at him. His mind was fuzzy, and it wasn't from the drink. Frowning, I pressed further, searched further, down his chest, his arms and shit...there…his stomach was externally fine, smooth and healthy. But internally, it was like he had been butchered, sliced and rearranged. Something was spreading there, winding around his veins and organs, travelling hidden within the blood straight to his brain.

What the actual fuck?

I needed to get whatever that was out of his body! It was killing him.

Taking another deep slow breath, I took a risk and pictured his organs healing, stitching themselves back together, rearranging to their rightful places. And somehow, I just knew that it was actually working, and the organs were doing exactly as I had wished. I moved onto whatever was swimming around his blood. It tried to hide from me, but I found it, sneaking around his body, causing more damage along its way. I mentally grabbed at it, held it within my mental grasp as I commanded it gone. Screamed at it to leave his body. To simply fuck off.

Cole groaned beneath me, his back arching off the bed as he held me tighter. He said he was poisoned with Darkness, but someone had put this poison there. Someone was doing this to him. And he had no fucking clue what they were doing.

Pulling back and opening my eyes, my head begun to throb as weariness took over. That took more from me than I had expected, but looking down I could see Cole's paleness was subsiding. His body grew healthy beneath me as his White magic now filled him with healing that it couldn't provide before. Whatever was inside him had stopped his magic from doing its rightful thing.

Who had done this to him?

I tried to wiggle from his arms, but he held me tighter before he opened his still glassy eyes.

They softened before he mumbled, "Gotta tell her, gotta tell Amaya...she's the only one. She can…" His eyes slid shut again as he mumbled incoherently.

"Tell me what!" I demanded as I finally extracted myself from his arms, ignoring my mark as it practically cried out from the loss of his touch.

I was the only one to what!?

"Cole" I tapped at his face in urgency, I didn't know what he was on about, but I suddenly felt like it was important.

"Cole!" I snapped as I tapped his cheek a bit harder this time. My chest constricted just as my breath hallowed out, a gasping wheeze coming from me as I began to struggle to breathe. That feeling of someone pressing on my chest once again causing me to gasp desperately for air.

What was happening to me?

Cole grumbled as he squinted up at me. "Amaya–" groaning he rubbed at his head before his arm flopped down to his side. "She's the only one that can go through the portals. Her magic...even if they are shut. She's the only one…her magic…can sense the portals…openings." He was out like a light, a small snore creeping from his throat as he lay still on Rí's bed of clouds, his blond hair stark against the black sheets.

I could go through the portal.

I could go through.

My heart slammed in my chest as my hands began to sweat. Wiping them on my jeans, I scratched my nails at my legs, pulling at the fabric as my mind raced with his words.

The pain within my chest subsided as I gripped my hair in my clenched hands. Did I get Rí? Ziel?

I couldn't wait.

I needed to see my boys.

Even if to check they were okay.

Then I could come back and tell my Mates.

Right?

I ran from the room, down the stairs and as I turned the corner, I slammed into a soft body before we both fell to the floor in the darkened hallway. My butt hurt as I dragged myself up. My heart still raced as my eyes adjusted to the darkness.

Bri glared at me as she rubbed her own rounded butt. "Amaya? Are you okay? Why are you running? I was looking for you. Hay your hairs floating! You look mag..."

I cut her off with the press of my hand to her mouth. I hated to see the spark drift from her face, but I had to rush. I didn't have time. I could see the boys. Now.

"I have to go. The portal can be opened!" Giving her no more explanation, I walked around her to the back door that was hidden in the dark hallway.

Bri grabbed my arm and stopped me, turning me to face her, "Stop. Wait!"

The horrid feeling of whatever was inside of Cole still slithered through my veins, but something about Bri's touch sent shivers down my back. Her usual warm brown eyes seemed cold, angry almost. The power vibrating through my body rebelled against her touch, unkeen to be in her presence.

Her faced changed, hardened as she straightened up, brushing her hands along her perfectly styled pink sundress.

Nodding to me she said, "Go. I'll distract your men."

Well, I wasn't going to argue with that. Nodding back to her once, I rushed out the back door, squeezing past empty crates of Ri's liquor glasses. I snuck down the back alley before I spotted the cobbled pathway to the Dead Village.

I knew they were going to be mad, but I just couldn't wait. This entire time if I had just accepted the Darkness within me, my powers would have appeared, and I could have gone back for them sooner. My stomach swirled with a coldness I only recognised as fear. My chest constricted and I knew, something was wrong, so very wrong and I knew they needed me.

I was getting my boys.

Thirty-Two

'Sirēn's Song- Sīrēn Carmen'

Rí

I dragged the Vamps from the bar, throwing them to the floor and snickered at their pathetic whimpers. They knew better then to cause trouble in my bar. It was a place for the misfits and shifters to come and wind down, relax in a place that didn't judge who or what you were, but these Vamps were constantly causing unneeded trouble.

I knew my Mate didn't find fear in the chaos that was around her. I knew she liked the idea of causing pain to those who deserved it.

So I didn't hold back.

I grabbed the greasy hair of the one closest to me, swearing in disgust at the feel of it on my hand, and slammed his head to my knee. The satisfactory crunch of his skull had my dragon chuffing with amusement.

Another greasy haired fucker ran at me, eyes blood shot, and teeth descended and sharp. Wrapping my hand around his throat I snapped a fang from his mouth, chuckling at his scream before spinning his head in a full circle, the skin of his neck now twisted and mangled.

The only way to kill a vampire was to rip out their hearts or burn them. I was just having fun for once. My Mate had taught me that bringing pain to others that really pissed me off could change my mood of the day entirely.

And she was, of course, correct.

"Having fun there?" rasped a glassy eyed Ziel as I snapped the arms back of the vampire whose skull was now indented and had tried to crawl away. I obviously ripped too hard, because the arms now hung useless in my hands, pools of blood gathering at my feet.

Ziel tutted as he pulled a vial from his leather jacket and collected the blood. "Its good money you know," he rasped as he popped the lid back on.

I clapped him on the back before informing him, "We don't need money."

My lair was full of riches that could fulfil even our great grandchildren and their children and so on and so forth. The thought of children with Amaya had my cock straining against my now stained jeans. The idea of filling her with my come, watching the utter bliss on her face as I filled her deep was arousing as hell. Great now I was hard whilst killing vamps.

Grinning wide, I threw the vampire with a missing fang his way, fully enjoying the burning smell of his flesh as Ziel released his blue soul-eating flames. He needed this, needed to let loose just as much as I did.

We were brothers now, connected to the one thing that would always come first to us both: Amaya. This was another bonding moment for us, another way to relish in the darkness that Amaya loved so much.

I knew Cole was in the bar somewhere; the strong smell of Cedarwood and White Witch had tickled my nose in an irritating way. I couldn't intervene, even if I really wanted to smash his pretty face into my bar. I needed to let him approach Amaya. I just hoped the prick would hurry up and make things right for her. My Mate deserved the world and more.

Once the vampires were nothing but ash and burning embers on the stone floor, we both frowned at each other and turned to look in the direction of my bar. A soothing melody floated from the open doors, its soft lyrical hymn wrapping around us like a warming hug. I had to get closer. I had to hear more. Nothing mattered but that melody of angels.

My legs pushed forward, moving me towards the doors as my hands became slack at my sides. My eyes grew heavy, and my heart slowed to match its soft hymn. I ignored the way my dragon raged inside of me, clawing at my insides demanding he get out.

Why would I let him out?

The melody was one of perfection, one of utter calm and peace. It was pureness in itself. And I needed to be close to it. I needed to find the source of it. It sung just for me. Only for me. I didn't care that others heard it. I could feel it soothing my body like a hot spring that lapped at my muscles

I knew a body beside me followed me into the bar; knew it also followed the hymn of angels. I knew it also ignored the thorned vines that slapped at its slack face.

Nothing could stop us; we had to be close to the music.

We stopped behind a crowd of bodies, each one stood with their loose expressions and swaying arms, basking in the pleasure the melody brought to us. Closing my eyes, I let the song seep into my very soul.

Thirty-Three

'Clarity-Claritate'

Cole

I had spent practically my entire life hiding who I was, hiding my pain and darkness from my father and the entire Council. I was poisoned with it, sick and cold. I hid it for so long, I did as I was told, went where they told me too, polished up on every possible Grimoire there was in Wisteria, dressed to the nines at all times. But Fates Above fucking damn it, the darkness was always there.

On my eighteenth birthday something within me broke. I thought the darkness had finally taken over, because I just couldn't fucking listen to my father and his relentless prattling about the good of the future anymore. What fucking future? We were all stuck in an endless cycle of life. Wake up, do as we were commanded, smile. Be a good little boy. Sleep. Repeat.

But that morning, my magic did something unexpected, after a typical tight-lipped command from my father as he walked out the front door of our pure white lavish fucking mansion, my magic…exploded. Every window, every glass every crystal from our over-the-top chandeliers shattered. The anger that clawed at my stomach was cold and oh so incredible.

It was only after I looked down at my father's still-beating heart within my hand, did I realise what had happened. *He* found me that morning and promised to help me, promised he would help remove the sickness that was the Darkness. But I know now, it was *him* that made me sick; it was *him* who poisoned me, filled me with black magic and allowed it to eat away at my mind, turning me into his version of a pure witch. Someone who he could command and train. Four fucking years I had undergone torture at the hands of someone I had trusted. Someone I had believed in.

And then there she was, so beautifully Dark. She was cold, practically soulless, so silent and so controlled. She was perfect. A Dark Witch. A powerful fucking being. And she was to be my Circle Link, my Mate. But I practically spat at her. Told her she was disgusting, that she was poison. At the time I genuinely thought she was. I thought she was putting a Dark spell on me, that she had planned to ruin all our progress of taking my sickness away. I told her she should have been ashamed of her Darkness.

I was wrong.

I was so fucking wrong. Having a darkness wasn't bad, not on her. Fuck me it was everything on her. It was a serene beauty that nobody could compare too.

But I had finally realised. I was never sick; I wasn't full of a darkness that wanted to overtake me. No, the darkness inside of me, that was Amaya; that was our Mate bond trying to connect us in some way. I believe it could have been her magic seeking help all the way from the human realm.

She had healed me, after everything I has said to her, after pushing her away countless times. After coming to her drunk and foolish and saying more vile things to her, she had *still* healed me.

I didn't know her, not really, but her magic called to me, her soul screamed for me, and her eyes: Fates Above be damned, her stunning purple eyes.

I remembered practically everything that was done to me over the years, remembered the hushed conversations between my father and the Council. I remembered their secrets they thought I would keep whilst poisoned and confused. I don't know how I managed to hand over that stupid White Witches' address, but I remember the anger that had boiled within me at the thought of Amaya being anywhere near him.

I needed to find Rí and Ziel. I needed to tell them everything. I was more focused than I had ever been. They were a good choice for Amaya: strong, powerful supernaturals. I was weak. I knew that now. I knew I had fucked everything up, that she would never accept me. But shit I would beg for fucking forgiveness if I needed too.

Dragging myself from Rí's huge ass bed, I steadied myself, allowed my eyes to focus. Her scent surrounded me, Dark fruits with the mixture of firewood cake; she had mated with the dragon. Inhaling deeply I commanded my magic to take the effects of the alcohol away, commanded it to finish its brutal task of healing me.

I rushed to the bar, gathering strength in my White magic for the first time in years. Stopping at the base of the stairs, I frowned as the lyrical humming of a Siren reached my ears, pulled at my heart and tried to take me under. Its silky touch dragged at me but somehow couldn't get a hold of me. Amaya's healing magic was still within me, still curled around me like a protective barrier. Grinning at the thought of her being with me even if it was just a touch of her magic, I prepared for whatever was in that bar. Unbuttoning my shirt sleeves, I shoved them up my arms, rolled my shoulders and stormed into the bar.

Every damn misfit and shifter, including Rí and that Death Warrior stood facing the bar, swaying to the low song of the Siren. She stood atop the bar swaying to her own music as she enthralled them all with her voice. Sirens were a rare Supernatural; they barely left the Mermaid Quay, choosing only to reveal themselves when they found their prey. They lured their prey to them with their song. Once they had someone within their grasp, they then ate the flesh from their bones and used what was left to decorate their underwater caves. It's said that the Fates Above didn't even create them, that they were from the Human Gods and had snuck their way to the magical realms.

I wound my magic around my arms, relishing in its use for something other than the Council, before pulling at the tight invisible string and releasing it in the direction of the Siren. White light flung from me, catapulting into the Siren and sending her flying behind the bar, smashing into bottles and halting her mid tune.

Rí and Ziel shook their heads, trying to clear away the fog that had clouded their minds. The dragon blinked his red eyes towards me before a deep angry rumble filled the now silent room. His eyes glowed brightly just as Ziel released his own angry growl, aiming his snarl in the direction of the source of magic: me.

Rí's canines grew as he roared his rage.

"It's a fucking Si-" I flew backwards onto a small table before it collapsed to the floor as his huge fucking weight pushed us down. He wrapped his massive hand around my throat and held tightly to stop any words from leaving me as he glared down at me.

I couldn't breathe enough to gather enough strength or magic to push his mammoth body off my own.

"Where the FUCK IS MY MATE!" he roared; my ears rang as all the glass in the bar cracked before shattering from his dragon's roar. That wasn't just Rí glaring down at me.

Shit.

The Dragon had come out to play.

"Get...the...fuck...off," I managed to squeeze out between punches to his forearms. This fucker was big.

"I smoke for two fucking minutes, and this shit happens." A raspy chuckle reached us as Ziel walked over and stood above us, a Mayfeaver hanging from his lips.

"This prick did something to me...where is she? WHERE IS SHE!" Lifting my head with his hands still wrapped around my throat Rí slammed me back down onto the broken table. Pain radiated through my skull as stars lit up behind my eyes. Bending down to my face, Ziel's empty eye sockets filled with a blue flame that had my mouth drying. Shit okay this was going south quickly.

"I don't...know...Siren…bar…" I squeezed out while trying my best to gasp in air through the small gap Rí allowed.

Growling at me, he lifted his hands and dragged me by my shirt towards the bar, slammed me into a stool and leaned over it.

"The fuck..." he rumbled as he jumped the bar and stared down at the Siren.

"Told you fuckers. Wanna thank me for saving your lives? Prick," I gasped and choked out as my magic tried to heal the bruising done to my throat. I sneered at Ziel as he prowled over and jumped the bar to stand with his Circle brother. My chest pinched at them standing together, accepted and united.

"The fuck?" Ziel rasped around his Mayfeaver as he bent down and dragged an unconscious Siren to her feet before slumping her over the bar. Her face and arms were the only things holding her up as her feet dangled down behind the bar.

I narrowed my eyes at her. I could have sworn I'd seen her before.

"Bri...wake the fuck up." Rí shook her shoulder roughly, pulling a groan from her unconscious form.

"You know her?" I asked as I looked to the crowd of frozen Supes.

"She's the owner of Bri's coffee," Ziel muttered. "Supposedly our Mates' friend." He wrapped her hair around his hand and lifted her head as she opened her eyes. Gasping, she tried to pull away as she realised her dilemma: three pissed off men looking for their Mate.

My Mate.

"Ha-Hay there dragon man," she stumbled out nervously.

I stood from the stool and got in her face. "Want to explain what the fuck you were doing and where the fuck Amaya is?"

Her nervous looking face straightened out before forming into a sneer as she laughed, causing us all to freeze.

"She's gone. Gone home to her precious boys." She laughed more as she slammed her head into Ziel's face, cracking his nose as she detached herself from him.

Licking the blood pouring from his nose, he growled out, "Stupid bitch" before snapping it back into place. The blood now coated his mouth as Ri reached to grab her once more.

"Ah, ah boys, hurt me and you lose any hope of getting your precious little Dark Witch." Walking around the bar and stepping back from us she grinned, looking every bit the deceiver she was.

"What have you done?" Rí growled so low it vibrated the glass that was scattered along the floor.

I had been too late. The Council had already employed a cover, someone to befriend the witch, someone to encourage her along her way to fully embracing her powers so that she could open the portals fully.

Bri was the undercover friend.

"You- it was you they employed," I snapped as I followed her steps. Each step back she took, I followed with a step forward.

She grinned as she smoothed out her too bright dress. Not answering, just smiling as if this was all some sort of game to her. The idea that this person had made Amaya believe she was a friend hurt my chest. It was another thing to hurt her, another thing to make her believe she wasn't worthy of everything she deserved.

"Cole, you better explain now, my dragon wants out and he wants out now." Rí's rumble was more dragon than man.

"The Council, they employed a misfit to play Amaya, to encourage her to embrace her full powers. To go back to the human realm alone. If she fully embraces it, she can open the portals fully." I braced myself for their wrath as I carried on. "I told her she could go through the crack. She's the only one that can enter the portals. Even if they're closed."

Vines snapped out from Ziel's jacket and wrapped around my wrists, slicing into my skin and pulling my arms behind my back before more followed and slithered around my neck. They tightened enough to make me choke out in an attempt to breathe.

"So you're in on it. Filthy fucking White Witch. You were against her every step of the way. She's your Circle Link. Your Mate!" Ziel's vines tightened, cutting off my entire course of air.

I didn't struggle. I knew I was a piece of shit. But there was more they needed to know.

Rí's angered roar pulled the misfits from their trance. They looked around at the chaos before blanching when they saw Rí's bright glowing eyes, and Ziel's vines wrapped around me.

What can I say, we had an air for the theatrics.

My vision turned black with the lack of air; my lungs burned as my throat constricted.

The misfits and shifters ran from the room; cowards that they were avoided our eyes as they scattered.

"Awh, are we having a little family dispute," the Siren Bri chuckled, unfazed by my current choking situation.

The vines left me in a pile on the floor, gasping at the sudden release as they whipped to her and wrapped her up in the same way.

"Tell us everything White Witch. Now," Ziel rasped as I saw his body fully turn to skeleton.

Standing to my feet, I rubbed at my bruised throat as I choked out the truth, "The Council knew of Amaya; they knew she was alive. They have been waiting years for her to come through. Planned to get her to open the portals. They wanted her under their thumb, married to a White Witch and doing as she was told. But they weren't expecting her to have Circle Mates." I shifted my feet, unable to meet Rí's eyes as I went on. "They planned the downfall of the Dragons, the Dark Witches. Everything was planned. For years. I was being controlled. Mind-fucked. He poisoned me, had me doing his dirty fucking work. Earlier, Amaya, she took pity on me and healed me. I remembered everything. Every damn thing." I sighed and rolled the tension from my shoulders and looked to the old wooden ceiling. I was tired, so damn tired of it all.

The silence of the room had me looking to the Circle brothers. I could have been part of that. Their bond was now unbreakable; they were mated or at least bonding with their Circle Link and had stood by her from the start. I sighed again. I was afraid of their pity, of their anger. They exchanged a look between them; unspoken words and they came to the same conclusion. Whatever that was.

"Who–" The double doors slammed open, halting Rí before he no doubt told me to fuck off and die.

I froze as the Council walked through, Mikhail and the twins, Fergus and Finnigan, strolled in as if they owned the place, their pure white cloaks laughable in the dim, glass-covered bar.

"Get the hell out of my bar before I let my Dragon loose." Rí stepped forward as he spoke oh so calmly: a sure sign shit was about to go down. Ziel stepped next to him, as his entire skeleton burst to blue flames. The room heated with both their anger.

Looking over at *him* I swallowed the lump in my throat. The fear that crawled up my spine and sent chills skating along my flesh was undeniable. I may have been finally free off the effects of whatever poison he pumped into my body, but the memories were still there. They were always going to be there.

Amaya was strong, so I needed to be. If I wanted to prove to her that I could be a worthy Mate, I needed to buck the fuck up. Decision made; I stepped to the other side of Rí and stared down the Council. My magic brewed within me, ready to be summoned.

"Now, now Misfits, we aren't here for a fight." Finnigan nodded to Bri and then to me. Finnigan smiled wide and fake as ever. "We are just here for our property."

My brows shot up high. Property? If I was anyone's, it was going to be Amayas. "I'm not your property. I'm where I belong. Leave." I bit out.

"Don't be stupid boy." He bit out, his calm facade snapping as he stepped towards me, his hands glowing in his usual sign of magic about to whip out at me.

"I. Said. Get. Out." Rí's dragon growled as his canines grew once more. His height increased as his muscles rippled, ready to rip apart and become one with his dragon.

Fergus grabbed Bri by the scruff of her neck and started to drag her away, the bruising around his healing mouth left over from Amaya's anger. Mikhail stood still, his eyes never leaving mine as Finnigan snapped a final, "You stay here boy, and we won't protect you."

Scoffing, I raised my hand and gave him the finger, "Eat shit."

"Where the fuck do you think you're taking her?" Ziel rasped as they continued to drag the Siren from the bar.

"My granddaughter is no concern of yours, Warrior." Mikhail snarled before turning and leaving the bar.

Thirty-Four

'Familiar Weakness-Nota Infirmitatem'

Amaya

The portal crackled with power. I hadn't even summoned my own magic and yet my hair stood on end, and my arms gathered goosebumps as my heart slammed against my chest. I didn't know why I was so nervous; I had spent my entire time in Wisteria looking for a way back and it was right here the entire time. I could have gone straight back through.

Shaking my head as I observed the small crack between realms, I sighed. I couldn't think like that, not now anyways. I had two Mates, two strong men that were now mine. I had a home for the first time in my entire life. I had a history there, a place to belong.

The black mist in the corner of my eye swirled closer, edging me towards the crack as I stepped away in shock.

What the fuck?

It had never done that before. Stepping away from the crack, I wiped my hands on my pants. I really needed to figure out what the hell the black mist was, but for now, I needed to work out how to actually get myself through the portal. The crack was barely visible to the eye; the vibration of magic from it was strong but it definitely wasn't big enough to simply walk through.

"Go watch my men for me?" I asked Ravioli as he watched me from his perch atop a fallen wooden beam.

Taking one deep breath and squeezing my eyes shut, I did the only thing I could think off-I threw myself at the crack.

The air ripped from my lungs; my face bled from the tiny pinpricks of needles that stabbed along my bare skin. I was compressed and squeezed through space and time. I couldn't gasp, couldn't scream in agony. I was nothing but an object now misshapen and abused. This was no portal between cities; no, this was a painful shove between entire worlds, realms apart.

I slammed to the ground with a thud. Bones crunched and snapped as my head bounced back from the cold concrete floor. The familiar smell of damp and blood filled my nose.

I was back in Lyal's basement. I had been away for such a short amount of time, yet here I was again, muscles seizing in utter terror at the thought of seeing his face again. I was waiting for the angry blows, the pain. But I wasn't the same as I was just a few weeks ago. No, I was Amaya of the Dark Mountain. I was a full-blooded

Dark Witch. I was powerful. And I was here for my boys.

I waited for the magic in my veins to heal the wound the portal had given me, but nothing happened. My body throbbed as the ache in my skull grew with each uneven breath.

Why wasn't I healing?

I shoved myself to my feet. The basement was dark, and I was barely able to see in front of me, just the small glow from the streetlight peeping through the filthy basement window casting a small orange streak across the floor.

Rushing to the rickety stairs I slipped and slammed back down to my knees, the pain vibrating through me as my hands slid in a warm stickiness.

What the fuck?

Squinting down at my hands, I tried to make out what it was in the dark. Rubbing my fingers to my thumb, I smeared it, its familiar thick wet slide, a memory I was never able to forget:

Blood.

My heart dropped down to my churning stomach as I closed my eyes and asked my magic to bring me light. Peeking through one eye, my shoulders slumped when the dark basement came into view.

Where were these damn powers of mine?

Shuffling on my knees, I reached up to the dangling string that pulled on the dull orange light above me. Bright red blood smeared all over my hands and pooled around my knees and legs.

A high pitch screech started to ring in my ears; this was not old blood. It was still liquid. Still warm.

I knew who it belonged to.

Everything slowed down. I couldn't hear through the screeching ring. My vision wavered as I stood to my feet.

Turn around Amaya.

Turn around.

Face it.

TURN AROUND.

Forcing my body to turn, I froze.

No.No.No. Nonono.

No.No.No. No

NO.

My heart ached; the blood pumping through thin veins circulated pain throughout my body.

Grief was supposed be a mental struggle, not utter torture that caused physical pain. This was a different kind of pain to being beaten within an inch of my life. This was a cold ache spreading and stretching through every morsel of my being. A hole was opening in my chest where the obsession and new happiness had been building. An empty dark pit that held nothing but loss. Loss and loneliness that only that one person could hold in their warm embrace, an embrace that was now cold, stale and lifeless, their body empty of the soul that swirled light and warmth.

A strange lump clogged my throat, a scream begging to be released and heard. The pounding of my shattering heart echoed in my own ears as my breathing became shallow. I couldn't move. Couldn't speak.

I didn't want to.

Didn't need to.

Blinking dry eyes I unclenched my fists. Wetness coated where my nails had dug in half-moon shapes into my palm. It didn't hurt, because all I could concentrate on was that coldness. I showed no emotion, just an expressionless mask, but inside I allowed the emptiness to spread and curl around my own darkening soul.

I always knew I was cold, dark and practically void of emotions. But this...this was something else entirely.

Breathing in deeply I expected to smell and taste the stench of death, but a nothingness greeted me. Nothing to smell, nothing to taste. There was nothing left for me here anymore. Swallowing the scream of utter agony that was my being, I forced myself to stare and take in every detail before me: the colourless blood that pooled around my frozen feet, the little toes that poked from beneath the stained sheet that covered the tiny, emaciate body, the lifeless soulless body of my best friend, my family. Everything was now a dull black, white and grey. Because my life had no colour left within it. It had floated away with his soul.

Had they felt every hit? Every kick? Did they cry out in pain? In fear? Did their little hearts pound in absolute panic? Did they know they were dying? Had they called my name and begged me to save them? Did their shitty little life play like a film before their heart stopped being? Were they greeted by warmth and love on the other side or were they just gone?

Were they nothing but an empty cold vessel? Is that why I felt a large empty pit opening up? Because they were gone and not there to fill it.

People said it got easier over time. Grief. That it was always hard to start with. But how true was that, when everything I did would remind me of them? Of how they once smiled flashing little dimples my way. Knowing that they had such an awful ending to their lives is never going to make that easier. It was going to stick to me like black poisonous tar. It would spread and curdle and fester. I could already feel its poison sticking to my bones.

The urge to follow them was strong.

How was I supposed to carry on? When I had fought for so long to get back? I fought to protect them with everything I had. Had only ever kept strong for them. Everything I ever had or was, was for them. I was nothing without them.

I failed them.

It was my fault.

I failed them.

It should have been me not them.

They were mine and I had left them there, alone and cold and empty.

I truly was a monster. Cole had been right; the entire time, he had been right. I was poisonous. Something that needed to be put down like a rabid dog. My venomous spirit had leaked my pores and sunk themselves into everyone's lives and caused absolute chaos.

I wouldn't leave them alone anymore. I would never leave them again.

A crack echoed around the room as the screeching finally stopped. I was on my knees again, looking down at the stained sheet. I slowly lifted it away from his face.

My boys were identical, but I always knew which was which. And this little soulless empty body was my little Elfyn. Smoothing back his curls, I rested my forehead against his cold one. I don't know how long I stayed there, minutes, hours-who knows? I still didn't move.

There was only one body here. But I knew, I knew Elyas was gone also. The swirling pit in my stomach that was usually filled with the deep obsession for them was empty.

My boys were gone.

Dead.

And without them, I was weak.

Worthless.

Pathetic.

Undeserving of the power within me.

I had waited so long to leave. So long to take my last breath and just be done with this god-forsaken fucking life.

I froze as the creaking of the floorboards above my head caused dust to fall onto Elfyn's body.

He was there: Lyal.

That disgusting, vile fucking scumbag.

He needed to be punished. He needed to feel the pain he put us through for so many years.

He *deserved* pain.

"I'll be back. I'll find your brother. And then I'll join you. We'll be together again," I whispered.

Pushing to my feet, my muscles screaming out after being sat in the same position for hours, I waited for the power to buzz through my veins. When nothing happened, I slowly walked to the rusty green pipe and yanked it from the wall.

I made my way up the stairs.

I was calm. So very calm.

No noise raged within, no clenching cold pit in my stomach.

Just utter calm.

I was finally allowing myself to do what I always needed to do, what I always wanted. What I *craved.*

Pushing open the basement door slowly, I stepped into the dirty kitchen. More blood greeted me, this one old and thick and smelling of rotten flesh. There, sitting at the old table with a bottle of cheap beer was Lyal, our foster father.

The monster who created a monster.

Next to him on the floor, laid in an awkward position was the social worker bitch. Her skull was caved in, and her eyes were open and bugged out as if the blow to her head had pushed too much pressure through them.

Lifting his heavy head, Lyal's watery blood-shot eyes widened in shock.

"Yo-you!" He slurred, throwing his half full bottle at me. It shattered in my face, piercing my skin. The fresh cuts burned from the alcohol as blood began to drip down my face.

I relished the pain.

Welcomed it.

I bared my teeth in Rí's fashion of a smile.

Rí. If I joined my boys. Then I wouldn't have my Mates. My men. My Circle.

I couldn't think about that. I had a monster to torture.

He sputtered in shock as I slowly walked towards him

"Sit back down." I was empty.

I pushed my finger into his food-stained chest as he fell back into his chair with fearful eyes.

Void.

Gone. They were gone.

"I–I–" Stammering, he leaned back against the chair, trying to get away from me.

"Where is he? Where is my Elyas?"

Ignoring my question, his bloodshot, watery eyes searched my face. Grabbing his stained shirt in my hand, I pulled him closer to me and let him see the empty coldness in my purple eyes.

He gasped as he realised my eyes were not normal and it was all it took for me to grit my teeth. He was ruining my calm.

"Where is my boy?" I gritted out.

He still flickered his eyes between my own. Just as I was about to punch him in the throat, he grinned. His watery gaze cleared, becoming more focused.

"What the fuck are you smiling at?" I snapped as I stepped back, an automatic reaction to my childhood monster.

"So you came into your powers?" I blinked at him as he stood up, brushing the lint of his now sparkling clean clothing.

What?

His usual stained, off-white top was now a pure white button down, tucked into sleek black slacks with shiny dress shoes. His balding greasy head was now full of salt and pepper hair tied into a knot at the base of his neck. His appearance changed before me.

He looked like…no.

He was "Mikhail?" I stumbled out. What the actual fuck was happening?

His laugh rang out in the kitchen, making me flinch with confusion.

"Mikhail? No, no Amaya. May I introduce myself?" Smiling widely he stepped towards me. His clean appearance was a stark difference to the dirty dingy house.

"My name is Lynel. Twin to Mikhail. White Witch of Wisteria."

What the fuck. What the actual fuck. Lyal was...Lynel? A witch? How?

"Ah I see the questions in those purple eyes of yours. You see, we knew your mother planned to hide you. So we made a plan of our own. I followed you through to this world. The *human* world." His face scrunched up in disgust. His obvious hate for the humans showed through. "We needed you Amaya. We needed your magic, but oh we knew it wasn't simply going to appear from living comfortably here! I was supposed to snatch you up and sneak you back to Wisteria. But then your kind had to go and blow themselves up didn't they. Shutting the damn portals and trapping me here with you. Without the portals, magic dwindles, puffs out. But one day, oh I found a way." Laughing, he stared down at me.

"I lost my temper and hit you. Lord the power that drifted from you and into me." Inhaling deeply as if he could smell the magic, he smiled again. He seemed too pleased with himself.

I was fucked.

I was confused.

I couldn't think straight as I stared at the identical twin to Mikhail. Not Lyal. Not a gross excuse for a human, but a White Witch.

"It gave me just enough magic to send word to my brother and the Council. I was alive. You were alive. And you had magic. I knew a way to get you to them. I just had to beat it out of you. But the plan changed, didn't it? Yes, it did." He acted as if I knew of his plan.

I stood there, so still, so confused. This was all their plan. My entire life. They had this elaborate plan my entire life.

"The humans, oh the humans. The answer is in their souls! So pure. So clean. So *perfect.* Their souls hold more magic than any White Witch could ever be born with. They just don't know how to harness it. But we do. The superior race. Us. Witches. Oh but the Dark Witches had to go and ruin *everything.*"

The drip of blood from my clenched fist pulled me from my confusion. Looking to my hand and the half-moon cuts in my palms, I watched the blood bead before dripping onto the floor by my black boots.

"Where is Elyas?" I whispered. My poor boys. Where did they come into it?

"Forget about him. Focus child." He snapped, his smile now gone and a frustrated look creased his greying brows.

"With your magic, we can open the portals, we can have everything we want. Have all the power we want. *I knew* you would come back for those boys, but they were holding you back. You need to focus on what *is* and not on what *was.*"

Stepping towards me once more I realised, I was now backed against the cracked wall, right against the small dent my head had created three years ago. I had forgotten to heat up the coffee pot and so I was thrown against this very wall.

"Where is Elyas?" I croaked out once more.

Sighing, he walked back to the crumbled table and sat in his chair.

"He's gone! Now focus! If you open the portal fully, I can get back through to Mikhail. We can–"

The walls shook; the glass cracked.

The screeching was back, its loud constant ring becoming louder as the stranger in front of me spoke with less ease, eyeing the shaking walls with caution.

"Where is his body?" My own voice sounded wrong…It was all wrong. Everything had gone *wrong.*

I wanted my boys.

I needed my boys.

I was so cold.

So empty.

Everything was wrong.

And it was all because of him, this monster. My 'foster father', Lynal the White Witch... He beat me, starved me, all because they wanted my magic. MY magic, to control humans and the power within their souls?

"Why did you hurt them; *they were innocent*" I managed to snap out. My throat was tight, my eyes stung and my chest aching. My body and my blackened damaged soul wanted me to cry.

"Innocent? If only you knew. Forget about them. They are gone!" He snapped back as he rose from his chair as dishes shook from the wall units and smashed to the floor.

Forget about them? How could I ever forget about them? He took them from me. Hurt them when I wasn't here to protect them. Looking to where he stood in his pristine clothes and annoyingly critical face, I suddenly knew what I needed to do. He needed to hurt as I did all those times, he needed to feel pain.

My erratic heartbeat slowed back to its calm beat as I stepped towards him, lifted the rusty pipe and swung it at his head with all my strength. His body fell with a thud to the dirty blood-soaked floor.

He cried out in pain and surprise before sputtering "Now, chil—"

"Child? I'm no child." Stepping away from his crumbled form I carried on, my voice now firm and clear, "but you knew that didn't you? Considering you hid my real age from me."

Walking behind him as he grasped at his bleeding head, I planted my foot at his back and pushed him towards the open basement door. He must have been woozy from the hit because he rolled with ease before flying down the steps with another cry of pain. His lint-free suit was now covered in blood and grime.

I slowly followed after him, walking down each step and relishing his painful gasps against the cold concrete floor.

And there he laid on his back, his salt and pepper hair now turning red with *my boy's blood.*

Smash.

Scream.

Smash.

Each swing of the pipe brought beautiful screams from him as I breathed heavily through gritted teeth. I leaned down and bent each of his clenched fingers back with force, snapping each one as his screams punctured the air. I relished in his pain and panic.

This felt so *fucking right.*

If only the twins had been able to watch me finally hurt this monster.

My heart seized.

His back arched with another scream as I slammed the pipe down on him over and over again, the bloodied welts ruining his lovely white shirt.

"Stop!" He screamed.

"Why do villains always retell their story and plans when they are obviously caught?" I wondered aloud as I breathlessly took a break and sat next to Elfyn, stroking his hair back from his cold forehead.

"Why do they do that? Like no one actually cares. You're caught. Yano?" Tucking the stained sheet under his chin and down the sides, I carried on stroking his little curls.

Looking over to Lynal as he gasped and gurgled on the sticky floor, I calmly switched my gaze to where the pipe usually sat and jolted.

Ravioli sat watching me. His black eyes held more intensity than usual.

He followed me from there.

How?

"You–you're a poisonous monster. You're a filthy Dark Witch!" Lynal managed to scream out as I continued to stroke back Elfyn's hair, my eyes on the crow as an odd panic began to fill my chest the longer I stared at him.

Lynal groaned and cried on the floor like a little bitch, so I stood up and swung the pipe on his knee. The loud crack and his screams were like music to my ears.

"Just-KILL ME ALREADY" he screamed as I stared down at him in disgust.

Already? He begged for death, already?

"You don't deserve the luxury of the release, you piece of shit!" I snapped. "Death is a paradise you should never be allowed to enjoy. The cold dark slip of death is a reward. Not a punishment!" My cool calm was beginning to fade at his weakness.

Standing over the weak little man I spat down at him. My spit landed right on his cheek before sliding down to his chin.

"I am Amaya of the Dark Mountain. I am a powerful pure blooded Dark Witch. And you can simply *get fucked.*" Lifting my boot, I slammed it down onto his spit-covered face, enjoying the crunch of his nose as it flattened under my foot. He lay there, pathetic and unconscious.

Turning to walk back up the stairs in search of Elyas, I stopped. There it was: the black mist in my peripheral vision. Floating and swirling. It moved, disappearing behind me. Spinning round, I gaped in shock as it stayed there, right in front of me. Clear as day in the dull light. The deep black mist swirled for a few more seconds before it began to form a shape. Swirling and whirling before solidifying.

Before me stood a person. covered in a large black hooded cloak. Its face was hidden by the black hood giving the eerie feel of coldness. It stood at 6ft with broad shoulders and the confidence of a king.

"What. The. Fuck." I whispered.

Thirty-Five

'You'll Crawl For Her-Pro Ea Tibi Serpere'

Ziel

I was going to kill each and every one of the Council members. I was going to play with their souls, poking holes into them before ripping them from their bodies and letting them watch me devour them. Then, oh then I was going to string that damn coffee maker up by her feet and have the Vamps come out to play.

How dare she play Amaya like that. How DARE she trick her with friendship and kindness. She was the fucking granddaughter of that stuck-up Councilman Mikhail.

I couldn't rein in my vines. My fire refused to go out. No amount of Mayfeaver helped. Rí was just as bad; his skin rippled and his hair stood at all angles as he paced back and forth, growls and rumbles spilling from his chest.

"We need to go to the portal, the one she came through," Cole spoke in a low tone, trying not to cause any more anger to Rí and his dragon.

"When we have her back, I want everything, and I mean *fucking everything* you know," Rí growled as he stripped his shirt from his back and strode from the bar.

Following behind, we stopped as Rí burst into his dragon in the street. The few late stragglers jumped back as his giant black tale swished as he lifted his massive head, giving a loud angry growl when we didn't immediately climb on his back.

Guess we were riding Rí tonight.

Cole looked nervous as he swiftly climbed on to Rí's back, the heat pouring from his scales already pulling beads of sweat down his pale skin. I knew he must be thinking that this was a ploy to fly him high into the night before dropping him to his death. I think I'd be happier if that was the plan.

But Amaya came first.

She was gone. I could feel it in my bones. The empty cold spot that her quiet presence usually filled ached with the knowledge that she wasn't in this realm. She had gone through the portal.

I gritted my teeth as my body burst into blue flames, and my stomach cramped with the need to consume a soul. I placed another Mayfeaver between my lips before it fell through my now skeletal form.

"*Fuck!*"

An ear-splitting roar of utter rage shook the ground. Stones fell from the old buildings as the closed stalls from the morning market collapsed in heaps of dust.

Rí felt her absence also.

"She's gone. GONE because of YOU!" I screamed at the pathetic White Witch as I threw myself atop of the dragon. I was barely able to grab onto one of his humps before he took off in a speed that had my empty eye sockets whistling.

"If any harm comes to our Mate because of you," I added with disgust, "prepare for my goddamn wrath, White Witch."

He stared out towards the trees as we approached the Village, his own fear and panic obvious on his face.

I jumped from Rí's back before he even landed then ran to the crumbled shack, that I knew she came from. I had made sure to know everything about her. Rí had told me about her human life, the abusive human who, if I got my hands on, would be tortured fully before I ate his soul and burned his flesh from his bones. I had retraced her steps from the crumbled shack to the forest to Rí's bar. Walking in her prints in the sand as she did, I had laid on the wooden door coated in her dried blood. I did this because I needed to be where she had been, needed to feel what she felt. Because she was mine. Ours.

I stopped at the shack; my glowing blue flames mixed with Rí's bright red eyes causing a purple hue to cast around the ruin.

It was empty.

She had gone through.

She had left us.

She had left me.

Gone.

I was going to fucking find her. And punish her.

I was going to bring her to the peak of utter pleasure before I splattered it with pain.

She was mine and she *left*.

"She went through. She did it." Cole walked around the ruin in shock, his face pale as he looked to us.

"The Council, they have something planned. I wasn't with it enough to understand…they have something planned to bring her to her full power. That...shit if she's at full power, the portals will open. The human–"

"Fuck the humans! Our Mate is through there. If one hair on her head, *one fucking hair* is hurt, I will BURN WISTERIA TO THE FUCKING GROUND!" Rí roared at him as his skin rippled once more.

Unable to contain his dragon, he stalked off, pacing the sooty dust beside the stain-covered pieces of wood containing Amaya's old blood.

"They planned all this. And we played right into their hands." I concentrated enough to regain my skin as I pulled a Mayfeaver out. Inhaling deeply and long, I hoped the drug would cloud my brain enough for me to actually focus.

"If she's the only one that can go through, then all we can do is fucking wait. She'll come back; she'll have the boys with her. So let's prepare for their arrival," I nodded to myself as I mentally planned for the arrival of two traumatized boys.

Clearing his throat Cole nodded back. "I'll beg on my knees for her forgiveness, but you have to understand that none of this was *me*. He did this to me."

Flicking the remaining ash from my smoke, I pushed him against the blackened wall. "You *crawl* on your damn knees. She's a fucking queen. My queen. And you'll do well to remember to treat her like one." My vines sneaked out and wrapped around his wrists, opening up his healing wounds from them last time.

"You keep saying he, he who? Who poisoned you?" Rí stopped his pacing and stood glaring at him, his canines peeking out from his lips ready to clamp down and tear into flesh.

Good, I'd fucking join him.

The words out of Cole's mouth next had me freezing. "Mikhail. It was always Mikhail. He killed some of the Dark Witches, took their magic for himself. I overheard him telling my father." Fuck. Mother fucking fucker.

We all knew what he had to do to gain magic from the Dark Witches.

He slammed his head back against the wall with a crack. "I thought I was ill, weak, being part of the Council and their blood line. They filled my brain with poison, and I never saw what they truly were, not until it was too late. By then, I was already fucked, already their pawn to move." Slamming it back again, he caused a wet smear of blood to drip down as he gripped his hair.

The Cole I saw and knew around the Light City was always immaculately dressed, well presented with a firm look of pure distain on his face. He looked down at anyone who travelled from the Shadow Land, even with him sneaking through for the good stuff Rí provided.

But this Cole looked every bit sick and deranged as I did. The scatty look in his eyes was bright with the sickness that plagued us all, smothered our souls and filled us with coldness. Chuckling, I stepped back, lit another smoke and stared at the spot Rí said the crack had been.

"We'll kill them all. We'll watch our Mate take her rightful place at the top of the pecking order and I'll hand her their bones shaped into a damn bird cage for her little pet."

It was as if Rí's rumble summoned the bird. It flew down and landed onto my bony shoulder, curving its sharp talons around the bone and scratching groves. Beady black eyes watched me as I stared back in trepidation. Something about this bird was definitely off. Because there it was again, that pull, that void that wanted to swallow me whole.

Flinging itself from my body it slammed into an invisible wall of pure electric power before disappearing into thin air.

Fuck me. The crack.

That damn bird flew through.

Looking back at the two equally shocked men behind me, I pulled the Mayfeaver from my pocket, lit it with my flames, smiled widely, and took a big risk by slamming my own body into the Crack.

There was no fucking way in hell, I was leaving Amaya to face that monster once again.

Thirty-Six

'Death-Mortem'

Amaya

"Hello Amaya." The deep voice was calm, smooth and utterly terrifying. Everything within me froze. I couldn't move an inch as an ice-like coldness spread over me. The dingy basement became so cold, the dripping, dirty window cracked from the change in temperature.

My black mist was a person, a man.

It had followed me everywhere the second I had landed in Wisteria.

I couldn't form words; my lips were paralysed as was my body.

Lifting its black-gloved hands, the cloaked man lifted the hood from its head revealing hair as dark as night, long and silky-smooth down to his broad shoulders, and eyes so black and cold, I shuddered. His pale face was so utterly handsome I swallowed thickly, even as I internally panicked.

Something about this man made me fear...well *fear*. I was afraid for myself for the first time in my life. I had always enjoyed the cold, the emptiness that sometimes clenched my stomach, but this feeling was like I was being consumed.

"I've been patient. So very patient, waiting for you to finally let go." The man calmly and slowly turned to look down at Lynal, still unconscious and covered in his own blood on the floor.

"I've had enough of waiting. Turns out I'm not a patient man." Chuckling to himself, he looked back to me. His black eyes stared into my own as if he could see into my soul.

"Who are you?" I managed to ask. My heart pounded in my ears making it hard to concentrate.

Something about this man was terrifying.

He smiled wide at me, flashing perfectly white straight teeth. He waved his hand in front of him and his cloak disappeared in a puff of black shimmering mist, leaving him stood in a black suit and shirt so dark he would be invisible to the eye had the room been in its usual darkness. He was so damn handsome it should have been illegal. He radiated power and strength like nothing I had experienced before.

"I am your king. Your Circle Mate."

No. No not happening. Another Mate? A King? Whereas I felt that instant connection to the others even if they were dicks to start with, this man gave me nothing but fear: an unwelcome cold terror that still held me frozen to the stairs.

"No," I squeezed out, unable to hold in the tremor of fear from my voice. I didn't want this.

I just wanted to be with my boys. But Rí and Ziel...could I leave them?

"Yes." Kneeling down next to Elfyn, he ran a pale finger down his bruised cheek.

"Don't touch him," I snapped, finally being able to move. I stepped down the rickety stairs, glaring at this stranger with a hatred I had only known for my abusers.

Tutting he stood back up, brushed invisible lint from his suit jacket and aimed those cold black eyes my way.

"Get out," I bit out, as I stepped away from the stairs, gathering strength from the need to get him away from my boy.

He stared at me, the silence so loud I regretted my words. Who was this man, so cold and terrifying? So much power radiated from him, my own magic practically hid in fear.

"Who are you?" I asked firmly, trying but utterly failing to hide the shiver his stare gave me.

"Your king." He answered with no emotion. Like that gave me any answers. I hated men that thought small answers were real answers.

"You said that. What king exactly? Why have you been following me?" I gave him my own emotionless mask, the one I had used my entire life, the one I permanently used, until Rí and Ziel. Until my Mates.

Tutting at me again as if I was a spoiled child, he circled me slowly, walking with a grace so perfect, he practically glided. His strong smell of ice and something

I couldn't quite figure out filled my nose. Not once did he remove his cold stare from my face. He looked at me with such possession and ownership.

"I am your king. Your Mate," he said stopping behind me. I froze once more as fear plummeted my heart, my chest ice cold as my stomach cramped with such a force my knees wanted to buckle.

One pale, ice-cold finger slid my long hair away from my neck as he leaned down and slowly inhaled before whispering into my ear.

"I own you. You are mine. I allow the others their share in you but ultimately, you are *mine.*" He walked back round so he stood in front of me. I stared at his suited chest, unable to look him in the eyes.

"I -No one owns me," I whispered, barely audible to human ears. But this man wasn't a human- no he was something else entirely.

"Your curse, your poison, your darkness, your *power.* I. Own. It. All."

Each word was spoken with such firmness as he used one hand to open the buttons of his suit jacket. Reaching into his pocket, he pulled out a black chain, thin and sparkling bright, even in the dull lighting of the basement.

My mark had not itched once, hadn't screamed for its Circle Mate. Not once had I felt its rope swirl in happiness at being found.

This man was *not* my Mate. And he certainly did not own me. Unclenching my teeth and watching the chain wearily, I spoke with my own firmness, surprising myself at being able to not sound like a weak little child.

"You are *not* my Mate. And no one will *ever* own me."

I begged my magic to listen to me, begged it to rear its ugly head and protect me from this man, because I suddenly realised one thing: I didn't want to die. Not yet. I still craved the silence it would provide me, but I had already lost my boys. Yes, I wanted to be with them; I wanted to surround myself in their souls, but I had Rí and Ziel, I had their marks, their protection, their *obsession.*

The stranger chuckled once more, causing chills to spread along my arms. That was not a happy sound. That was a pissed off laugh.

Shit.

"Oh I own more than you think Little Witch. I not only own you, but your Mates, your precious Dark Mountain and the entirety of Wisteria. I am not just your king, but the entire damned universe's." He wrapped the chain around both his hands as he spoke, pulling it tight with each twist of his hand. "I allow people to live and die as I wish. I allow them to have Wisteria and their little magic tricks. After all, this place and Wisteria is just a world and you're just living in it. Because I ALLOW it!" He snapped the chain tight one last time before wrapping it around my throat before I could even blink.

Its tight coldness pressed against my neck, I expected to panic and struggle to breathe, but instead of choking me, it wrapped around my neck like a necklace.

"A gift, Amaya. For my Mate, my wife, my *Queen.*" He smiled wide, his white teeth flashing at me. He shrugged on his cloak that appeared in his black mist. I was speechless. Unable to form words or argue back. This man was insane. He was utterly terrifying and probably going to kill me and everyone I now called mine. So why did the sick, unwell part of me preen at the chain now around my throat?

A crack of magic sounded in the room as a slit of blurry water drops appeared in the air above the pool of blood at our feet.

"It seems our Circle is attempting to get to you."

He walked to Lynal laying on the floor as he started to stir, a groan of pain escaping him as he tried to open his swollen eyes.

Satisfaction coursed through my body at the mess of him.

I did that.

Fucking prick.

"I will deal with this…" He curled his lip in disgust. "Peasant in a way that I see fit."

Frowning, I managed to mutter, "He's mine to punish."

The stranger tutted at me again. "Yes, but you are *mine.*"

He nodded to Ravioli still sat in the corner; at his nod, the crow flew over and clung his talons to my shoulder.

Did he know my Ravioli?

"Enjoy my gift."

My hand reached up to brush my fingers over the chain, and he threw his head back in a laugh.

"Not the chain, my Queen."

Another crack filled the basement as Ziel jumped through the crack of a portal, landing smoothly on his feet, his knees bent and vines out at the ready for attack. His skeleton head swung to me, before his skin appeared, and grinned at me. The grin quickly slipped from his perfect face as his green eyes then landed on the stranger.

His skin paled, and eyes widened in utter shock as he fell to his knees and pressed his head to the sticky concrete.

He was…bowing?

The stranger chuckled once more before he disappeared in a puff of black mist, taking Lynal's body with him. I crashed to the floor in shock or was that fear? I didn't fucking know.

I looked to Elfyn's body and stared at him once more. The distant murmur of my name was being called, but I couldn't look away. He was truly gone. And his twin wasn't even with him.

"Amaya!" I blinked Ziel into focus as he slapped my cheek with force. The sting was a welcome feeling to the numb that was quickly building within me. The numb was something I could deal with, a familiar feeling I wanted to remember but couldn't.

"We have to go back through. Rí and Cole should have been through by now." I nodded, but continued to stare at Elfyn's body, his little blond curls, his now colourless lips.

Ziel looked back at him, before reaching over and lifting his body into his arms cradling him close.

"Come on." He reached out one hand; I looked to it. I saw his unmarked smooth skin, no vines, no bones. Just skin. My Mate, Ziel. I gripped it and allowed him to pull me to my feet. Wrapping his arm around my waist, and cradling Elfyn in his other arm, we shoved through the portal. There was no pain, no suffocation as we were forced through the barriers of the cracked portal.

Landing on our feet, I was pulled into huge arms and lifted from my feet. Rí held me tightly, muttering soft comforting things in my ear. I didn't hear him. I pulled away and as he gently lowered me to my feet, Ziel lay Elfyn's body down on the sand outside the crumbled shack.

"Fuck...fuck is that..." Rí rumbled behind me as I knelt to my boy, stroking back his hair once more. I had no words. I had no anger.

I was empty.

"We couldn't go through, after you and the bird, it zapped at us." Cole spoke to Ziel as he shifted on his feet. Cole was uneasy and most probably waiting for my reprimand. There wasn't one.

Because I was empty.

"I don't know what happened. He was there. Fuck he was there." Pulling a Mayfeaver from his jacket Ziel lit it up with shaking hands and drew in deeply. I looked to him as he knelt to the other side of Elfyn.

"Who? You bowed to him. Who was he?" I muttered. I was unable to put any firmness in my voice. Ziel knew who that man was. He'd also been afraid, he'd bowed, and I'd seen him tremble.

Who was that man that made my power hide and Ziel tremble in fear?

Who was he that he made me fear, *fear?*

Rí crouched down beside me and smoothed my hair, Cole stood with his arms crossed, obviously unsure where he stood with me. Ziel looked me in the eyes as he drew in deeply, holding the drug within his lungs before releasing it in a shaky exhale.

"Death. That was Death."

To be continued.

Please leave a review of My Dark Obsession on Amazon! It allows me to keep writing books.

Book 2 My Dark Possession out soon.

ABOUT THE AUTHOR

Amber M. Clark is a Dark romantasy writer who loves to include tropes of Morally grey girls bringing the men to their knees.
She lives with her husband, two children and doggy best friend and loves reading as much as she loves writing.

Hang out with her on Social Media!

@Amberclarkauthor

@Amberclarkauthor

THANK YOU

A huge thank you to my Beta readers who
made the time for me.
To Carly for being an amazing editor.
To my husband for listening to me talk
nonstop about my ideas.
And lastly, thank you to my mother, for
introducing me to Dark Romantasy and being
the one to encourage me to write.
I wouldn't have been able to do this without
you all.

Printed in Dunstable, United Kingdom

67032190R00201